I0666258

Tightly Bound

A selection of Short Stories by Vonnie Giles.

Following Vonnie's successful short story compilation 'Acid Rain' and her contributions to the anthology 'Picked and Mixed', Vonnie has collected together another selection of her unique and quirky short stories.

'Tightly Bound' delves into her eclectic collection of dark and esoteric tales and promises to entertain and surprise.

Meet more of the darkest characters ever to send shivers into your dreams.

Author of **Acid Rain**

See all Vonnie's books on
www.uppbooks.com
www.vonniegiles.com

First published in Great Britain in 2017 by U P Publications
St George's House, George Street, Huntingdon, Cambs PE29 3GH

Cover design copyright © G Griffin Peers

A CIP Catalogue record of this book is available from the British Library

ISBN 978-1-908135-07-0

Also published as an ebook by U P Publications under
ISBN 978-1-908135-08-7

FIRST PAPERBACK EDITION

Published by U P Publications - Printed in England by The Lightning Source Group

www.uppbooks.com
www.vonniegiles.com

Tightly Bound

Vonnie Giles

U P Publications
2017

Dedication:

For Martin with Love

Contents

Furniture Talk 7

The Lotus Eaters 14

The Naughty Shepherdess 21

The Self-Contained Scientist 32

Tightly Bound 40

A Very British Murder 48

Mealtime 54

A Random Journey 62

Butter Me No Parsnips... 71

Dear Reader 82

First Meeting.. 88

For Your Ears Only 94

Guitar Man.. 100

Lavender Bags 110

Mrs Tabernacle's Obsession.................................. 117

Needlepoint... 128

Reunion... 135

Rivals 142

Shadow Love 149

Dead Art.. 155

The Wise Woman... 162

A Kiss from Alice 169

Congratulations 176

The Billionaire's Yacht 182

Sleepwalker 188

Stormy Weather 194

The Abandonment 201

The Bartered Bride 210

The Doormat 218

The Goddess and the Gambler 225

The Second Coming 231

The Time-Shaper 237

Totally Divine 246

White Noise 254

Womankind 260

Little Brat 271

Pumpkin Baby 279

Ralphie 286

The Battle of Bosworth 297

Anticipation 309

Aqua Tofana 316

Hybrid Dream 327

Blue Imperfection 333

Too Tightly Bound 338

Furniture Talk

The seamstress, surrounded by deep-orange painted walls, sat in her tall chair, completely at one with it – the pattern of its upholstery was even imprinted on her face and neck, while the shape of her hands and arms – yellow silk-covered – mirrored exactly the chair's curved oak-wood arms, so that they seemed to merge. She was painfully thin and so tightly bound in on herself that there was not an ounce of flesh to spare. Her tiny, tiny feet, peeping out from under her dress, seemed to have transmogrified into two small slivers of wood to match her chair.

Against the flamboyantly coloured wall, stood another chair, identically upholstered, but this one was without arms. It was busily using an elegantly shaped leg to tidy the bottom drawer of a highly-decorated chiffonier, where the seamstress always kept her handkerchiefs.

Nestling up against her, and annoyingly nudging her, was a sewing basket standing on spindly legs. Odds and ends of yellow silk hung out untidily from its top and, inside, was a jumble of thimbles, scissors and reels of brightly coloured cotton, all eagerly waiting to be used. One spindly leg had sinuously wrapped itself around a chair leg and, so as not to be outdone, one of the chair legs was exploring the inside of the sewing basket.

Familiarity breeds contempt, and the chair and the sewing basket had spent so long next to each other that there was a constant tension between them, especially since the day when the seamstress's yellow dress had been produced.

"Surely you can see the soft, subtle colour of my upholstery, its intricate design," the chair had remarked in its usual overbearing manner. "That yellow material is so cheap-looking and doesn't blend at all with the decor. It's just not a fit material for a fine seamstress like our mistress to wear."

The room's floor – polished, plain wooden planks – was obviously in need of repair; a ginger cat was eyeing the seamstress up and down through one of the broken boards and meowing furiously.

The seamstress said, "Why do you all move around so much and make so much noise when all I want to do is to think and have some peace? And please stop arguing, for everything is really quite satisfactory."

Seemingly slightly embarrassed, the cat stopped its complaining, but the scissors were sorely offended for they were just about to begin cutting the yellow silk remnants to make her a frilly mop cap, which they thought she would like; the needle was already threaded and the pins standing to attention. The seamstress was very sorry that they were all out-of-sorts with her, but her mind was on other things. With her head aching, she stood on her little feet and, tip-toeing with difficulty, moved to the next room. The ginger cat scrambled out of the floor and followed her.

The next room, windowless, was one of several completely different rooms; opening upon opening with not a door between them. Each room gazed at her through a pair of heavy-lidded, bright green eyes set high in the walls like wide, shallow lamps. The whole scene was one of muted greenness, so much more restful than the intrusive orange of her sewing room. Her eyes were beginning to fail her after so many years spent sewing thousands upon thousands of precise, neat stitches, but she couldn't close them, couldn't sleep, seemed destined to have become the epitome of insomnia.

"I feel so tired," said the seamstress.

"So tired," echoed the cat.

"I just want to sleep," said the seamstress.

"To sleep," echoed the cat. "Forever?" it asked.

"Yes, perhaps forever," answered the seamstress.

"I will help you, mistress," it said and plodded purposefully back to the orange room.

In front of the seamstress, amid all the greenness, stood a small three-legged oval table on which was a candle stick with a flame flickering at its centre, but radiating from this, like a corona, were exquisitely thin filaments that sparkled like a star.

Back in the orange room the ginger cat smiled

wickedly and jumped onto the seamstress's chair, which was hers and hers alone. He knew that this would cause mischief and, indeed, the chair rose slightly at this insult and, in a fit of pique, banged its four feet on the floor.

"So, what do you think you're doing?" it said proudly to the cat, arching its tall back so that it reached its full height. The cat, however, had not been ousted by this sudden movement, having dug its claws deeply and painfully into the upholstered seat. He then rolled over and, to the chair's further annoyance, a thick patch of ginger hairs appeared, which would be a serious problem to remove.

"With my mistress absent, I've decided to take her place. You can complain as much as you like, but it will make no difference."

He then began to sharpen his claws on the chair back until the material was virtually ruined and hung in shreds. He was well aware that he'd be in serious trouble when the seamstress returned, but all he had to do was to hide himself again in the hole in the floor; in that little refuge, there was no way that she could reach him.

Very rarely did the seamstress ever leave her orange sewing room. However, now that she was in the suite of green rooms, the three-legged table decided to indulge in a tantrum while it had her there. It was a vain, proud little table and longed for nothing so much as a fine mirror where it could admire itself and bask in its own glory. Tears began to fall from its surface and it started to grizzle and moan.

"I can't see my reflection, mistress, which is a desperate situation. Here am I, a true picture of sparkling beauty, and yet I can't see myself. Please, please," it said pitifully, "arrange for me to have a mirror, a gorgeous one in a fine gold frame so that I can enjoy the loveliness that others can see."

On hearing this the green eyes on the wall lifted their lids in exasperation.

Mayhem is the best word to describe what happened next. The three-legged table, realising that its words were falling on deaf ears, deliberately and very rudely, pushed its way in front of the seamstress, then trundled through into the orange room where it had always been forbidden to go. The first object that immediately caught its attention was the chiffonier on the front of which was a mirror. From that moment, it was impossible to stop it pirouetting and preening, mesmerised by its own beauty.

Hence, the side-chair was now prevented from performing its task of tidying the drawer and putting its mistress's handkerchiefs in order. It did this time and time again, every day, every minute of every day, for it was never satisfied with the result.

What ensued was an unfortunate entanglement of curving, wooden legs curling around each other; pulling, shoving, kicking, there were no holds barred. The chiffonier was eventually pushed over, its mirror smashed, its woodwork scuffed and ugly. Being of

French extraction, it uttered a long list of foreign expletives that floated through the room.

The oval table by now had only two legs and limped back to the green room, its wondrous show of lights extinguished, its surface scratched; it was never to recover its former glory. "My beauty is ruined, I can no longer bear to look at my reflection. My mistress should have had more care for my welfare. I feel disappointed and deceived."

Meanwhile, events in the orange room were about to become more dramatic. The sewing basket was in the middle of its worst fracas yet with the seamstress's chair: the poor chair looked decidedly worse for wear and the cat still hung onto it for dear life.

As the seamstress once more entered the room to see what on earth was happening, the sewing basket lurched into her, causing her frail, little feet to slide across the slippery, wooden floor; they ended up splintered and doubled up under her. Her chair, in the meantime, reeling from the pain caused by the cat's claws, lost its temper, lifted the scissors from the sewing basket and aimed them at the ginger menace, running once more towards his hiding place. The cat, skilfully, had calculated the scissors' trajectory, so that they missed their mark and ended up protruding from the poor seamstress's heart as she lay on the floor.

By the time she died, the cat had reclaimed his place on the by-now rickety chair. "Enjoy your long sleep, mistress. It is, after all what you wanted, isn't?"

With a smug smile on his plump face, he purred contentedly, thinking that this was far better than living under the floorboards.

The Lotus Eaters

It was simply too divine. Finally, to have a cake and with icing on the top, as well: in fact, oodles of icing! What more could one possibly ask from life? For the first time ever, Camilla had enough money to do whatever she wanted. *Thank you, Ernie – I never thought that you would come up trumps.* A million-pound win from a bond that had been purchased years ago costing a mere one-pound sterling!

Camilla, however, was suffering from a bad case of greed – of much wanting more. She was, luckily for her, a very sharp cookie with plenty of ideas whirling around in that clever little mind of hers, one of which would surely come to fruition. Mummy and Daddy naturally knew of her good luck, but they didn't know the depths to which she was soon to sink to enhance her fortune and would surely go bananas when all was revealed.

Her childhood had been spent in a house of faded elegance at a time when, apparently, there were no funds to restore it to its former glory. Nevertheless, this hadn't stopped Daddy from being a long-standing member of the best golf club in the area. As for

Mummy, well, she was in a constant battle against age and wrinkles, embracing invasive surgical procedures: Botox, beauty treatments of all kinds, anything that would stop the advancing years. She lunched at least twice a week with her so-called girl friends in a mad frenzy of dry martinis and Nouvelle Cuisine.

She also had a pretty good idea from where the money came to indulge in her extravagances …but more of that later!

Camilla had a younger brother called Craig who was a total waste of space, always leaving his spliffs around the house, soggy with his saliva: disgusting! Camilla often suspected that Mummy, too, enjoyed the odd hit of marijuana. Craig was in a continual state of lust, always directed towards older women; some really old – anyone younger than forty-five could forget it!

His other addiction was eating so, not surprisingly, he was somewhat on the podgy side. Being flabby and lazy, his work history was hit and miss but occasionally, or so it seemed, he made the effort to earn some honest pennies doing odd jobs: a bit of building work here and there, even shelf-filling in supermarkets, which was why he seemed to spend so much time absent from the house at night …well, that was his story and he was sticking to it. Nevertheless, despite all his faults, Camilla adored him. He was the one person she could trust and to whom she would tell all. In fact, she hoped he might even help in a managerial capacity once her business got going and after he'd had some training.

Gerald and Eliza – Mummy and Daddy – despite their social aspirations, didn't deceive anyone in that rural, snobby corner of England and all their friends knew that they were playing a part. With accents that were just too perfect, they gave away their humbler origins but, as they appeared to have plenty of money, they were forgiven. The house, too, saved them from being ignored, for it was shabby-chic and in unbelievably good taste, in the same way that stately piles were often the worse for wear. Bitchy was the best way to describe their circle, with noses that both turned up and looked down, depending on the circumstances.

Everyone was of the opinion that Craig was definitely not a suitable name to be passed down through the centuries, if that was what Gerald and Eliza were hoping. For example, all the eldest sons in the Manor House had, for the past five-hundred years, borne the name of Humphrey and would continue to do so until England sank under the briny when the big tsunami finally arrived, or until the whopping death-bringing asteroid from space hit the village.

As she surveyed the Mediterranean, Camilla, stretching luxuriously, took her dry martini from the tray presented to her by a gorgeous hunk of a waiter. Many options were open to her, but she was in no doubt as to the type of business she wanted to open. She had the management skills, marketing knowledge and, above all, the imagination to make her million work for her.

The first priority was to find the ideal premises: in London, she thought. Then there was the problem of an under-manager, as she herself didn't intend to work every day, or even every week.

She thought that Craig would fit the bill wonderfully: easily manipulated, too idle to nip out and neglect his post and a voice loud enough to put the fear of God into the workers if things got out of hand. Also, as a family member, he would, she hoped, work for less pay, because, let's face it, a million pounds may sound a fortune, but it's soon spent. There would, of course, be staff members; the interviews would be great fun. One would have to be mindful that a range of personal tastes needed to be satisfied. She first thought of out-of-work builders, big chaps, who would make most women tremble with desire. Then there would have to be the more intellectual, Lord Byron/ Mr Darcy type who could hold a good conversation, as well as fulfil his main function.

Among Mummy's circle, she knew at least a dozen frustrated women who would love to find a stud to give them the action they didn't enjoy at home. Discreet publicity, mostly by word of mouth, would soon ensure a good return on her investment. Yes, a male brothel for the discerning woman – that was definitely the answer.

Meanwhile, back home in the village, Craig was still slouching about, poking his nose where it didn't belong, which annoyed Mummy and Daddy no end. He was forever opening drawers and cupboards to have a root around. "Nosey little sod!" was how Daddy put it.

As for their *Dear Daddy*, Gerald …what a sly one he was! While his daughter was considering her future, living the life of Reilly and his son was prying and enjoying his spliff, he was seated behind his desk at Spotters Bank, PLC, having a very intense conversation with one of his best buddies. Gone was the upmarket accent. Now it was more *EastEnders*. This little chat involved all sorts of corruption: money laundering, extortion and any scam you can imagine. Gerald was a successful con-man, and working in a bank was the ideal position for him. "I think we're definitely on the right track here, Gerry, my mate," said the grungy little man sitting opposite him. "One more scam like the last one and I think we'll be able to say that we've well and truly made it."

Gerald's mind, however, was somewhere else, for there was no way this small-time crook was going to share in any of his success; a bullet through the head would be the best solution to that little problem. He'd do the deed himself: far safer that way and no opportunity for blackmail.

Camilla was full of excitement at the prospect of setting up her business. There would be all sorts of services offered, some of them way out of the ordinary, in fact, downright weird.

Well, each to his own, and she would make sure that all tastes were satisfied. If you'd been able to see inside the crates that were trundled in you'd have seen a variety of the most extraordinary contraptions, which

I'll just leave to your imagination. Suffice to say no strange fetish was ignored.

It was in her choice of staff that Camilla came unstuck: illegal immigrants with no papers (although the clients loved the foreign accents) and the others who were British to the core, but whose undeclared earnings would not be too popular with the taxman if he ever found out. As long as it saved her money, Camilla wasn't bothered about the legality of it all. Undoubtedly, none of the men would squeal because that would mean deportation or less pay, so it was to everyone's advantage to let these illicit arrangements stay hidden under the proverbial carpet.

Craig proved to be a very good choice as under-manager and Camilla was positively amazed by his dedication and change of attitude. He spent far less time sitting down, changed his diet and interacted well with the staff, talking to them and finding out about their backgrounds. He refused, however, to work nights for he had other fish to fry.

So now you can see the family set-up – not very pleasant people, were they? As the years passed, Gerald's shady deals grew more and more lucrative. As for Camilla, well, her business became even more successful than she had hoped.

It was a wet, windy Autumn day in the village, brown leaves sticking to the old, stone houses with their pretty gardens and thatched roofs …any American's dream of England, unless, of course, they'd actually been there! That was the day when Gerald and Camilla, snug in the family home, met their Nemesis and began to pay for their illegal activities.

A police car, with no lights flashing or sirens blaring, discreetly rounded the curved drive and stopped quietly outside the fine, oak door. This, after months of investigation, was going to be a triumph for the police; a conman and murderer, plus a daughter who thought she could get one over on the fiscal system, were about to be rounded up and charged.

Flanked on either side by two constables, a hefty, smartly-dressed Detective Sergeant rang the bell and was admitted by the open-mouthed cleaning lady who just couldn't take her eyes off him. The family was now complete and gathered in the chintzy sitting room: a cosy scene, with a large basset hound snoring loudly on the rug in front of the log fire.

"Good morning," said Craig, surprisingly dishy in the plain clothes he was allowed to wear as a Detective Sergeant. "You can guess why I'm here," he added, staring at the two guilty parties.

He watched Mummy crumple up and faint completely away, her head coming to rest in the dog's basket. The words coming out of Daddy's mouth were far too scatological and shocking to be shown here. Camilla, however, as the handcuffs were put on her wrists, merely said a simple, "Fuck you, Craig!"

The Naughty Shepherdess

The music was ethereal and the darlings sounded absolutely divine, which was only right under the circumstances. They were singing their little hearts out, probably better than ever before. However, as some of the singers were well into their eighties, it was never going to be perfection, but ten out of ten, ladies, for trying.

Nevertheless, was this really the best they had to offer, thought Virginia? Wouldn't they prefer Justin Beiber or something similar? They'd all find it so much more fun!

Virginia was in her postulant stage at the convent where she had been for six months, and was thus still wearing normal clothes, the only sign of her eventual intention being the cross that she wore around her neck. She didn't think that she would ever reach the novitiate stage. It was a pity because the thought of being bride-like, wearing a white veil and wedding dress was the one thing that had kept her going; it all sounded rather attractive and romantic. She did tend to forget that it was God and not gorgeous Reggie Trent who was going to be the bridegroom.

She was coming up to forty years of age, rather old for a prospective nun. Nevertheless, she was still extremely attractive, which had been noted by one or two of the sisters who perhaps should not have been in a convent. Virginia vaguely hoped that their obvious prurience stayed only in their minds, and that they didn't approach her in an unseemly fashion. After all, this was intended to be a monastic, cloistered life, not a girls' boarding school with rampant hormones whizzing around all over the place. Not, personally, that she really gave a damn!

She knew that Mother Mathilda must have recognised her unsuitability early on, but had rather tetchily persevered with her. She knew, too, that she had no business in this dark, gloomy place, living in a small cell, sleeping on a bed with a straw mattress and pillow, and eating awful food – especially after what she had always been used to.

She regretted her decision to come here almost straight away and actually, strangely for her, felt guilty, because her mind was too preoccupied to give much thought to God and the saints. Although, to be honest with you, she wasn't sure that she believed in any of them. At the time it had seemed the easiest option open to her: free food, somewhere to lay her head, not too much work to do (just a bit of cleaning now and then). She had companionship too, although it was of a rather silent, contemplative nature. There would even be someone to care for her if she ever became ill, which would be jolly handy as she'd been forced to give up her private health insurance due to of lack of funds.

Darling Reggie Trent had abandoned her, left her on the rubbish heap, declaring that she'd outworn her usefulness as a sexual object; that she was, in fact, the most boring woman in the whole world, bar none.

She'd last set eyes on him outside a nautical club – she thought it had been in Cannes, but she couldn't quite remember. She wasn't sure, for the simple reason that they had driven all over the Riviera having such a splendid time that she couldn't remember the exact details. Well, at least she thought it had been splendid – she just didn't realise that she was about to receive her marching orders because Reggie's boredom threshold had been reached!

She had stood in front of him in her favourite white dress, the one decorated with green-leaved pink roses, and, tucked around her head, she had swathed a pale pink scarf. Her feet were clad in bright-orange high heels that didn't really match, but which, for that reason, gave the impression that she was totally laid-back and at home with herself. Although, in fact, she would spend hours on her appearance before ever stepping over the threshold. All this was topped by a pair of fashionable, and very expensive, white sunglasses. She had thus achieved the archetypal Hollywood-star-look to perfection, although, back home it was definitely the 'Sloane Ranger' look that prevailed.

During those last world-shattering moments, she and Reggie were standing against his to-die-for silver sports car; he was a sturdy hunk, terribly good-looking in a George Clooney sort of way. Wearing a smart navy blazer with white trousers and soft, cream shoes, he looked the cat's whiskers, and didn't he know it! He gazed thoughtfully at her through his dark glasses, one hand on her waist and, with no warning whatsoever, dropped the bombshell.

"Well, Virginia, I'm sorry to tell you that this is it – adios, ciao, arrivederci, goodbye etcetera, etcetera... All good things must come to an end and I've truly reached that point. You're just such a bore, Virginia!"

"But, Reggie..."

"There are no buts, my sweet. I do so hope that you will find somewhere comfortable for the night. Go to a bar, look around and see who you can pick up. An older man I suggest, taking your age into account."

The sarcastic bastard then drove off, without even a peck on the cheek, just a casual wave that said it all – that he just didn't give a toss.

In an instant, for Virginia, the glorious Mediterranean sun disappeared; black clouds came out, a cool breeze began to blow, and all the palm trees drooped.

As she came to the end of her time as a postulant, the convent was becoming more and more of a struggle for Virginia.

In that particular spot, dozens of martyrs had died for their faith, and much time was designated to praying for their souls. Surely, she thought, after all the years that had passed since their martyrdom, they must have, by now, occupied enough of God's time and it was other people's turn to have a prayer or two. For example, Mother Mathilda needed everyone's intercession in her fight against obesity and to forgive her transgression for being such an overbearing old bat. You can see that attitude-wise Virginia didn't seem to be doing too well on her spiritual journey towards being a fully-professed nun.

Where, for example, she asked herself for the umpteenth time was that skunk, Reggie Trent? This thought, very inappropriately, was passing through her mind while she was supposed to be spending a quiet hour in prayer and study.

After he bade her his sudden and unexpected farewell, Virginia had wandered off to have coffee at a little bistro, the outside of which, was surrounded by holly bushes – quite appropriate for someone who felt at that moment that thorns were tearing her heart. Sitting on the chic blue and white upholstered chair with a coffee cup on hand, she looked inside her handbag, checked with a conveniently sited ATM machine and discovered that she had just about enough money to see her through the next couple of weeks. Even though her situation was precarious, there was no way that she would stoop to look for employment.

Kind fate, however, was on her side; she picked up and started to read a newspaper that, by chance, had been left on the table. She wasn't left in peace for long, for a black cat suddenly appeared from behind a holly bush, jumped up onto the table and started to nuzzle the newspaper, demanding her attention. He placed his paw over one of the articles, which almost seemed a sign that she should read it – after all, black cats were supposed to be lucky, weren't they?

As she read, the sun suddenly reappeared in all its yellow glory, bringing warmth again to the earth, the clouds drifted off to visit another part of the sky and the palm trees revived from whatever had ailed them. Here was the perfect answer to her dilemma. Enter a convent! Become a nun! What a dramatic gesture that would be!

She could almost smell the incense wafting through the holly bushes. She could see herself slowly walking along the cloisters in an attitude of prayer, with beautiful, angelic music drifting with her. Now that her true path in life had been revealed to her, she knew, finally, that Reggie Trent was unworthy of her and too worldly.

She returned to London and made her way to the headquarters of the Order of the Little Shepherdesses of the Cross. She had already written to them and contacted them by 'phone, so that when she arrived she was expected. Mother Mathilda, her mounds of fat moving alarmingly, welcomed Virginia, who immediately wanted to give her advice on how to lose weight. *Too many carbs and too much sugar, darling. You'll just have to try harder, for nothing comes without a price where dieting is concerned.*

Mother Mathilda, with no idea of the silent criticism she was receiving, sent her in the direction of the vocation advisor, Sister Ursula who was ninety if she was a day.

Well, this was easy-peasy and all Virginia had to do was to lie like hell, at which she was an expert: always had been …in her pushchair with her Norton nanny, at boarding school, at finishing school and certainly would continue to be so, here in the convent. She assured Sister Ursula that yes, she prayed regularly – yes, she had felt the call and yes, she had indeed talked to many sisters to find out what life might be like within a convent. So, the interview continued. *Yes, yes, yes* – where appropriate and *No, no, no* – where 'yes' was not.

Her only problem came when she was invited to supper and asked to say grace. She'd had absolutely no idea what words to use, so she suddenly let her body go limp, and slid dramatically under the bench where she sat, so that – like a female James Bond – her cover wouldn't be blown.

Meanwhile, Reggie Trent too was making his way to London. Not, however, in the car that Virginia had so much liked, but by plane: cattle class, no less. The wonderful, silver roadster had not even belonged to him... It was his brother's, that ace entrepreneur Teddy, dripping with money. No wonder then, that Reggie, despite his self-confidence, felt second-rate in comparison. He just didn't possess the business acumen, the pizzazz that Teddy had. Poor Virginia had picked the wrong brother, which was a pity because Teddy preferred silly, vacuous women like her; his two ex-wives had been of the same ilk: so much easier to manipulate than a blue-stocking with a mind of her own.

How Virginia managed to pass muster and proceed to the next stage, becoming a novice, was a mystery, but that is the way the other shepherdesses had voted. Therefore, on one dark, overcast day with the lights shining in the chapel, the whole order of shepherdesses sat on the hard benches, giggling excitedly and twittering away like birds. Their black and white habits seemed such a heavy burden to bear that perhaps they needed this moment of lightness.

On this occasion, Virginia was to be the only bride of God. Although her family and friends would have been welcome to attend the ceremony of dedication, there had been no one to invite, so she was completely alone with only the sisters to pray for her. Through the small, arched, lead-glass windows they could all see and hear the rain falling heavily: as it turned out, not a good omen.

Having for months looked forward to this day, she was absolutely appalled at the so-called veil, a very short piece of lace that looked more like something a housewife would wear to keep dust and cobwebs off her hair – not at all Kate Middleton! The dress was even more of a shock: a pale blue satiny affair that looked distinctly worse for wear. Tears came into her eyes, for she knew that within a few minutes her stylish hair would be cut off and placed in something that resembled a bread basket. Even Luigi of Bond Street, that hair-stylist *par excellence*, wouldn't be able to do much with what was left. She looked hard at the prie-dieu where she must kneel to take her vows and thus, in effect, become dead to the world.

Alarmingly, within her chest, she felt a flare-up rising to the surface rather like Vesuvius in AD 79. She dug her nails into the palms of her hands, and tried taking deep breaths, but she had lost the battle, and nothing was going to stop the eruption. A noise, like a kettle beginning to boil, welled up in the back of her throat and exploded into the air. This turned into a full-blown scream and she began to stamp her feet. She then picked up the little, neatly-arranged table on which lay her novice-dress, veil and wimple, plus a Book of the Hours.

Flinging the table at the altar, the crucifix fell to the ground, causing horror on the faces of those watching her. "I don't want to become Sister Agnes Mary," she howled, "I just want to be me, plain Virginia Octavia Smith-Hyde-Jones." The annoying sound of clicking beads, which she hated so much, increased in volume and did nothing to disperse the flaming, black cloud hanging over her head.

The mayhem increased as she picked up one of the gold candle-sticks from the altar and sprinted towards Mother Mathilda who, unsuccessfully, wobbled away to escape the onslaught …too late, however, for a determined Virginia was a Virginia who would not be denied.

As Mother Mathilda lay dying on the lovely rug that had been brought out from storage for today's ceremony, it entered Virginia's head that she might deflate like a punctured bicycle, now that there was a candle-stick poking out of her enormous stomach.

"Why couldn't you have bought me a decent wedding outfit, you old cheap-skate? If you'd given me the say-so I could easily have popped into Harrods or Harvey Nicks and found something truly spectacular."

She had completely lost the plot… "God took Reggie Trent away from me and what did he offer in return? – the life of a pauper, with not a penny to my name and the most disgusting food known to man, always being told to do this, that and the other, not even allowed to have a man in my room. A poor show I call it! And I'll certainly wring that damned black cat's neck if I ever meet it again." This last little gem, of course, completely mystified the shepherdesses.

Virginia stood looking down at the corpse: bemusedly wondering what it was doing there.

As the priest had disappeared to take cover behind the altar it was left to that valiant, ancient fossil, Sister Ursula, to hobble from the murder scene to call the local police with trembling claw-like fingers.

Without much further ado, two burly constables escorted Virginia from the chapel, still shouting as she made her final exit from the scene. "I want you, Reggie

Trent! I love you, Reggie Trent. I promise never to bore you again, if only you'll come back to me."

Destiny decided that Reggie Trent and Teddy Trent would not, after all, go to visit the naughty shepherdess in Fieldgate Prison for Women, as they had intended. They had read of the amazing events in the papers and could still hardly believe that the person involved was Virginia: a silly, empty woman, but surely not a murderess. Snow had fallen during the night, making the roads particularly slippery that morning and Teddy, at the wheel, drove far too fast. He lost control, the car swerved and ultimately exploded at the bottom of a ravine.

Virginia, now condemned to existence in yet another cell, was given the news that her visitors, after all, would not be coming, then or at any time in the future. "I loved you, Reggie Trent," she whispered. "I loved you more than I'll ever love God." The rest of her life was thus spent worshipping his memory, lying prostrate for hours on the cold, stone floor, a candle permanently lighted in front of his photograph, her shorn hair lying nearby in a prison bread basket.

The Self-Contained Scientist

How would you feel if you lived on the very edge of the universe, fearing that at any moment you and your abode would tumble over some vast, cosmic cliff into heaven knows where, perhaps into a completely alien corner of space with different laws of physics?

Ezra, that strange-looking young scientist, with his square face, broad square head with cropped, blond hair standing up like a cornfield, had a body that was also on the square side. All this, together with his oblong glasses, gave him a rather geometrical appearance. He was feeling anxious and afraid and, with each second, he became less light-hearted.

He lived in a high-vaulted room, with a door-less, arched entrance as its one and only exit: a rather untidy room, one has to say, with bits of abandoned experiments lying all over the place. If he peeped out of the arch, his view was limited because one false step and he could have floated away easily. Actually, all he could see were misty swirls of cloud that hovered on the threshold. He sensed, however, that disaster was imminent. "Dearie me, dearie me, what a fine kettle of fish this is! How will it all end?"

Biting his nails nervously, he sat in front of a table that was covered with a creased and crumpled, blue cloth. Near the table stood a large, silver chest, which had once held hundreds of crystals of all shapes and sizes, but their number had declined considerably. Ezra, in his frenzied experiments, had spilled many of those unused onto the floor and couldn't be bothered to sweep them up. It proved to be a serious hazard as he frequently cut his feet on their sharp edges, but that was only a minor problem because of the magically rapid healing-time of his wounds and scratches, which meant that within a few seconds he was always as good as new.

Things were beginning to change and deconstruct, so he knew something extraordinary was undoubtedly about to happen. For example, the tiles were beginning to come away from the floor and he had to move with care, because he had tripped over them many times. He had, indeed, broken most of the bones in his body. Of course, this didn't much matter because they knitted together almost immediately.

The room was never tranquil, because birds of one sort or another were constantly flying backwards and forwards through the thin arch; one little sparrow had even pecked its way into the back of a leather-covered upright chair, where it had built a nest. Ezra would have loved to talk to the birds so that he could ask them what was outside, but they seemed purposely to ignore him, being far too occupied with their own business.

"Don't you realise how very impolite you are,

using my home as a glorified roosting place, without so much as a please or a thank you? Why don't you go and bring up your families somewhere else; this isn't a nursery, you know? And please, please don't bring your leaves and twigs in here!" The only response was angry twittering, but it was better than nothing. It appeared to be a very lonely existence, but, in fact, the tools of his trade were remarkable, for they included two ghost-like, ethereal entities that hung from the wall above his table.

They never spoke but could communicate their ideas to him through a spiritual pathway, which was quite usual in that strange border between one universe and another. Whatever he required they would miraculously provide: test tubes, retorts, gears and pulleys, plants of all sorts, vegetables, fossils, even orreries. He needed the latter, especially at that time, because he was studying the motion of a far distant solar system. It was small and beautiful – you know the one I mean! It is situated somewhere in a galaxy known as the Milky Way, but please don't ask me how the entities managed to acquire all those objects because your guess is as good as mine!

On his table stood the remains of his last, but unfortunately, failed experiment. He absolutely loved music and had been aiming to create the most sublime notes in the universe that didn't yet exist and had, thus, never been heard before. He'd constructed an upright frame strung with five horizontal wires to emulate a musical stave. On the frame, he had arranged various small objects to represent notes, one on each wire: a knobbly potato, a blue feather, a pink (artificial) hydrangea, a series of hieroglyphics printed on a scrap of paper and, last of all, a piece of shining glass.

Nothing had happened, however. There had been no results, not a tinkle, not a sound, so he had abandoned the experiment and was now more interested in a blue marble that he'd seen on one of the orreries; he wondered what would it be like to live there. It appeared to be such a beautiful, peaceful place where there would be no need for confrontation.

As the days passed, Ezra's sense of isolation gradually grew. It was a rare emotion for him; he felt the need for company, even for love. There was no beautiful girl to take in his arms, no loving words to console him. Like everything else about his life, things were beginning to fall apart, not just the floor tiles; even his ghostly helpers were beginning to slide down the walls, leaving flakes of paint all over the place.

Their minds seemed preoccupied and they were so slow in providing him with the objects he needed that his experiments were becoming a burden – indeed, even a bit of a drag to put it more bluntly, "I'm starting to lose patience with you two and, if you don't buck up, I'll scrape you off the wall and chuck you out into the abyss. That'll teach you!"

There was, of course, no response.

For the first time, ever, science had become a hit-or-miss occupation for him and frustration set in; previously, he had been so successful. He was particularly disappointed not to have provided the universe with new music and, even today, adding a treble clef at the beginning of the stave, had not helped one jot.

He left his place at the table abruptly. Nervously he popped his head out of the arch as far as he dared. Because desperation had set in, he shouted at the top of his voice, "Please, please, bring me someone to love!" As he did so, he felt the room tilting and knew that, at any moment, everything in the universe was going to tip over the edge of the horizon and propel him towards a new one. His chair bumped across to him, nearly pushing him out into empty air, and he could hear crystals tinkling as they slid along the floor. Simultaneously, his musical frame burst forth into a symphony of true harmony with the most beautiful melody that had ever existed. If only he were not alone!

The potato, the feather, the hydrangea, the slip of paper and piece of glass were moving rhythmically back and forth, with great enthusiasm, along the wire stave. Alongside were five sparrows, like a chorus line, swaying to and fro, singing along with it: in tune and in pitch perfect. When a strong breeze whooshed through the arch he was whisked away from danger, swiftly.

To his amazement, when he looked back, he saw the strangest sight. Floating through the arch came a woman on a penny-farthing bicycle. She was pale and thin, but wore a wondrously exotic hat covered in flowers of every colour; it was a true work of art. Her body was clothed in black satin, which showed off the hat to perfection. The penny-farthing seemed not to have any pedals: an example of thought-locomotion, not an unknown phenomena, there, on the edge of nowhere. "I shall move into this room and share it with you," said Hagar. "You need looking after. And what a very untidy place you live in! Did your mother never teach you to tidy up after yourself?"

"How do I know? I never had a mother."

"Don't be silly, Ezra, everyone has had a mother of some sort." Ezra thought that it was just not true and that he had been placed in his room fully-formed, complete with all his scientific knowledge. His whole life had been spent in that tiny spot. *Confined in a prison* is how Hagar would have described it, but she would set him free and take him out on her bicycle, at that moment leaning again a wall. Ezra thought it looked terribly out of place as, indeed, did she …he just wanted her to leave.

He was beginning to feel peculiar and he saw that his hands resembled a jigsaw puzzle coming apart. Amazingly, his whole body looked the same! Every one of his component parts was crumbling into small pieces and the jigsaw puzzle was utterly ruined. In fact, he had unexpectedly died. He did not, however, pass instantly through a portal or membrane, or through a tunnel with a light at the end into a different existence. There was nothing spiritual about his departure; in other words, he was just plain dead.

His last sight was of the lady cyclist smiling down upon

him and it flitted through his mind, as the darkness of death enveloped him, that she was not someone he could ever have loved.

He would never know that her name was Hagar, but she had known all about him.

"You fool, Ezra," she said aloud to what was left of him, "you have wasted so much time and missed so much fun by not having the courage to exit through the arch." Truly, he'd been too self-contained, too afraid to branch out into the unknown. "Why didn't you show more bravery, Ezra? Why didn't you go beyond the boundary of your experience? You would have found the answers to so many of your questions. I've been everywhere, except, of course, beyond the edge, into the unknown. It's too late for you now, far too late, you silly man. You should have been more like me!"

However, Hagar was in for the shock of her life as the house suddenly toppled over, before she could even grab her bicycle, with the result that she, the bicycle and everything else, including many jigsaw pieces, fell into space.

She shouldn't have been so smug, so self-satisfied about her zest for exploration, for this was truly horrible. Bricks, plaster, chairs, birds twittering in panic, Ezra's two ghostly friends screaming for all they were worth (an unearthly sound, if ever there was one), the chair with the built-in sparrow's nest, the musical stave (now sounding flat and completely out of tune) …they all followed her. The terrible, spine-chilling journey was long, which only delayed the total horror of what was to come at its final destination.

Waiting for Hagar were sights that no human mind could imagine. Believe me, no one had ever before seen anything as horrific. It all looked so frightening, so disgusting, so much worse than your most nightmarish of dreams. There were, for example, leafless, brown trees covered in thorns and spines with translucent sacks hanging from them whose contents were so awful that I'm not competent to describe them. The birds suffocated to death and Hagar's heart almost stopped beating with fear as huge, slimy, green tentacles came towards her.

Ezra, the self-contained scientist, now a broken jigsaw puzzle, had joined in the mayhem as his ruined home had flown around in the open air like a whirlwind. However, he had been most fortunate and truly blessed not to have been alive; death was a far better option than having, like Hagar, to endure the dreadful experiences that awaited anyone who went beyond the edge of the universe.

Tightly Bound

The water was all around him and the tight, plastic sheet that had bound his body so that he couldn't move, was unwrapping itself. Jimmy could still see, but he knew that his eyes had gone and that only empty sockets remained. The crabs and small fish of the sea had had a feast. Soon only his skeleton would remain and the plastic sheeting would eventually float away.

A small octopus approached rapidly and wrapped its tentacles around his wrist seeming to enjoy this human contact. His next inquisitive visitor was a grouper fish that looked as though its blubbery lips had suffered a bad cosmetic job. It took a bite out of his nose and he could feel pain pulsing through his body, but, in some strange way, he enjoyed it and wished it would happen again. It showed, at least, that some of his nerve endings were alive and instilled a modicum of hope into his dire situation. Then an old woman's face, at the front of a fish body, glided past him; she grinned – her small, yellowing teeth seemed to offer him a threat. As bubbles gurgled out of her mouth, she seemed to be laughing. He didn't recognise her at all.

The sea was now growing more turbulent, its

colour darkening and an unexpected movement of water turned him over. Below him, he glimpsed two green reeds entwined as though making love and, on one of the pebbles where they were rooted, sat a gold ring with a sparkling diamond in the centre. Why it was here he couldn't imagine, but it somehow looked familiar. *Just let me wake up he thought and then I can perhaps make some sense of all this.* If he didn't wake up, however, if this wasn't a dream, if it wasn't some terrible nightmare, then why was he here? Who had done this to him? Had he been murdered, or had he simply died and been buried at sea? Was he going to be here forever? Was this what was meant by life after death? Was this hell, because it certainly wasn't heaven. Perhaps, limbo then!

The time for pondering came to an abrupt end. Incredibly, he felt his spirit, or whatever one liked to call it, rise above his ruined body. Thus, he witnessed it being battered, feeling no pain when it was thrown against the rocks underneath the towering cliffs that for many years had been so familiar to him.

This wasn't home; it was where they always used to spend their summer holidays. Every year he, his parents and his sister picnicked on these very same rocks and watched the waves rolling towards them as the tide came in.

After more thrashing and pummelling, the waters at last abandoned him like flotsam on a small stretch of wet sand, his gradually-loosening plastic shroud rustling and moving in the puffs of wind coming off the sea. How horrific he looked. Was this really how he had ended up? In the meantime, the story seemed to be continuing; he could hear voices calling out to him, so perhaps this wasn't his final fate after all. "Jimmy, Jimmy!" whispered the voices. "He's coming to get you. Hide yourself deep in the sand. Enclose yourself within the cliff face. Take refuge anywhere that comes to mind, but understand that there will be no escape so do not struggle too much against your destiny."

Gradually, the wind-blown words faded and ceased. Jimmy didn't understand because there didn't seem to be much more that anyone could do to him. The only mystery was the identity of his pursuer and why he was being pursued. He watched in fascination as the dreadful corpse disappeared into thin air. It might never have existed, and he became aware that the world had changed.

He now had a different body and, raising his arms he saw, with amazement, two smooth-skinned childlike hands. Their sand-encrusted finger-nails appeared before his eyes. A sound behind him made him turn and, stomach lurching, he saw a familiar red and white gingham cloth there, spread on a large rock. His parents and small sister were seated on rugs, tucking into sandwiches and cake.

"Come on, Jimmy, you can search for crabs later. Just sit down and have something to eat," said his mother gently.

Jimmy started to weep. "What on earth is the matter with you?" asked his father sternly.

"I just feel funny. Something's very wrong," he answered with hiccupping sobs. Something, however, was always very wrong in Jimmy's life.

So there the four of them sat, laughing and enjoying themselves before returning to their modest hotel – well, you never knew who might be watching. After all, a factory foreman must be seen to be doing well and looking after his little family, whatever might be passing through his mind. Such a happy little family, weren't they? So safely cocooned within their own little world, just like the seagulls nestling above them in the cliff face, feeding and protecting their young?

However, behind closed doors, with no one to watch them, no one to complain about what they might see, dynamics change, people adopt different roles, the play-acting stops and the characters become themselves. Dear little Carol, toddling on her baby legs, was suddenly swept off the carpet and thrown onto the sofa, her soft head hitting the hard, wooden arm, a piece of kitchen-roll stuffed into her mouth to silence her cries of pain. For poor Jimmy, there came a slap across the head: his punishment for not sitting down immediately at the picnic!

A torrent of whispered, ugly words escaped between clenched teeth so that no one else could hear them! All this was the harsh reality of Jimmy's carefree, childhood holiday, for his father was a beast of a man.

All at once, Luke – so unsuitable a name for such an unsaintly man, don't you think? – grabbed Audrey by the hair. "Take the bloody ring off. How many times have I to ask you the same thing, you silly cow?" Jimmy's mother began to weep. "Take it off, Audrey, or else …"

"You know it was my mother's and one day I want to hand it down to Carol."

"Don't you ever listen? We need the money" By this time he was almost breaking her wrist, twisting it with his large hand.

"I can't get it off, Luke!"

"In that case I'll have to help you, won't I?"

If a knife had been handy at that moment, such was his anger, that he would have simply cut her finger off and claimed the ring without giving it a second thought. Instead, he wrenched it off so roughly that blood flowed: the flesh torn, the bone broken and exposed.

Jimmy, shocked and appalled at the sight, gathered up all his courage, picked up the gory ring and ran with it, his heart about to burst with the effort. Luke, meanwhile, his arthritic legs hurting like hell, was no match for Jimmy and gave up the chase, waiting instead for his return when rough punishment would be meted out in a way that Jimmy would never forget.

Much later, in a coat closet, Jimmy was subjected to the most obscene treatment that a father could ever commit with his son.

"What did you think of that then, Jimmy?" Luke asked, the sweat running down his face. "That's called sodomy, Jimmy, the correct retribution for the little sod you have always been."

The gold ring, now washed clean by the sea near their picnic area, was protected by the two green embracing reeds like an egg cared for at the feet of its penguin parents. On that spot, it was destined to remain lost forever and a day.

Time, having no beginning, no end, going in whatever direction it chooses, forever altering speed, suddenly changed, for standing gazing down into the water where years ago he'd thrown the ring, Jimmy looked at his hands. They were bigger now, older, the nails carefully manicured. He touched his face and there was stubble.

Under the midday sun he could see his father crouching immobile behind a boulder, a blood-covered hammer in his hand. In front of the boulder was plastic sheeting held down by rocks so that it wouldn't fly away in the wind. Then he saw his father drag the body of a young man, about twenty-years old onto the plastic where it was tightly bound. He then shoved the whole bundle into the water. "Well, Jimmy, there will be no family skeletons coming out of the closet now?" laughed Luke, proud of his nasty, sick joke.

So, thought Jimmy, that's how he had met his end; now he understood. He was just another piece of garbage, fish-fodder, tossed into the great rubbish tip that the sea had become. The worst piece of garbage, however, was still on land, watching his son's corpse disappearing out into the ocean.

The story was not over however. In another part of the circle of existence, time, being uncertain, had moved forward. Now he could hear the sirens of police cars, see their red lights approaching through the darkness, faint moonlight shining on the water. He watched Luke being hustled out of one of the cars, saw him pointing out to sea, witnessed him babbling as though he couldn't stop. The words '*diamond ring*' carried towards him on the wind.

Was it perhaps a relief to Luke that his crime had been discovered? Had Audrey, in a moment of courage, told the police of the unspeakable abuse Jimmy had suffered as a child, of her suspicions over what had become of him since his disappearance all those years later and where his body might be? For surely, he was dead by now!

Luke had, of course, as a family member, been a main suspect as the police had searched for Jimmy, but it would seem that his glib tongue, easy ways and, above all, any lack of concrete evidence saved him until now. The investigation, by this time, had run cold and the case quietly shelved, put on the backburner, presumably until Audrey had said what she should have said a long, long time ago. So, the second time around things had changed. It would not now be the sea's buffeting that brought him back onto dry land, but an underwater search team.

Time, however, took a sudden detour and swung round on itself, taking a backward or, perhaps, it was a forward turn. It was such a nebulous, unquantifiable force that one could never tell, and events that repeated themselves were not always an exact replica of what had gone before. For example, Jimmy was somehow saddened when the little octopus this time seemed not to want to make contact and the blubbery-lipped grouper fish simply turned away from him.

So here was Jimmy again in his watery grave, but the reeds had grown: the ring and the pebbles now completely hidden. The fish with a woman's face, Audrey to a tee, again swam past him, this time not in the least threatening, but laughing with happiness. Behind her came a smaller fish, swimming frantically to keep up with her: surely it was Carole, carefree and dancing in the waves. How they had come to be here was just another mystery that perhaps, when the circle of time had turned again might be solved, questions answered.

A Very British Murder

Sabina, despite her rather exotic name, was British to the core and inordinately proud of the great favour that destiny had bestowed upon her. During her thirty years she had several times left these hallowed shores to see something of the world, but it had all been nothing but a disappointing failure – too hot, too cold and, let's face it, even the flora wasn't anything to shout out about! Why go to the tropics, when there were palm trees in Bournemouth?

What more could you possibly ask for?

To get a taste of South American jungles steaming with heat, or dry desert places, you only had to buy a bus ticket to Kew Gardens and there it all was!

Sabina was a pretty enough woman, but not a great beauty and certainly didn't feature in any young man's fanciful dreams. Thus, her social life was bleak, saved only by the Young Conservatives of which she was a fervent member. This gave her the outlet she needed to feel useful and to meet other people.

Who but the Conservative Party could possibly raise the standards that had been allowed to lapse so sadly during the last few years?

Queen and Country was Sabina's motto and the sooner the Empire was re-instated the better for everyone!

Fortunately, or unfortunately, depending on how you feel about that sort of thing, nature had given Sabina a strong libido and, as her hormones were usually racing at top speed, it was something that she could not easily ignore. Colin, therefore, who lived over the road and was a quiet, unassuming sort of chap had his definite uses. She had first met him at a Young Conservatives' jolly and discovered their political views to be pretty well in tune.

Poor Colin, however ...pasty looking, sensitive, and very clever, was your typical nerd: with glasses and clothes that were too big for him. He lived alone, which was convenient for Sabina: she had only to worry about his cat, Guy, who had a huge body with a personality to match. He was, actually, a damned nuisance, for he was very vociferous and made her sneeze.

The room was stiflingly hot, the fireplace being full of flaming logs. Colin had turned the lights off and there was just the gentle glow of candlelight coming from the shelf where he usually kept his collection of science fiction books. The shelf now looked like an altar, for on the wall behind the candles, hung a framed portrait of a rather odd, kingly figure with pink lips and rouged cheeks, his crown slightly askew. Across his royal robes someone, presumably Colin, had written in red felt-tip pen a very disgusting scatological opinion of him.

Under this painting, as though on guard, lay Guy his yellow eyes gleaming, keenly watching the action.

Sabina, in the meantime, was tied by a strong rope to the top of the dining table, which was covered with a Union Jack. She was completely naked as Colin, in an unusual moment of frenzy, had excitedly removed all her clothes. Her imagination by this time was in overdrive wondering what he was going to do to her next. As she was lying on her stomach she was hoping that it would be the latest fun trick that she had taught him …and the rope, well, that was an added piece of ingenuity. Perhaps Colin was finally becoming more enterprising in his old age.

He'd taken off his jacket and was bending over the table, his hands outstretched in front of him. The flickering light shone through his white shirt-sleeves, illuminating his thin arms like some winged insect against the rays of the sun.

"You should not have done that, Sabina. It was a very un-British, very foolish thing to have suggested and I am deeply disappointed in you. So, my dear, you will be punished accordingly."

Colin's voice was most definitely no longer that of a nerd. His tone was now totally suited to the judge's wig that he had placed ceremoniously upon his head at the start of the proceedings. The cat had wondered if it was something edible! Colin suddenly lifted one hand and pointed towards the hearth. There stood the fireside companion set, with its tongs, shovel and poker: especially, its poker.

"Oh, no! Please don't, Colin. I didn't mean any harm by it and you've always so much enjoyed it before." She had an inkling of what this gesture had meant, but surely, he wouldn't, he couldn't really carry it through – could he?

"Well, I've changed my mind and today I feel shocked, shocked to the core. The sins of Sodom and Gomorrah have no place in this house or, indeed, in Britain. Let dirty foreigners keep their dirty, little sexual habits in their own dirty, fly-ridden countries. We don't want them here in this God-fearing, sceptred isle."

"Don't be silly, Colin, you don't really think that we are the first couple to have done that, do you?"

"You tempted me, Sabina, as Eve tempted Adam, and I fell for your wiles. I have sinned gravely and one day will probably go to hell for what you made me do."

"Really, Colin, haven't you ever watched "Sin in the City" – they're all at it there!"

For this he slapped her hard across the face. "American filth!" The cat waved his tail excitedly at this; he obviously enjoyed watching a bit of the rough stuff.

"No, just a reflection of what some people get up to!" shouted Sabina, despite her stinging jaw. "Anyway, Colin, what's this all about? I feel rather like a sacrificial lamb. And what did the man in the picture do to upset you so?"

"How very perceptive of you, Sabina, for a sacrificial lamb is exactly what you are."

Fumbling in his pocket, he took out a rather crumpled, black hanky that he placed over his wig. "You have been condemned to die, for polluting this green and pleasant land, in exactly the same way as the sodomite in the picture, King Edward the Second."

"But Colin he died when they put…"

"Exactly, Sabina!" As he spoke, he placed the poker in the fire, holding it there until it was red hot.

Poor Sabina, her screams of agony must have been heard all over the town. At least her suffering would have been short-lived and, as compensation, she had shared her fate with a king of England: for her the most sacred place in all the world.

The Daily Balderdash, both on line and in the press, had an absolute field day with this story, for news was a little sparse at the time. They were grateful to Colin for filling up their website and keeping their readers happy. The gruesome murder scene, Colin's trial, the life and times of Edward the Second and the *naughties* that his subjects got up to, plus his burningly painful death, all made great copy and perhaps, more importantly, made a lot of money for their advertisers.

Even an animal therapist was brought in to write an article on the trauma that the horrific event would have caused Guy. Well, anything about animals is always close to British hearts, isn't? Why, Guy even had his photo on the website which meant that hordes of school children and loads of doddering, old ladies sent him goodies accompanied by hundreds of letters with lots of kisses at the end.

The police had no difficulty in putting the facts together and there was certainly no mystery surrounding the murder, which was a bit disappointing for the Daily Balderdash. Though, as recompense, they'd had plenty of blood and guts with which to entertain everyone and what they didn't have they could always make up!

Mealtime

George was chomping away at his supper. His mother had tried to instil all sorts of good manners into his head, but to absolutely no avail. The meat was raw, which was how they all liked it, so his chin, as usual, was covered in blood and juices.

They were a very dysfunctional family. There didn't appear to be much kinship among them, as if they were three separate beings who had just happened to cross each other's path. Mother was a plump, moody character who, like George, was a big eater. Whenever there was food around she would shovel it down as though there were no tomorrow. Savouring a lovely taste didn't enter the equation for her.

Father, an expert huntsman, was definitely the head of the household and would almost growl with greediness when food was present; the other two always had to wait for their turn until he had satisfied his hunger. Only then would he slow down and allow them to share what was left.

Eating and love-making were his two most important impulses, but it was lust not love, pure basic sex that he desired. Not surprisingly, more offspring were soon on the way, which pleased neither parent. George was livid when he discovered the truth. Food was his main concern, and more offspring would mean less stomach-fodder for him.

Detective Sergeant Clarke, standing on the front step, rang the doorbell and heard someone scrambling towards him from inside the house.

"Where is she?" screamed Minnie's mother hysterically. "Has someone taken her? Help us, please! Just tell us that everything will be all right." Minnie's father, white as a ghost, was more controlled but, even so, was shaking like a leaf as he put his arm around his wife's shoulder.

"Believe me, we are doing all we can to find her. No stone will be left unturned"

DS Clarke had a bad feeling about this case; Minnie was the third little girl to go missing within the last couple of months. The other two had been found dead in shocking circumstances, sexually assaulted and with deep scratches all over their bodies.

Minnie loved everything that was pink. In other words, she was a typical little girl, pink socks and shoes for her feet, pink slides and Alice bands for her hair. The last time her parents had seen her she was wearing her favourite, flowery, summer dress. The happy little family, full of love for each other, had gone into the forest to enjoy a picnic. Delicious food of all sorts had come out of the basket – sandwiches of almost any filling you could imagine and, finally, Minnie's favourite pink cupcakes. Now, however, it seemed as though the forest had swallowed her up. She was only six-years-old but modest in her behaviour, and so had disappeared alone behind a nearby bush to spend a penny.

Nevertheless, Minnie didn't evaporate into thin air, for the picnic had been observed by big, bulky Terry who loved little girls. He would often take day-trips down to Weston-Super-Mare so that he could watch them on the beach, taking photos of them in their cute, little bikinis or, better still, wearing nothing. More additions for his vast pornographic collection! On the other hand, little boys were quite safe from his prying eyes and his dirty mind. Terry really was a nasty piece of work!

One hour after he snatched her away, Minnie was mercifully lying dead, buried in the earth, under a pile of leaves that hid any signs of disturbance.

It was George who was instrumental in finding her.

"It's about time you stopped lounging around and went out into the forest to practise your hunting skills, such as they are," ordered his father. He was frightened of his father and there was no way that he would disobey. So, with his bushy tail and pointed ears in a state of alertness, he left the foxes' lair. All at once he yelped in triumph for he had found something – a substantial something. Father was delighted with his find, which was pushed and dragged back to the lair.

That evening they had a wonderful meal and, for virtually the first time ever, father praised George, even smiling at him, if you could call it that! Then they all tucked into the tender meat until all at once mother began to choke, gasping for air and desperately trying to catch her breath. Father got up and hit her hard on the back which made her suddenly spit out what was caught in her throat. It was a pink hair slide. Mother was so upset that she told George to take the wretched thing outside the lair and to leave it on the ground so that it would cause no further problems.

"Why didn't you notice it in the first place, you stupid boy?"

"I didn't think about it. And what does it matter anyway?"

"Don't you dare speak to your mother like that!" roared father. George earned a painful bite on the neck for his insolence.

Why Terry had turned out to be such a bastard was anyone's guess. His mother had at first thought that like all teenagers he was simply interested in the opposite sex. He also did horrible things to animals, but again she thought that this too was probably quite normal in a growing lad. As the years passed, however, she could see that there was something not quite right about him.

Now at forty-two he had no friends, no feelings towards others – in other words he was a loner, completely antisocial, spending hours in front of his computer with the door locked.

Little girls were easy prey and gave him a feeling of power that he did not experience anywhere else. Pretty little girls like Minnie were especially appealing and, unfortunately for her, he now needed to kill his victims to complete his satisfaction. Somewhere Terry had a father, but his whereabouts were a mystery, so it was only his mother who gave him any love. It was because of this love that she was frightened to take him to see anyone about his little peccadilloes in case it all turned out to be true. Words like psychopath and psychotic would perhaps have best described his mental state, but to his mother, a simple woman, they might as well have been double Dutch.

"Mummy, can I ask you something?"

"Of course you can, my sweet one!"

"Is it wrong to like little girls?"

"If it was wrong, people wouldn't want daughters, would they?"

"That's not what I mean, mummy. I mean . . ."

At that moment, she stopped him and put her hands over her ears to shut out his voice.

Terry's interest in small girls had not gone unnoticed in the area; the way he stood watching them through the school gates at playtime, the way he gave them sweeties. The police had interviewed him, but nothing had come of this. He was just one of the town's misfits

Jo-Jo, the white horse, went up to the paddock fence because she recognised her visitor. It was Terry who will surely have brought her a couple of carrots before taking her out for a slow ride through the forest.

Her owners were used to Terry and knew that he loved Jo-Jo almost as much as they did. He wasn't much of a rider, but good enough not to come to any harm. They were the only people with whom he ever had any real human contact except, of course, for his mother.

For some unaccountable and perfectly above-board reason Terry had always loved horses. One day, walking past the paddock on the road leading to the forest, they had all started to chat and, recognising his enthusiasm, Jo-Jo's owners had agreed to teach him gradually how to ride.

Four days had now gone by and DS Clarke knew that by this time there was only an outside chance of finding Minnie alive.

Her parents were wretched with despair as their hopes of a happy outcome slowly waned. Throughout the area there were flyers posted on tree trunks and in shop windows and naturally the media were full of it: in the newspapers, on television and on the radio. Neighbours and friends organised themselves into groups, methodically scouring the area. Every garden shed, every likely nook and cranny was searched, but it was all to no avail.

Minnie's mother, heavily sedated, prayed for her return. "Come home to mummy, baby. Please, come home. We love you so much!" she whispered, her heart breaking.

It was an overcast day as Terry set off on his ride and he could feel drops of rain wetting his shirt. As he rode through the forest he bent his head to avoid the tree branches. He thought he might see if he could identify Minnie's grave – he wasn't a hundred per cent sure that he could remember its exact position, but he knew that he would eventually find it. It would be such a pleasure to recall the event and he just hoped that it would not be long before he could repeat the experience.

On his next visit to Weston-Super-Mare he might try following a little girl onto the dunes and there, hidden from prying eyes, he could follow the strongest impulse he knew. It seemed only fitting to choose Weston-Super-Mare where he had enjoyed so many erotic sights on its various beaches: Sand Bay Beach, Uphill Beach, Brean Beach and so forth.

This would never happen, however, because being a mediocre horseman it only needed a fox called George suddenly to cross his path, causing Jo-Jo to rear up. Terry lost complete control of the horse. Perhaps Minnie lying in the earth heard the satisfactory sound of his neck snapping in two, severing his brainstem.

Heaven only knew how many more small souls George had unwittingly saved. Naturally his only thought had been of how proud his father would be of him – his second big find within only a few days!

"What happened there, then, George? I could smell the meat! So where is it?"

George went to a corner of the lair and put his head between his paws trying to avoid his punishment.

The police, overwhelmed with sadness at finding Minnie's pink hair slide and what remained of her body, nevertheless tried to think positively; it was the only way they could possibly face a job like theirs. At least the murderer had been identified and would do no more harm. Minnie's parents and Terry's mother were the ones who were going to suffer the agony most and for evermore.

The only happy ending to the whole sad story was that Jo-Jo had been unhurt and was led contentedly back to her paddock where she enjoyed a meal of oats, carrots and even a sugar cube or two.

A Random Journey

Miss Witherspoon was a devoted existentialist. If you had asked her what this meant, she would not have had the foggiest idea how to answer you. Well, having left the local Secondary Modern School sixty years ago with only a vague knowledge of reading and writing, it was a pretty sure guess that she knew absolutely damn all about Jean-Paul Sartre and existentialism. The only type of philosophy known to her was of the home-grown sort, but she did sometimes hold in-depth discussions with Mouser her cat, which did perhaps verge on the philosophic.

"Now where did the time go, Mouser! I love crime films, but they go so quickly. *Midsomer Murders* is over in two minutes, but the news just drags on forever! Why do you think that is?"

Mouser gave her a bemused look.

"There's no rhyme or reason to it, is there? It must be pure chance, just like life in general. Everything is completely random."

Mouser thought she was getting out of her depth here. She was a nice old biddy, but a bit eccentric with no logic to her thinking.

"When I'm dying, will it all drag on a bit, rather like the news, or will everything whiz by? Will there then be silence just like there is when I turn the telly off? I suppose really, it's just a question of chance, don't you think? Perhaps some people go on forever into another life, because there's no other way for it. Do you think death will be rather like music where one note simply has to follow another?"

"Hold on" thought Mouser, "we're getting in a bit deep here, aren't we?"

Suddenly the rather scuffed and battered ancient grandmother clock told them that it was ten o'clock: in other words, time for bed.

She had to be up early in the morning for it was washing day. Also, Dr Sycamore, emeritus professor in mechanical engineering at Swilgate University who was her next-door neighbour, wanted her round at his house at nine o'clock on the dot, to give the place a good clean. She'd had a very bad bout of flu and so had been unable to do this for several weeks.

Miss Witherspoon, like Mouser, always did exactly as she wanted – no one could ever persuade her to do otherwise. Rules and regulations were a lost cause for her. "It's my life and I'll do what I want with it," was her prevailing thought. This of course was limited by her finances.

It was sometimes rather difficult for Dr Sycamore to put up with her, but she was such a good worker that he was prepared to accept her little peccadilloes. Also, having her living next door was very convenient as she was always prepared to cater for any little tea-parties with his old university chums.

The next day it was with a rather heavy heart that he watched her tottering up the path with a whole collection of new cleaning materials in a sparkling, blue bucket. Nevertheless, he felt a certain excited anticipation at the sight of her because he had a little scheme up his sleeve that she might quite enjoy – or not as the case may be! He noticed too that as usual Mouser had come along, which might make the experiment he had in mind even more interesting.

Dr Sycamore had a soft spot for Mouser, because sometimes, looking into the cat's eyes, he could see a mysterious something that for the life of him he could not define. He was a cat, who like his mistress, knew what he wanted, and Dr Sycamore hoped that Mouser would agree to come on the journey that he had in mind.

Looking at the house closely Miss Witherspoon could see that it needed a bit of tender, loving care. There were cobwebs on the ceiling, some with spiders still in residence and lots of dust on the furniture. The kitchen and the bathroom were spotless as was only to be expected from Dr Sycamore.

"I'm delighted to see you again, dear lady. If you should begin to feel a little under the weather, just tell me and we'll go and have a little drink of something in the study. Perhaps a sweet sherry wouldn't go amiss for you, though how you can drink the stuff I'll never know" He was actually hoping that he might be able to draw her into the study so that they could sit there together and have a little chinwag. "Give me a gin and tonic anytime!"

"Mornin', Dr. S. 'Ow are you doing then? It's good to see you again, too. I think Mouser would like something to drink, if you don't mind and perhaps one of those wafer biscuits 'e likes, if you've remembered to get some in. If you 'aven't 'e won't be too chuffed and 'e'll want to go back home."

Naturally there were wafer biscuits for Mouser, for he never forgot to buy them, and also a new bottle of sweet sherry.

Many were the cups of tea and plates of sandwiches consumed by Doctor Sycamore's academic guests. They were cucumber sandwiches, of course because this was deemed by Miss Witherspoon to be, what she termed *'the poshest of all fillings'*. Horror of horrors if you were suffering from diverticulitis and the seeds got stuck in the little pouches in your colon! Well, that was just your bad luck! It was cucumber or nothing!

These tea parties were incredibly tense and, if things went as hoped, would change the world, not just in the present, but also in the past, so that nothing would ever again be certain and assured.

Eventually, so great was Dr Sycamore's excitement that he could wait no longer and invited Miss Witherspoon and Mouser into his study, a small room where nothing was ever out of place. Today, however, a strange machine stood on his desk, somewhat like a large computer. Red, green and yellow lights flashed and winked on its surface and the whole thing was humming and throbbing. Also, there were sparkling, silver wires lining the four walls of the room – what a strange sight! Whatever did it mean?

"What in the world is this, Dr S?" asked Miss Witherspoon as he poured her out a sherry.

"It's a time machine!" the doctor declared, his voice rising in excitement.

"Where's the Tardis then?" she asked, thinking she was making a joke.

"We're in it now, but we've named it Timon – short for the Time Machine of Now. My colleagues and I have been working on it for a long time. But we've not advanced enough in our experiments to be to be able to calculate with much accuracy where we might end up in our little journey through time. To be quite honest with you it's all a bit of a gamble, the destination a completely random one."

"Rather like life in general!" Miss Witherspoon thought.

"My companions aren't too keen on accompanying me and think we should wait until everything is at a more advanced stage. But I want to go now, Miss Witherspoon, and was just hoping that you, dear lady, might like to come with me, or may I perhaps call you Winnie after so many years of knowing each other?"

Mouser flicked his ears and tail at this familiarity, sensing a momentary sense of discomfort emanating from Miss Witherspoon. What on earth was he suggesting? Nothing improper, nothing inappropriate, hoped Mouser who was quite a prim and proper little creature.

"Your friends 'aven't got much sense of adventure, 'ave they? Life is what we make of it! And yes, you may call me Winnie, Dr. Sycamore.

Well, that reply certainly allayed Mouser's fears.

"What era would you choose to visit, but just remember that there is no guarantee that's where we would end up?"

"That's easy! I just love *Upstairs, Downstairs* and *The Duchess of Duke Street* and, of course, *Downton Abbey*. So, for me it must be Edwardian times."

Doctor Sycamore personally favoured a meeting with Gutenberg, the inventor of the movable-type printing press, so it was back to the fifteenth century for him. He thought that in some mysterious way the fact he knew not one single word of German would not be a problem and that he and Herr Gutenberg would be able to communicate with no trouble at all.

No one, of course, asked Mouser if he had any opinion on the subject which he most definitely did.

Professor Greystones who held the chair of philosophy at Swilgate had suggested that perhaps the power of the mind would be their greatest help and that focusing their thoughts on where they wanted to go was perhaps their greatest chance of success.

"We're ready to go, are we? Don't be afraid of the noise!" said Dr Sycamore.

The study shook and trembled and there was, indeed, a most horrifying sound. Cement and bricks flew in all directions as the room was torn from the rest of the house as the time machine sent them on their way. The neighbours were in a complete state of panic and when the police and the television crews arrived it all became headline news, especially in the Daily Balderdash Online that changed its opinion by the minute as to what had happened.

The Edwardian era passed by, as did fifteenth century Germany, so where on earth were they headed – hopefully not to their death?

All at once the study lurched and everything then became quiet and calm – obviously their destination had been reached. Miss Witherspoon realised that Mouser was missing and hoped that nothing bad had happened to him.

She and the doctor clambered through one of the holes in the wall, all the while calling out Mouser's name. They had finally entered into the unknown, only aware of the smell of incense and the sound of chanting. The dusty gloom, aided by the flaming torches on the walls of the temple, gradually dispersed. Seated in front of them was Mouser the demi-god wearing his golden earrings, a golden scarab on his forehead and his neck adorned with lapis lazuli and with even more gold. His fur was brushed and scented, his eyes gleaming in triumph and satisfaction. By his side sat his master and companion, Tuthmosis, crown prince of Egypt.

Bald-headed priests dressed in their simple, linen robes and papyrus shoes knelt reverently before Mouser. He'd certainly fallen on his four paws here, thought Dr Sycamore. Mouser, himself, was so pleased that he'd had enough mental strength to rise from a state of mere existence to find his true essence and had been able to direct the time machine to this magical world. Most humans were so stupid and blind that they couldn't understand the superior power of cats.

When the time-machine returned home, they would find that the course of history had been changed. Well, when you interfere with time that is bound to happen. Mouser knew that the hour to leave was upon them. Dr Sycamore, however, would have liked to remain there longer to discover further wonders of the ancient civilisation, but that was just not possible – too much harm would be done.

Miss Witherspoon was so pleased to have found Mouser that she just wanted to get home as quickly as possible, while all three of them were still safe and sound. Dr Sycamore inspected his rather battered study, but it didn't look too bad and should be able to make the return journey successfully.

The next day The Daily Balderdash, the police and the neighbours were very surprised to find that the house seemed to be in perfect order – had they dreamed the disaster, had it not really happened at all? However, on the inside it was a different matter. The demi-god was now human-size and very, very plump. Between his two claws he held one of the doctor's cigars and drank a strong gin and tonic, both lit and poured for him by Miss Witherspoon.

In houses all over the world similar scenes were occurring- the best armchairs now occupied by large, lazy felines. There were not even any stray cats around searching for scraps to eat, for they were now all worshipped and adored. Perhaps it is always better to leave history alone and simply let it develop naturally. This, at any rate, was Dr. Sycamore's conclusion. There would be no more journeys through time for him.

Butter Me No Parsnips

The cat, his head full of wisdom, sat on the window sill and pondered upon the stupidity of mankind. The state of the hovel was disgusting, he thought; he, himself, was forever licking and tugging at his fur to make sure that it was in pristine condition and so did not understand these awful conditions.

Perched atop the back of a splintered, wooden chair was a moth-eaten owl who had definitely seen better days, but seemed unwilling to do anything to rectify his lack-lustre look. He just sat there staring into space, unconnected with what was happening around him, not even interested enough to blink. The cat simply did not understand this strange creature who, to his way of thinking, was emitting a very strange smell that he did not recognise.

Grime was engrained in the walls, on the broken-down furniture and in the tattered curtains. The stone floor was scattered with leaves that had blown in through the door, which was half off its hinges and there were mouse-droppings decorating the top of a rickety, very ancient table leaning precariously against the wall, its legs just about to collapse under it.

Surveying the fire crackling in the grate, the cat thought that he might later move nearer to it, for a strong draught was making its way towards him. He needed warmth, and the smell of meat boiling away in a cooking pot over the flames was making him feel hungry. His fastidiousness did not extend as far as being put off by the filthy fingernails of those doing the cooking.

"You know you can do it, Abigail," muttered Cressida, jealous that she had not been the chosen one.

"Your spells are darker and more potent than ours. Therefore, you must do it if we are to succeed," chimed in Esme, with an unctuous smile.

"Please, Abigail, for you're the most able of the four of us," begged Mercy. "And we will loyally follow your instructions to the letter. Just tell us what to do."

"Kind words butter no parsnips, sisters! Just let's see if I can really do this. On second thoughts, I am wondering why none of you wants this challenge, for we've all suffered at the hands of this accursed knave. May his soul one day soon be in the fiery pit of hell."

"So mote it be!" was the other three witches' response.

They were all seated in the middle of the room at a small, round, three-legged table. Abigail was feeling anxious, hoping that their buttering her parsnips had not been in vain and that she was up to the task set before her. With elbows resting on the table top, heels tapping nervously upon the flagstones, nails digging into her palms, she firmly set out their agenda.

"Matthew has cruelly mocked our sisterhood and our arcane mysteries. He must, therefore, be punished; I truly believe he should pay for his sins with his life. Do you not agree, sisters?"

"Yes," Esme whispered. "He shall be banished to another world, to a world of eternal nightmares."

"So mote it be," they droned in unison.

The cat was wondering what the owl thought of this turn of events, but the owl just stared vacantly into the distance, giving no hint of his opinions.

Esme was studying her Grimoire, her Book of Shadows with its pages stuffed with spells and recipes that would cover all eventualities. She would not be using her broomstick any time in the near future, so she had placed it down by her feet, hoping that the cat would not paw at it or gnaw at it, as it sometimes liked to do when in a playful mood. As she turned the pages, her eyes suddenly alighted on the very thing needed for their purpose and she handed it over to Abigail for her perusal.

Abigail became excited and announced that the solution for banishing the miscreant to the flaming furnaces of Hell had been found. Setting her pointed, black hat even more firmly on her head, her ugly, wizened face with its long, beaked nose and equally long chin became even more repulsive. The cat shook for he did not like any of this one little bit.

"Well done, my beloved sister, my Esme full of guile and mischief. Go, Cressida, fetch paper, ink and a quill. I shall inscribe the sacred spell onto this parchment." At this point the wind whistled ominously down the chimney, the fire spluttered and the candle standing in the middle of the table threatened to extinguish itself, leaving them all in darkness.

Abigail dipped the quill into the ink and carefully copied the deadly spell to make sure that there were no mistakes; then she would cast it. Thus wrote Abigail:

My sisters and I beg our great Master Lucifer to send our enemy Matthew, our denigrator Matthew, to deepest hell for scorning us, for laughing at us, for doubting us and all those who follow the paths of witchcraft.

By the power of our sorcery

To Matthew bring death,

Bring him surely to his doom

Before the setting of the moon.

"So mote it be!" she said aloud, thus completing her prayer.

"So mote it be!" the others repeated.

They all unsteadily dragged their cast iron cauldron in front of the fire. Exhausted by this effort, they then sat down again at the table where they imbibed a good swig of March ale. Abigail, in danger of burning her hand from the flames, cautiously lit the piece of paper, their petition to Satan, and dropped it into the cauldron where it disintegrated into ashes.

Meanwhile her fellow sorceresses screeched, their voices croaking and scratching the air, "Die, Matthew! Die, Matthew, die, die, die!" This became a chant and they tottered to their feet, repeating it over and over and over again. They attempted to dance, but were somewhat the worse for wear, having consumed a hefty amount of the March ale.

Cressida's wrinkled face, already disfigured by large warts, became even more contorted as she started to scratch her face in agitation. In fact, her ravaged visage looked as though it were moving: a trick of the light, no doubt, but the cat knew differently, for he had watched the witches so many times in the past. She almost fell over and her face shifted even more. It was an horrendously ugly sight, which quite put the thought of food out of the cat's mind, although he realised what was causing it.

There was something not quite right, he thought, about this whole affair for they were all acting with an evil intent and true viciousness that he had never witnessed before.

By the time the ritual was over they were almost hysterical and the cat, beside himself, jumped onto the rickety table by the wall, which collapsed under his weight onto the floor making a great clatter that added even more drama to the whole occasion.

The cat was almost frightened to death and scampered back onto the window sill to see what would happen next.

The owl remained untouched by it all and sat calmly perched on the back of the chair.

The tension and theatricality of the scene was suddenly broken by the ringing of Cressida's smartphone.

"What have you always been told about switching off your phone?"

"Don't speak to me in that tone of voice, Abigail. Are you so perfect, then?"

"It's not about being perfect. It's about breaking the atmosphere. There's no way now that we can possibly recapture the moment. You've spoiled it completely." The silly tune coming from Cressida's phone was annoying all of them. Even the cat was of the opinion that it was truly awful: a real caterwauling.

"Well, why don't you answer it, then?" grumbled Esmé.

None of them realised just how much this was going to change everything; they would never forget the movement of Cressida's hand opening the pink cover of her phone and swiping the screen to access the call. As in a dream they would forever recall her removing her warty witch's mask and seeing the ashen colour of her face. She stood immobile, silent, lost and then sat down heavily on one of the wooden chairs. A tortured sound escaped from her throat.

"He's dead ...Matthew is dead ...my brother is dead." She gazed ahead, seeing nothing, her eyes filling with tears. For some unaccountable reason, she would always remember the taste of the salt that her tears left on her tongue.

Mercy, wanting to know the whys and wherefores of everything, was the first to speak. "But ...how? It just can't be true."

Abigail, shocked and stunned, was overwhelmed.

What powers did she possess, what demon had taken over her mind and body to allow her to bring about such a tragedy? It had all been a game, an innocent piece of fun, nothing serious, just an excuse to dress up, do a bit of play acting, have a few drinks, eat a pleasant meal. The thought flitted through her mind that her parsnips had been too well-buttered.

A sudden, completely unexplained heart attack had killed the unfortunate Matthew, but surely it was a sheer coincidence, they reasoned, that this should occur while they were trying to send him to hell. He'd been a very naughty boy who, at eighteen years of age, should have known better than to taunt four friends who just loved their witches' frolics, so he had been made the butt of their games. After all, they had not teased him about his collection of Star Trek memorabilia.

Cressida remained slumped on the chair, her hands loosening their hold on her phone, which slowly slipped to the floor. She began to sob piteously.

Mercy removed the pointed hat from Cressida's head, washed her grubby face and hands with a wet wipe and cleaned her grimy fingernails with the file that she always carried in her bag.

She then, almost ceremoniously, stacked their broomsticks into a pile knowing that they would never return.

Esme put the stuffed owl into her duffle bag. It was a fine example of the taxidermist's art and greatly prized by her grandmother from whose house she had taken it without asking. She also added the Grimoire: in truth, an empty notebook.

The cat was disappointed that they were leaving, for knowing that there was usually food about when they were there, he always sensed when their visits were imminent.

Mercy and Esme touched the cauldron for the last time: a farewell to an old friend. They said a sad goodbye to the hovel and everything contained therein. "So mote it be," they intoned sadly, all the while wondering what evil they had let loose.

The cat did not follow them. He was a stray and valued his independence. As the witches had not eaten the succulent-smelling meat, he sat cosily in the hearth near the dying embers waiting until the cooking pot had cooled sufficiently for him to be able to partake of an exceptionally good meal.

The years passed quickly, but no one forgot that terrible evening. They had to live through the funeral and all the dreadful sorrow associated with Matthew's death.

At the service Abigail was forced to bite her lips and clasp her hands firmly together to stop herself rushing up the aisle towards the coffin and announcing that she had caused all this misery; she was the instigator, she was the Devil's daughter who had made this perpetual void in Matthew's family's midst.

Tarot cards, fortune telling, the reading of palms, Ouija boards, in fact, anything that hinted at the supernatural was simply no longer tolerated. Why, even magic turns on television made her change channels and, as for auditioning for a part in 'Blithe Spirit', well, that was definitely out... That is, until the day when she decided that she had had enough of her whinging husband. Nothing she did ever pleased him. Her lover was a much better proposition: richer, more handsome and easy going.

"I adore you, Abigail, truly, truly adore you," said her lover.

It was while she was lying in his arms that, in desperation, she decided upon a solution for her marital problems that would not fail. She would dispose of her husband; not with a knife, not with poison, not with a bullet. Why should she not use her devil-given gift and cast a spell? There would be nothing, after all, to connect her to the crime; it would all be so simple.

The cat was old, but still full of wisdom and common sense. He watched her enter, wearing a newly purchased Halloween witch's costume.

"Hello, cat. You still here, then?"

"Yes, I'm still here," he said silently to her, "but I see that you have not brought a basket. Where's the food, then?" The broomsticks still lay piled up on the floor, the cauldron still stood in front of the fire. Abigail took a candle out of her bag and lit it with her cigarette lighter.

Then out she crept into the dark night, the moon lighting her steps, to collect twigs and branches with which to make a fire. Above her an owl hooted and she saw him swoop to the ground to sweep a rat away in his talons. It crossed her mind to wonder if Esme had inherited the stuffed owl from her grandmother.

The flames sparkled and danced in the hearth and the cat moved nearer. He watched Abigail writing her petition to the Devil, this time using a Biro. He could sense spirits gathering around her as she performed the task.

See him in deepest Hell,

Ring, ring the tolling bell.

Lord of Darkness hear my plea.

May his soul quickly flee

Into the fiery pit, Near the throne, Devil Lord, where you sit.

Abigail said quietly to herself, "Well, it's not exactly Shakespeare."

The discerning cat, who knew about those things, thought to himself, "Well, you're right there!"

The petition was burned in the cauldron. Then Abigail picked up one of the broomsticks, held it out wide and, as it shed years of dust, she danced around the hovel chanting her incantation.

What worried the cat, however, was that she had not actually named her victim, so who, he wondered, was very soon going to die: a husband, a lover, a friend, the butcher, the baker or the candlestick maker?

It was not until later that same night when she received the eagerly awaited phone call that she realised her mistake; it had all gone so tragically, horribly wrong. Worse still, she had knowingly condemned someone to death. Hate or love him she had begged the Devil to take his soul.

The cat was never to know whom Abigail had dispatched to the great hereafter. Suffice to say she wept profusely, eaten up with guilt at what she had done – again – and rightly so.

"That was a very dangerous game you played," the cat thought, watching her tears fall, "but if that's what you really wanted to achieve, so mote it be."

Dear Reader

Dear Reader,

It's not usual for a writer to address himself directly in the form of a published letter to his public. I am an exception, however, because I've been a bit of a naughty boy and feel that I should confess. Who better to be my confessor than you? – however many of you there may be! (It's only when I receive the royalties that I shall have an approximate idea of your number).

Being an author means that you spend an inordinate amount of time alone, ensconced in that refuge of a computer room, or study, or whatever you might like to call it. Because of this, your friends and family don't have to wonder where you are, because they assume that they have a pretty good idea. If you want an alibi for your whereabouts, become a writer.

I'm a travel expert with a weekly column in a national newspaper, which, in principle, is the same as being a proper author – apologies to my fellow columnists! Again, it's a good opening for creating alibis – people expect you to be elsewhere, doing travel blogs or researching foreign climes: Rome, Tokyo, Timbuktu – who knows where?

I always insist on doing my work alone. I don't want to be traipsing all over the world with my family in tow, cramping my style, knowing what I'm up to. I need to be able to concentrate without their mithering me – well, at least that's my excuse to them.

I'm finding it quite liberating talking to you, so you are doing me a valuable service. Therefore, thank you in advance for listening to my confession. Confessing to a priest wouldn't, I'm afraid, work for me, for I'm an unbelieving sort of chap.

A few weeks ago I was spending what I hoped would be a very productive and satisfactory week on the Costa Blanca of Spain. My confession proper starts from the point when I finally arrived in Benidorm, which people who don't know it well, think of as being cheap and cheerful, brim-full of drunks and the worst class of tourist. How wrong they are! I can tell you that it is positively wonderful and one day when I'm too old to look after myself and death is on my tail, which is all coming too fast, I shall take my creaking bones across the sand and into the blue Mediterranean. There I shall simply let myself go beneath the waters, warm as a bath, and not come up again.

Anyway, back to my confession. My wife thinks that Benidorm is quite awful and, therefore, it was easy to suggest to her that she doesn't want to waste her time lying on one of the cleanest and most interesting beaches in the whole of Europe. Neither does she wish to eat disgustingly delicious tapas nor drink disgustingly palatable Spanish wine. My goodness, me – how she's got it all wrong, which was good for what I'd got in mind: my little murder plan.

So, there was I in my beautiful, small, stylish hotel, gazing down upon the iconic little island that lies just off Benidorm and upon the skyscrapers with their thousands of windows. I knew that somewhere behind one of those windows was lurking that arch-bastard, Zachariah Glerg, my son-in-law, my victim: perhaps even expecting my appearance. He married my sweet daughter and ruined her life: a controlling tyrant and a player away from the family nest. I too play away from home, so I understood that need. However, I have never wanted to be the uber controller of anyone, being, I hope, a fair-minded chap who thinks that everyone has the right to freedom of thought and action and certainly the freedom to give in to their little weaknesses now and then.

I lay on my bed looking at the sea and planning my strategy. In the room safe, I'd placed a pistol and a garrotte in the form of a piece of wire: neither a very subtle method of murder, but, at the very least, effective.

My wife, like most women, would have preferred poison. She too is on Zachariah's tail, but lacks the actual determination to finish him off. I certainly don't want her to find out what I'm doing, because she would get it into her silly head that our daughter is carrying faulty genes and would cart her off to a therapist to pre-empt her, too, from carrying out any funny business.

I did know the precise window that separated the loathsome Zachariah from the rest of humanity. He had a lovely, minimalist apartment on two floors, with a real Hollywood-style, lush terrace looking out to sea. Nothing but the best for the greasy swine.

I took a taxi to the exclusive apartment block and hid myself among the verdant palms, exotic plants and brilliant flowers in front of the entrance. I looked up at Zachariah's large balcony and could see him leaning over the parapet to admire the view and smoking a cigar, with a glass of wine to hand.

He was not alone, and I could hear raised voices. I rang the buzzer and announced myself. I heard him laugh as he let me in. I then stepped into the smart, sparkling lift and went up to the penthouse, which was on the third floor, the building being low-rise. He had his front door open and stood back to let me enter. I was ushered towards the curved, railed stair case that led upstairs. So up I went and into the sitting room. The sliding glass window that glided into the wall was fully open so that the balcony and the room became one.

The view was phenomenal and you felt that there was no boundary between you and the sea – as though, with very little trouble, you could just dive down into it. A moment later that was exactly what Zachariah did, as my daughter, Julia, bounded out of the kitchen wielding a rolling pin and rushed at him, toppling him over so that, in his surprise, he lost his balance and miraculously fell over the parapet. He failed, however, to make it into the sea and instead smashed his head on the rocks below. Manslaughter, an unpremeditated occurrence was the true cause of death, but Julia smirked, looking positively triumphant, so I did wonder about her!

The police came, forensics came and someone from the British Consulate came. Being frisked and found with a pistol in my jacket pocket, there was little doubt in their mind that it was a case of homicide and who the guilty party was. In their opinion, I'd obviously changed my modus operandi and had flung Zachariah over the parapet.

As I'm dying from some ghastly, terminal illness that will finish me off quite soon, I didn't want to leave the world before I'd told the facts exactly as they had occurred. As things stand (my being in prison, that is) I see little chance of making my way to Benidorm, to the beach and then into the sea which, as I've already told you, is how I wish to die. My trial will not be for some weeks by which time I will already be dead.

Nevertheless, by telling the tale I have at least been able to relive a time when I was in paradise by the Mediterranean. This public account of the events, however, is giving me hope, because, dear reader, if you were to act very quickly and start up a petition on my behalf, I would perhaps be released early enough to be able to get a cheap Easy Jet flight to Alicante and thence, by taxi or the Beniconnect Shuttle, to Benidorm. Please help a dying man to fulfil his last wish!

As you can see, I was perfectly innocent of the

crime of murder and my only niggle is that I've now landed my daughter, Julia, in the cart. Her look of triumph at the scene of Zachariah's demise, nevertheless, makes me think that he perhaps had an excuse for treating her the way he did. After all none of us truly knows what goes on behind the closed door of a marriage, do we? Is my daughter perhaps a monster in the making?

As for you, Julia – so sorry, my darling – but a chap has to do what a chap has to do.

By the way, dear reader, if your petition is successful and if, by any chance, I don't make a very good job of floating out to sea, for my illness has badly affected my sense of co-ordination, would someone please give me a shove in the right direction?

Thank you, dear reader, and please forgive a dying man's ramblings.

Sincerely yours,

Saul Jenkins

First Meeting

The rain is tumbling down with a vengeance, the sea is a veritable maelstrom, I've read most of the books in the library and the entertainment is total sparkle and glitz, without even a modicum of talent to go with all the razzmatazz. So, you will easily be able to imagine how very, very tedious I have found this cruise.

What has really bored me to the gunnels, to use an appropriately nautical expression, is having to share my meal-times with the same awful people every single evening. Hour upon hour of inane conversation, everyone trying to outdo everyone else: their wonderful holidays, their expensive cars, their sumptuous houses, how superior they are to everyone else, how brilliant and extraordinary are their children!

Then, of course, there's that frightful table steward with his beady eye upon us who plonks this garbage down in front of us, this disgusting food, which, after a while, all tastes the same; in fact, it has no taste ...and please don't try to remind me of the starving millions! He's probably at this very moment working out how big a tip he'll receive from each of us at the end of the cruise in those little white envelopes, with which we will so thoughtfully be provided. Yes, I know he only earns a pittance but he might get more from me than he bargains for, if he doesn't wipe that eager, ingratiating smile off his face.

It's all been so unutterably boring, but suddenly you've turned up to join our happy little band… Mr Swansdown, isn't it? Looking at you, I do believe that with you here, for me at any rate, things are going to take a distinct turn for the better. We have, this very minute, all introduced ourselves to you, but I know full well that I have disappeared already from your conscious mind for, as well as being easily bored, I, in turn, bore other people – to death, you might say. I don't quite understand why, but I can never think of anything to say, at least nothing of great importance and, whenever I do manage to dredge up something passably acceptable from the depths of my mind, the chance to speak has long gone and I've probably forgotten what I was going to say anyway. Sadly, my social skills are lacking, to say the least.

My great problem is that I'm just not noticed by other people – for most of the time I doubt they even realise I'm here; I suppose it's called merging with one's background – which is what I do well. People are only half-aware of this brown blob hanging around the fringes of their world.

That's me – a brown blob: brown hair, brown clothes, brown shoes; only the extreme whiteness of my skin relieves the brownness. I am unobtrusive and take up little space. A nothingness, that's what I am: boring, and therefore, harmless.

Heavens, Mr Swansdown, I think this could be a defining moment in your life... I do believe that your eyes, for a second, looked in my direction – but I don't think that I actually registered with you, did I? I always know the moment I set eyes on a man whether he's the right one for me, and there's something indefinably right about you, Mr Swansdown, especially in that first look you gave me.

At this moment, I mean absolutely nothing to you, but one day soon, I promise you, I'll fill your whole world ...in fact, I'll *be* your whole world. You see, there haven't been all that many Mr Rights for me. However, when I say I will be your whole world, I am not, as you will discover, suggesting a long-term relationship or anything of that kind – that would be too boring for words!

By the way, I should tell you before I go further that I bear grudges – other people seem to be able to take insults, sly digs, criticism, et cetera, in their stride but I cannot do that – it's not in my nature – they must always be dealt with ... which is why you, Mr Swansdown, really shouldn't have made that very, very silly face at me when you said "hello". I don't quite know what it meant, but I didn't care for it.

I'll tell you one more thing for free – something you won't have guessed. I'm a butcher – I don't mean I cut up cows and sheep etc. Actually, I'm vegetarian – can't stand cruelty to animals – poor defenceless things! No, what I mean is that I butcher people. Well, perhaps butcher is too strong a word, making it all sound too dramatic, but I do dispose of people. It's a little hobby of mine that, at times, can become a bit of an obsession, but usually I manage to keep it in check.

You know, you really are annoying me, little man – there's that same silly look, sent again in my direction – so, you have noticed me! A drop of cyanide in your wine at this point wouldn't go amiss, but I don't think I'd get away with that one. Added to which, of course, I just don't feel attracted to poison, although I know it's supposed to be a means of extermination favoured by women.

No, my weapon of choice is undoubtedly the knife – I just love the moment itself, when the blade goes in – steel and flesh meeting – you really should try it sometime. I so savour the glorious moment of recognition – the surprise and fear in the eyes when there is nothing in their world that isn't me – which is why I do like to get to know my victims. Otherwise, it might feel rather impersonal and random. I do think it's important to have built up some sort of relationship, however tenuous, with the person one is sending off into the great beyond. Nevertheless, I have to admit that occasionally, very occasionally, I'm a bit of an opportunist. Actually, it depends on how things pan out – it's just a question of being in the right place at the right time and, of course, being in the right mood.

I usually favour men as my victims, probably because I find them so totally useless. On the other hand, I always remember my first visit to Rome – and that was during a cruise – a five-hour excursion which ended in St Peter's Square. There was the Pontiff in all his papal pomp, holding his Wednesday public audience and there was I in this bastion of Roman Catholicism, surrounded by placards and banners, by the fervent, by the devout, by the curious and by the photo snappers. I was not in the best of moods, I can tell you – I don't approve of organised religions or, indeed, in religion at all – believe me, all that you see around you and feel within you is nothing but a random event in a cold, uncaring universe.

Then, to add insult to injury, I was suddenly roughly jostled by this extremely large woman; it seemed to me that the pushy bitch took a perverse pleasure in doing so... Well, I'm afraid, no-one does that to me. Before the papal holy homily finished, out had come the knife from my handbag and there was one more soul winging its way to where silly people seem to think souls go.

After finishing her off, I merely slipped away while a crowd gathered around her, wondering, I presume, how such horror could happen in such a holy place. Well, that might have taught one or two of them that nothing is sacred and religion is a farce that won't save them from anything. One could say it had been, at the same time, an example of a first and last meeting.

However, with you, Mr Swansdown, I'll have plenty of time at my disposal and be able to spend many a pleasing hour planning, imagining the scenario, considering all the options open to me, but I think that once we arrive in Venice the hours that remain to you will be numbered.

Poor Mr Swansdown, it really wasn't your lucky day when you were allotted a place at this table, was it? At least you have no idea what is in store for you, so for the moment ignorance really is bliss. By the way, if anyone reading this is thinking of going on a cruise in the near future, I do advise you strongly to look out for me and, if you do see me, to be beware. I will, of course, be the little woman dressed in brown – yes, I always must wear brown – it must be something within my psyche calling to me – brown, brown, brown, it says.

In all likelihood you'll most probably miss me completely against the pattern of the carpet. That, however, does seem to be my allotted role in life: to be walked over, that is.

For Your Ears Only

With wheels screaming, Paul drove recklessly up to the front of the hotel. He virtually threw the car keys at the valet who would park the snazzy, little sports car in its usual spot – then staggered across the lobby.

The valet thought he had, undoubtedly, had too much to drink and certainly should not have been on the road. All the women who saw him took a second glance as, indeed, did some of the men – think *James Bond* and it saves me having to go any further with my description. Paul was nothing to do with the Secret Service, however, and the only spying he ever did was of a pornographic nature, setting up his cameras in one of the hotel's bedrooms that had a small hole in the wall, and then making a nice bob or two from blackmail: the sleazy world of sex and prostitution was his metier, not that of saving his country.

As he passed by, he quickly glanced at Georgia behind the reception desk. She winked at him as she licked her biro and moved her fingers up and down it provocatively. She looked at him intently for she knew what his little game was – exactly the same as hers. They were totally in cahoots in their desire to make money; and to enjoy themselves together under the sheets while watching what had been filmed.

Paul came down most weekends, nominally for the sea air, but mostly for this, that and, especially, a bit of the other. This little trip to the seaside, however, was of a slightly different ilk and, for once, he had not come alone. He had brought the wonderful Dolly with him and if he'd ever loved anyone it was she – beautiful, intelligent and, needless to say, sexually accomplished.

As Paul ran rather unsteadily towards the lift, like an ailing bat out of hell, he patted his jacket pocket to make sure the little, beautifully-wrapped, gift was safe and sound. He just couldn't help giving a giggle which is not exactly the sort of reaction one expects from men – a guffaw yes, but surely, it's women who giggle. However, giggle he did, in a rather girlish fashion, and kept on doing so until he reached his room, receiving some very odd looks on the way.

He used his card to open the door to the penthouse suite – nothing but for the best for Dolly. The first thing to reach his eyes was the sight of her smooth, gorgeous legs and the fantastically expensive, strappy shoes they had bought one wonderful afternoon in Paris: all this framed by the sea in the distance. Her immaculately pedicured red-painted toenails were shown off to perfection as she rested them on the table – he'd always had a bit of a foot-fetish and his body reacted accordingly. She was holding an extinguished cigarette in her hand, which was draped over the arm of the chair. Her wine glass was empty, as was most of the bottle.

Popping his head round the glass doors that led onto the balcony to speak to her, he giggled again. He found it all so screamingly funny; such a strange scene was playing out before his eyes, swishing and swashing around his brain. Then the image had gone, but it would reveal itself again. You couldn't forget something like that, could you?

"Well, my darling Dolly, I've brought you a little present that I think you will like very much. It's just your style: something to match those gorgeous, blue eyes of yours."

As he sat down opposite her, glancing out to sea, he inadvertently kicked a large ball of rubbish and tutted with annoyance as it rolled under the drinks trolley. Heaven only knows what it was, but his favourite shoes were now stained. He'd make sure the hotel paid for a new pair; he'd have a word with someone on the staff.

This didn't improve his temper, for he'd been feeling distinctly under the weather all day, bumping into things and feeling confused – perhaps he was in for a bout of flu. He sat down wearily, opposite Dolly, lit a cigar and cursed her silently for having finished off the wine. He satisfyingly inhaled the smoke and looked more closely at her – there was something not quite right about her; he giggled but couldn't quite put his finger on the problem. "What's the matter with you, Dolly? Look at yourself in the mirror. Tidy up a bit. It's not like you to let yourself go."

As he glanced at the cigarette smoke drifting away,

he happened, out of the corner of his eye, to see the rubbish ball. He hated untidiness, so up he got, bent down to grab the curly, blonde hair and pulled Dolly's head out from under the trolley.

"What on earth are you doing, hiding down there, Dolly? Don't be so silly!" By now, his white shirt-cuffs were covered in blood and, when he glanced up at her sitting in her chair, he realised what was wrong: some bastard had cut her head from her shoulders and left what looked like a torn, red ruff around her neck. She looked exactly like Anne Boleyn – all that was needed to make the scene complete were the grey walls of the Tower of London and the green lawn on which the scaffold had been built.

Suddenly, a distinct feeling of excitement passed through his body – why, he'd forgotten to give Dolly her lovely gift. He went back to his chair, placed his legs together and carefully arranged Dolly's head on his lap so that her blue eyes were staring into his. He fluffed up her curly hair in the way that she liked to wear it and, bending forward, gave her a kiss.

From the gift package he took out a beautiful, leather box and held up the sapphire earrings so that they sparkled in the sun. He lovingly placed them in her earlobes; they looked as beautiful as he'd known they would when he'd first seen them. "You look wonderful, my darling!"

Then, with the blood still trickling from her throat, he took her head into the bedroom and held it up in front of the dressing table mirror, so that she could see how true this was. "Now to find the murderer and the murder weapon!" he said with another giggle.

He first tried to place Dolly's head back on her shoulders, but with no success, as it just kept rolling off. He even had a go at securing it with a length of string, but it was useless. Frustrated, giddy and confused, almost falling over, he staggered outside to the balcony, where he nonchalantly chucked the head over the railings. As fortune had it, it landed on the driver's seat of a parked open-top car; someone would be in for a nasty shock. Luckily, at the time, no one was around, so there were no hysterical scenes from passers-by – not that his befuddled mind would have cared a jot.

Leaning casually with his arms on the railing, he felt his foot touch something and heard a clink of metal. Looking down at the tub of geraniums, he saw a knife on the floor, its blade stained almost the same shade of red as the flowers. His memory was suddenly jogged and he knew, in that split second, that it was he who had created what he now realised was an horrific scene of carnage – why he had done it he had simply no idea!

Hysteria took him over and his unstoppable giggling sounded like a babbling brook. That was the moment Paul decided to end things – life simply wasn't worth the effort any more, so he dropped over the balcony railings, braying with wild laughter as he fell.

Gravity carried him, and the large brain tumour that the autopsy would reveal, towards the hard, unforgiving pavement. The air was damp with rain that was starting to fall – surely tears for Paul and Dolly.

Georgia, on the other hand, needed no tears, for she had come into her own. All their seedy, ill-gotten gains would be hers.

Guitar Man

He was wonderful; the crowds adored him and, in his broken English, he told them that they made him so happy, that playing for them was his life. The applause was deafening – it made them feel good that they were so important to him; he was brilliant, so charismatic, his playing totally tantalising: rock music at its best. He was truly at one with his audience, with his guitar; his face reflecting the intensity of his emotions – eyes closed, facial muscles twitching: his body movements poetry in motion, nothing suggestive but, even so, sexually charged.

The venue for this high-quality performance was not high profile – he just didn't want that sort of existence, fame and fortune were not his aim. Born in Spain, but now a legal, one hundred percent American citizen, he just wanted to lead a stress-free life where he could earn sufficient money to support Maria Angeles and their small daughter, while at the same time doing what he was born to do.

It was a very warm, sultry evening in down-town Phoenix and the interchange of feeling between the guitarist and his audience was at its height. The palm trees and the topiary balls and spirals all added to the wonderful atmosphere. Enjoyment was the name of the game; everyone out to have the best time possible. His usual fans were there, plus pale English bodies now dressed in summer-wear and exposed to the setting sun.

They danced, sang, drank cocktails served to them by smiling, smoking-hot waitresses and sat listening intently to the signature pieces, which demonstrated his God-given talent. It was a happy, friendly, aggravation-free atmosphere with well-heeled people of all ages, diamonds and gold glittering, as the subdued lighting came on.

Without his guitar he looked almost insignificant: thin and dark – not someone you would normally give a second glance. His name was Chico Chimera and he hadn't a care in the world. Fate, however, sometimes has a way of doing the dirty on happiness and this time it was Chico's turn.

When the gig was over he stood on the small stage, putting all his electronic bits and pieces away, covering the speakers that were positioned in the trees protected by black plastic bags.

Great stars, of course, had people to do all this for them, but he was happy to do it himself, while the waitresses cleared away the empty glasses and detritus of the evening: everyone working as a team.

As he picked up his guitar case, his cell 'phone rang.

Against all odds Maria Angeles was still alive; the car

that had mown her down at the crossing had truly been a machine of destruction bringing horrific, life-changing injuries, but she was so sedated that she was floating on a cloud, feeling little of the trauma. That would come later. Chico had been unable to take in the words that he had heard on his 'phone and just dropped his guitar on the stage and ran for the exit, leaving it for someone else to keep safe for him.

He sat at her side for days and weeks, with Father Bennett helping him to intercede with God to save her. Their prayers were answered, but her recovery would be painfully slow and very, very expensive; he just didn't know how he would ever pay the medical bills.

"God will help you. He will show you the way to help Maria Angeles. He wanted her to survive and so he will provide," said Father Bennett in annoyingly unctuous tones. It was not God, however, who provided. What brought him the means to solve his problem was a hand placed firmly on his shoulder. A Mexican voice spoke behind him as he sat holding Maria Angeles' hand.

"You need pasta, Chico, money to let this beautiful young woman recover her joy for living, to be a mother to your little girl. I can help you and you'll be surprised how easy it will be." Chico immediately had a bad feeling about this. The man's appearance alone was enough to make him feel nervous. He was small and fat like a toad with an incredibly ugly face, his features a strange mixture of Mayan god and oriental gentleman: not – at least in his case – a good combination. He desperately needed a shower, his clothes were shabby and yet Chico could tell that the gold he wore was worth more than a dollar or two.

"Nothing illegal!" said Chico naively.

"Naturally not!" lied the Mexican.

So, there was Chico in an old 98 Ford Explorer loaded with .38 calibre hand guns, the weapon of choice for the bad people, on his way to the Mexican border to deliver his cache. After two years of this he had never been caught or even stopped, his journeys always carefully orchestrated by the cartel for which he was trafficking. The monetary reward was amazing and would certainly more than pay for Maria Angeles' care for as long as it was needed.

His luck, however, was bound to run out one day and so it did, on a particularly sweltering morning, after he had passed once more across the dry, shade-less Indian reservation that led directly into Mexico. Here, there were fewer resources to man an efficient border control but, nevertheless, the police were waiting for him.

A small group of native Americans was his audience; they were a resentful bunch, fed up with the lack of respect towards their sacred places, tired of having their homes regularly trashed by these illegal travellers. He was dragged out of his car and stood shaking with fear and melting in temperatures well exceeding one hundred degrees, the dust filling his mouth and nose. He and other couriers doing the same run were rounded up and eventually sent for trial.

Each morning all the hundreds of prisoners were herded out of their shambolic cells where there was little privacy as there were no locks on the doors; the pitifully small rooms were like pigsties, as tidy as each occupant cared to make them, which in most cases was not at all. Then, in the large courtyard, among plastic tables and chairs and little stalls where he could have bought all sorts of things, Chico waited for his name to be read out. As this happened, the prisoners one by one returned to their rooms. This was prison – Latino-style. There were even wives and children there.

This was Chico's future for the next eight years – an appalling place where he had to fight, literally and metaphorically, for every moment of peace. His guitar was one of the first things he lost; it was stolen, then returned, then destroyed by someone who hated his guts. Money was always changing hands among the prisoners, between the prisoners and the guards, favours were exchanged or extorted – it was a hotbed of intrigue, with opposing gangs whom you really would not have wanted to know. The only possible advice was to avoid looking at them, keep your head down, your mouth shut, your anger under control – then you might escape the worst of the trouble. Chico's body, nevertheless, bore bruises and scars that showed he had not been a hundred percent successful. His guitar had gone, but at least he had a photograph of Maria Angeles.

The small, toad-faced man, not surprisingly known as El Sapo, was driving towards the Mexican border accompanied by Tony Benito a.k.a. Father Bennett, both leading lights in the cartel. Drug smuggling, people smuggling, gun-running, prostitution plus all sorts of dark goings-on was their business.

"You know, I'd almost forgotten Chico Chimera's existence. Well, eight years is a long time. Anyway, we'll pick him up in the morning and return him to Phoenix," said the faux priest.

So, they strolled into the prison completely unhindered, questioned by no one. They kicked the cell door open and even they were shocked by what they saw; Chico looked as though he were wasting away, his hair was thin and grey and his teeth had mostly gone, the gums red and inflamed. Eight years of yearning for home, with no decent food or vitamins, no medical treatment, too many cigarettes, the occasional soft drug to ease his misery had made him into a wreck. He was now a different person.

Chico stared at them with a blank, haunted look in his eyes. "Maria Angeles, how is she? And my little girl?" he asked.

"They're both okay," replied El Sapo, somewhat vaguely.

"What exactly does that mean?" Chico wanted to grab him round the throat, but thought better of it. Anyway, he'd very soon see for himself how things were.

Having now seen him in the flesh and how he had deteriorated, the two men decided there was no way they would use his services again. The first-time round it had been because he was desperate and thus they were sure of his loyalty and commitment. That was, of course, how it was intended to be after one of their hoodlums had knocked Maria Angeles down at the street crossing making sure, however, not to kill her. Chico had had a suspicion about this because rumours of all sorts constantly flew through the prison like birds on the wing. He knew too that Maria Angeles, despite the time that had passed, was still a long way from a full recovery.

Sometime soon he would, of course, carry out the plan that had passed through his mind every night as he fell asleep. Hatred was now his prime emotion and he knew that one day he would have his revenge.

In the music business in Phoenix there was much support for Chico; they knew what he had done and his reason for doing it. It would have broken anyone's heart to see Maria Angeles in her wheelchair with their daughter, Julia, like a shadow always at her side. Her speech was slow and her mind not as quick as it had been. There was a live-in carer, but it was Julia who had virtually sacrificed her childhood to loving her mother and keeping her company.

One of the great moments had been when Julia had placed a guitar in his hand; she herself could not even remember hearing him or seeing him play, so for her it was a fantastic moment. It had been almost eight years since he had plucked the strings of a guitar, but, even after so much lack of practice, the magic was waiting to cast its spell.

By the end of six months he had almost recovered his health and his fingers were now moving more easily over the guitar. The music within his soul was once again awaking – shivers of emotion travelling through his body as they used to do, until that fateful evening so long ago.

One morning, as dawn was breaking, he crept down the stairs and out through the front door, closing it quietly behind him. He drove through the deserted suburbs until he came to Tony Benito's house. He had learned through careful study the mobster's routine and the route he and El Sapo would take. The car was sitting on the drive and silently Chico unlocked it, one of the many tricks of the trade he had learned in prison. He carefully placed half a dozen guns under the back seat, adding a stash of narcotics for good measure, and relocked the door.

Later in the day an anonymous 'phone call was received by the border guards.

"Where have you been, daddy? It's ever so early."

"Well, Julia, I've just been settling some unfinished business!"

During his years in prison Chico had changed for the worst; he had learned bad habits, doubtful morals and his heart had hardened.

One day, Maria Angeles, hardly able to move her lips to form the words, asked him if he still loved her.

He hesitated, for the honest truth was that he was beginning to feel that she cramped his style; it was rather like being in prison again. Nevertheless, like a coward, he would not tell her how he felt. It was better to let his absence, when it came, speak for itself.

"I've loved you for a very long time and always will, but people and situations change …" He let his words die away and did not continue. However, she had received the message loud and clear, and now knew what to expect at some time, probably soon...

It was at one of his fantastic gigs that he had first met Ana and thereby was lost, for she was vibrant, intelligent and very beautiful: long, black hair, startling green eyes, a woman of the world. Moreover, she was very rich. Truly, for him she was a dream from which he hoped he would never wake up.

Cuddling and kissing under the palm trees, he told her what she already knew: that he wanted her desperately. "Come away with me, Ana. I can't live without you."

"But you can't leave your wife, Chico. She's only just got you back after such a long time apart. She needs you."

"And I need you. Believe me, I can, and I will leave her."

So for the sake of Ana, he left Maria Angeles, he left Julia, he left Phoenix and, taking his collection of guitars with him, moved into an opulent art-deco condo in Miami: a fantastically expensive love-nest. Once he had been selfless, but now he thought that life owed him big time, so why should he not take what he wanted? After all, he had given up eight years of his life to ensure Maria Angeles' well-being – what more could be expected of him? His only regret, his only stab of conscience was leaving his daughter behind, but one day she would understand and forgive him … wouldn't she?

Lavender Bags

I think I might organise a little orgy for this coming weekend – it's about time we all had a bit of fun! I know we've all got our own areas of interest and our own little peculiarities, shall we say, but I'm sure they can all be accommodated! I like orgies! Don't you?

Well, that's got your attention, hasn't it? However, I'm afraid I've been rather deceitful here! You see, I wrote the above because I thought that it would arouse your interest, because we all like a little bit of naughtiness, don't we? Wouldn't be human otherwise, would we? And, of course, you're still reading – I hope!

Which all goes to prove what they always say i.e. that when writing a story, you should have an arresting opening. And perhaps if I'd continued I might have been the one to be arrested because I'm sure that there must still be a law or two about producing pornography. I think I'll look that up on the Internet before I go any further and then I'll come back to you......

Well, here I am again and it seems to me, having waded through several websites, that I could probably write pretty much whatever I wanted – as many salacious descriptions as I like. But, you know what, this has rather taken the gilt off the gingerbread, because I've always been a bit of a rebel really, doing a lot of things only because other people disapproved! Rather naughty, that, I know, but that's little me for you! So, from now on I think this story is probably going to be pretty tame! I could jazz it up a bit, of course, but it's probably better to stick to the truth and tell it as it happened.

You might find it rather unseemly, of course, that someone who is eighty-two years of age should be so focused on all this prurience – but it never goes away you know – this interest in sex. I put it all down to Jilly Cooper – she's the one to blame. If you haven't read any of her books you really should do so! Jackie Collins too, of course – she's even worse! How I look forward to Thursdays because that's the day the mobile library comes!

I know I could always look up naughty things on the web, but I have this sneaking feeling that Big Brother is watching somehow and knows what I'm doing. Bit of a shame, but never mind!

Anyway, all this has been a complete red herring and has absolutely nothing to do with what I'm going to tell you, except, of course, that it does involve the mobile library that I've already mentioned – the source of so much pleasure! Oh dear, there I go again!

What I'm doing at this moment (in case you're wondering) comfortably ensconced in my small sitting room, is making lavender bags. Here I am, surrounded by bits of gingham and lace and ribbon, all green and mauve of course, because those are my two favourite colours. As you can imagine the scent of lavender is overpowering – all, I may say, out of my own little garden. The fruits of my labour are destined for the village fête, where I'll sell the lavender bags in aid of the church funds. Just as I did for last year's fête ...and thereby hangs my tale! So, if you're settled with a nice cup of tea and a large slice of cake, (I don't believe in stinting oneself) I'll begin.

It was a Thursday morning and the faithful readers of Mulberry-under-Marsh were all there, standing on the Green. We were awaiting the arrival of the mobile library. My shopping bag was laden with an interesting selection of returned books (better than usual, in fact! – if you see what I mean). It hadn't rained for ages, even though it was late October, but suddenly down it came. I love it when it's been dry for a long time because the rain really brings out the smell of herbs, especially of my favourite, the lavender. We could see the library in the distance, trundling merrily towards us through the puddles.

I suppose, in the manner of the best stories, that at this point I should wax lyrical and describe to you the lovely countryside where I live but, to be quite honest, I just can't be bothered. Anyway, it's not going to make the slightest bit of difference to what happened, so if you *are* into descriptive, atmospheric writing I'm afraid you're going to be left wanting. Anyway, to cut a long story short I was hovering at the side of the book case, in the mobile library, keeping a close eye on things, as

I usually do, when I became aware of whispering. Peeping around the corner of the non-fiction section, I saw the vicar's wife, her hand cupped over her mobile phone, having a very intense conversation. Of course, with ears like mine, I simply couldn't help but hear what she was saying.

"The fur coat, Bertie darling, the fur coat. The white fur coat!"

Well, I was quite intrigued... Who was Bertie, because the vicar's name was Archie? And what had this Bertie or, indeed, the vicar's wife, to do with fur coats? I mean she'd always been dead against foxhunting and most certainly would never have worn a fur coat. Or so I thought!

"Just you make sure it's genuine," she said, "the real thing you understand. None of that imitation rubbish!" Then she suddenly she giggled. "Oh Bertie, you are naughty! Naughty, but nice. Look, sweetie, I'm going now because I think Mrs Nosey Parker is up to her usual tricks!" *I suppose she was meaning me! Well, they do say eaves droppers never hear any good of themselves or words to that effect!* "Anyway, Bertie, see you later at the fête! Byeeee!"

Well, that had certainly given me plenty of food for thought, so having checked out my new books at the desk (a new Jilly Cooper and, even better, a new Jackie Collins!) I couldn't wait to get home to arrange all the pretty lavender bags in a satin-lined basket. What I do, you see, is, I dress up in a sort of Little Bo peep costume and wander round the fête selling the lavender and collecting the money in a white, woolly, lamb-shaped bag. It's amazing, the gossip and tittle-tattle I manage to pick up while I'm doing it. Well, I can tell you that the vicar's wife was certainly going to be closely watched!

She's quite a sweet little thing in her own unspectacular way – a bit drab and unadventurous in the clothes stakes, but perfectly adequate at visiting the sick, making cakes and doing flower arrangements in the church! However, after what I'd overheard, it seemed she might have hidden talents – another mind perverted by the contents of the mobile library!

Albert Foswell …well, who would have thought it …not the dapper, lady-killing Bertie of my imagination, but Albert from behind the counter at the Post Office! What a let-down! And what was that large paper parcel he was handing across the cake stall to the vicar's wife! The white fur coat, no doubt!

"Why, how kind of you, Albert," she said primly and winked at him. Then seeing me, she blushed! Yes, Mrs Vicar, I know what you've been up to! I think.

However, as it turned out, there had been some slight confusion on my part because I hadn't realised that not only did the mobile library bring books to our little village, but, in the last week or so, it was also providing us with DVDs. Moreover, if you were friendly with Charlie, our so-called librarian – well – under the counter he has DVDs of a rather different variety. Not the sort of thing a vicar's wife could very well ask for herself, so it was left to her very good friend, Albert, to obtain the rather unsavoury material for her.

All this came to light because Mrs Huggins who 'does' at the Vicarage twice a week, happened to see Albert sneaking in there (while the vicar was conducting a funeral service) and glimpsed the pair of them watching this rather shocking piece of cinematic art entitled, yes you've guessed it, "The White Fur Coat." I mean the imagination positively boggles! The reason that the DVD had to be genuine was because the DVD player is new and the vicar's wife thought that a copy might harm it. The parcel? Well, who knows what else that might have contained?

Anyway, we villagers are just loving all the shenanigans between Albert and the vicar's wife, because a year later it's still going on. In fact, it's a wonder that the path between the Vicarage and the Post Office hasn't worn away, the number of times they both find a pretext to visit each other.

The vicar, of course, has no idea what's going on under his very nose and I think I'll leave it just a little longer before enlightening him. Although, when I do, my goodness, the drama that will ensue will be even more riveting.

Of course, what I've forgotten to tell you is that there is a Mrs Foswell, Bertie's other half, and you wouldn't want to get on the wrong side of her, so it's all going to be terribly exciting when the cat's let out of the bag. Heaven only knows what the Bishop will say when it reaches his ears which I can guarantee it will! Talk about fireworks!

Just before I end this little tale I must tell you that the mobile library has suddenly taken on a different dimension and is now becoming even more scrumptious than before. This is all thanks to E.L. James and her wonderful, simply wonderful Fifty Shades Trilogy... I really am sleazy, aren't I? Sleazy and tacky! I should be more discerning at my age.

Anyway, I've just finished making all my lavender bags for this year, so now I'm going to make myself a nice cup of coffee and I'm sure that you could do with one too, couldn't you? Then perhaps we could settle down and watch a DVD that I've just managed to get my hands on, at last ...and no prizes for guessing it's title!!

Mrs Tabernacle's Obsession

The rather delicious Mrs Tabernacle was obsessed by self: herself. Well, she would be, wouldn't she, being the only person who existed? Everyone else was a fabrication, produced by her mind. Who had put these strange images into her brain was a bit of a mystery and why she was so unique she had no idea. She thought that probably there must be a God or some sort of Overseer in charge of things; which meant that she and he were the only two beings in existence.

She did not believe that she was the one who had created the universe because surely, she would have remembered doing so. Anyway, she was a bit of a lazybones and to have made all those swathes of matter and the shining stars would, from her perspective, have needed an awful lot of concentration and meticulous thinking which just wasn't her forte ...but then, of course, the swathes of matter and the stars weren't real anyway, were they? It must be, therefore, that the Overseer, the One Other, had made everything just for her and that existence was a sort of film being unwound in her head, which continued in her dreams even when she was asleep. Perhaps God was her own personal slave, a sort of divine punka wallah wafting images in front of her eyes for her sole edification. She did not, however, always like what she was shown and often wished that her cerebral cinema would screen different movies.

War films, disaster films and films about cruelty and starvation were definitely not her cup of tea. God must realise that she did not like that sort of thing, so why didn't he do something about it? Why, just last week she'd seen poor little Jamie from down the street being badly bitten by a dog, which had been horrible. Of course, it hadn't really happened, for there was neither a Jamie nor a dog, but that's not the point, is it?

Existence was all a bit of a mystery: topsy-turvy, like that book, *Alice in Wonderland,* that she remembered holding in her hand a long time ago, and had imagined reading. However, mysteries are mysterious, unknowable. One can't explain them in any other way.

In the past, before she realised the truth, some people had truly mattered to her, until the day when it hit her that it was all a lie.

There were oodles of what she called ghost people whom she couldn't stand and now she had come to the terrifically wonderful conclusion that she could finish them off, remove them from face of the earth with no harm to them or to herself – in fact, it just didn't matter a damn what she did!

Most importantly of all she could murder that phantom, Mr Slade, who supposedly lived next door but, of course, lived nowhere. He was annoying the hell out of her through the party wall, his dry, old man's voice forever chanting mantras – he must be into one of those strange eastern religions or else he was mad. She had never seen him, in fact, but could imagine his withered body sitting on a prayer mat surrounded by mounds of fairground-type ornaments and other tasteless tat.

She would go there later in the day and sort the old chap out, so that she could have a bit of peace and quiet. Mr Tabernacle had been such a staid, well-behaved man who had never caused her any trouble, but at the time she had not realised that he was merely a character in the One Other's cinematic production. It was strange to think that she had loved him for so many years, but that he had obviously been unable to have the same feelings for her, although he had acted them out very well.

She had loved dear little Arnold, her beloved cat, even more than Mr Tabernacle. He had been a fantastic actor too, purring and gazing at her in adoration.

Anyway, she would make herself a nice cup of tea and think about Mr Slade's demise. Suddenly, once again, she heard him starting his infernal chanting. Why couldn't he just put a sock in it? If only she could learn to co-exist with these non-existent mirages, but then, why should she? She was the most important person, in fact, the only person in the universe? She had asked her divine slave very politely to stop Mr Slade from being so annoying, but he had simply not listened to her.

Mrs Tabernacle took out a piece of paper from the

sideboard and listed the possible means of extermination: poison – but which one to choose? Perhaps rat poison because it is easily available; stabbing, for her mother had left her a small, razor-sharp, Toledo steel dagger; shooting, but obtaining a gun would be a problem; assault and battery, for which she could use Mr Tabernacle's old cricket bat. Thus, she continued to ponder, all the while tapping her fingers on the table in time to the mantra.

In the end she decided that assault and battery was the best solution. Mr Slade was old and would not be able to put up much resistance and, with a bout of fierce battering, she could rid herself of her pent-up anger. On went her faux, fox-fur jacket, as it was cold outside, and then she slapped on a bit of make-up, for she could never step out of the front door without looking reasonably smart. Obsession with self must surely include pride in one's appearance. A quick spray of perfume and so, with the cricket bat in hand, she was ready for action.

As she put out her hand to ring Mr Slade's door bell, she was surprised to notice that her fingers were trembling, which was really quite ridiculous. There was nothing to fear in a non-existent environment from a non-existent man.

She heard strong, confident footsteps approaching and, as the door opened, so did her mouth. Her first thought was that she was so glad that she looked nice, for Mr Slade was an absolute wow, as hulky as she was foxy: dressed in a black leather jacket with a stylish tattoo on his neck, his rather sparse hair drawn back in a ponytail. She discreetly dropped the cricket bat behind a thorn bush.

"I'm terribly sorry to disturb you, but wondered if I could have a word with you. My name is Tabernacle and I live next door. I thought that after so much time living cheek by jowl, as it were, I should come and introduce myself. It's been very remiss of me not to have done so earlier." By this time Mrs Tabernacle was positively simpering, feeling short of breath with her heart working overtime and Mr Slade was looking at her very approvingly.

"Do come in, my dear, and let us introduce ourselves properly over a nice gin and tonic, shall we?" So, Mrs Tabernacle entered the house of Mr Slade and what an eye-opener that proved to be. It was like something from an interior design magazine: chic, minimalist furniture, everything sweet-smelling and sparkling clean, with not a nick-knack in sight: only modern pieces of sculpture dotted about and amazingly bright surrealist paintings on the walls.

Ensconced in a deep-cushioned, black sofa they sat cosily side by side, sipping gin and tonics so strong that it seemed as though the tonic had been forgotten, in the same way that Mrs Tabernacle had for the moment forgotten that she was living a fantasy orchestrated by the One Other.

Mr Slade told her of his work as an antique dealer, about his travels to exotic places, his interest in eastern religions, but was equally mindful to ask her about her life.

From then on, in spite of the fact that she knew Mr Slade was a mere puff of smoke, his chanting didn't seem to worry her any longer, for she rather liked listening to it, and she most definitely liked him.

Mr Slade, however, gradually realised that she had some very odd ideas about existence and particularly about her place in the big scheme of things. She was definitely a tad eccentric, but then, he thought, everyone has a little quirk of some sort.

However, her whole way of thinking was about to undergo a great change. Life had been progressing very pleasantly, thanks to her new friendship with phantom Mr Slade, when she had suddenly read a most fascinating and enlightening newspaper article. It told of a scientific theory that proposed that everything that existed – and that included the unique Mrs Tabernacle – was a simulation generated by aliens by way of a giant computer on the edge of the universe. Apparently, we were either all part of an experiment or even just some sort of cosmic game.

What a revelation that was and Mrs Tabernacle fell completely for the idea, for it meant that she and Mr Slade were on an equal footing and that she could again like people and treat them as equals.

Now she was as real or as illusionary as everyone else, which in a way was a great relief, for it took any pressure she might have felt away from her. It was nice to be normal, because she had occasionally wondered about her sanity. She just felt a bit sorry for her divine punka-wallah who was now surplus to requirements.

From then on, she spent a fair bit of time pondering on those aliens. What were they like? Did they resemble the Roswell alien? Were they perhaps spider-like? As they were clearly very intelligent, did they perhaps have a huge head to accommodate an outsize brain, or two heads, or perhaps even three?

Aliens were now Mrs Tabernacle's new obsession.

The former First Lady of the universe had decided to prepare a cosy little supper for Mr Slade. His home was much smarter than hers, so that was where they were going to eat.

Around the supermarket went Mrs Tabernacle, filling her basket with all sorts of goodies. Scallops, beef Wellington and crème brûlée were on the menu, all beautifully cooked and perfectly presented. Luckily, as it turned out, there would be more than enough to eat.

The only thing now needing to be done was for her to choose a couple of bottles of good, red wine. Fortunately, the supermarket was fairly empty so, undisturbed, she was able to stand for several minutes making her choice. Suddenly she jumped when she felt a hand on her shoulder and a voice whispering in her ear.

"Don't turn around. Don't be alarmed. I mean you no harm. I am your friend. And be careful that you don't drop the wine. If I were you I would put it in the basket."

So, into the basket it went.

"Now I want you very carefully to turn to me, but please, please do not scream. Remember what I said. I am your friend."

Mrs Tabernacle was somewhat surprised by what she saw. Having spent hours reading and thinking about aliens, there she was, actually face to face with one. Well, that was not strictly true because he was a good twelve inches shorter than she was and so it was his grey, shiny, bald head that she first saw. He was a Roswell alien to a tee: a little, thin thing with huge eyes.

"Where have you come from?"

"Nowhere that you would know," he said, rather rudely.

"You look thin. Are you hungry?"

"Yes, I am a bit hungry."

"I think you should come home with me and have some food. Mr Slade won't mind. He's like putty in my hands."

By this time the other shoppers were beginning to stare at this rather good-looking woman talking to herself. Some people did, of course, talk to themselves: for example, while mentally going through their shopping list, but they did not leave pauses for some sort of reply and were less animated than this poor woman. She should not have been allowed out by herself they thought.

When Mrs Tabernacle reached Mr Slade's house with the alien tottering behind her, she plonked the shopping on the work surface. Mr Slade gave her a peck on the cheek.

"I hope you don't mind, but I've invited a new friend to share our supper. May I introduce you to Grimtoad Grey from outer space? I met him in the supermarket."

Mr Slade's face paled as he thought to himself, "She's got to be kidding!"

Mrs Tabernacle was surprised that he did not show more surprise on meeting his very first alien.

"Look, delicious one, why don't you let me do the supper? I'll pour you a lovely dry Martini, shall I? Just relax and forget all your worries."

"Don't forget Grimtoad! ...Grimtoad, sweetie, would you like a drink of some sort?"

The alien pointed to a bottle of rather awful sweet sherry; he obviously didn't realise what he was choosing.

"I tell you what, Grimtoad, have a dry Martini instead – it'll buck you up no end after your long, long journey."

Grimtoad slowly scratched his chest with both hands and lifted his head as though in deep thought. He eventually answered, "That sounds yum-yum. Thank you."

Mr Slade, also known as Absalom, set about his barman's duties, handed Mrs Tabernacle her drink and sipped his own. The alien started to tap one of his feet with impatience.

"Absalom, didn't you hear Grimtoad say that a dry Martini would be yum-yum? We must show him how welcoming ordinary earthlings are before he is taken to meet our leader." She had high hopes that perhaps she might become the earth's special envoy to wherever it was he came from.

Mr Slade could see that the end of his very amicable relationship with Mrs Tabernacle was in sight. She was obviously far from well. He had never noticed her imaginary conversations before and it was all rather worrying. As the evening progressed, events worsened. Grimtoad seemed to lack any social skills and started throwing his beautifully prepared meal all over the place, meat and pastry soon decorating the walls and carpets.

It was at this point that Mrs Tabernacle began to shout at him. "You bad, bad alien, naughty, naughty Grimtoad! How could you behave like this? Perhaps on second thoughts you shouldn't have had three dry Martinis. However, I shall not be inviting you to spend the night here."

"Right, my gorgeous darling, I'm calling an ambulance," said Mr Slade.

"But, Absalom, it's only because he's not used to alcohol. There's really nothing wrong with him."

The ambulance carried Mrs Tabernacle off to the hospital where her mental condition was carefully studied, but it was obvious that her obsession with aliens was going to be long-lasting, for she insisted that Grimtoad should accompany her to the residential psychiatric unit, and that a small bed should be prepared for him in her room.

Mr Slade wondered what the next obsession would be, but he had made up his mind that he would not be around to see it. As far as he was concerned, she and her obsessions were now on their own.

Needlepoint

The earth's mantle was worn out and in desperate need of up-dating. No one had bothered with its renovation for thousands and upon thousands of years and it was a real disgrace that things had been allowed to get into this state.

Rivers and seas were so full of detritus that they could hardly move, so tides were negligible, with the result that the moon felt superfluous to requirements and, diva-like, was sulking. Trees were dying in their millions and the snow at the two poles of the world desperately needed topping up, for the land there had become arid and brown. Even the volcanoes had just about given up trying and were eerily dormant and silent …and so on and so forth and what have you.

The sheer shabbiness of the earth instigated a competition whereby an expert team of sewers would be chosen to right this terrible oversight. The new mantle would be sewn quickly and carefully onto a good stiff canvas, using a super-strong woollen yarn so that it would last a very, very long time.

The golden needles would be of the very best quality.

The women, each one a tiptop embroideress, sat in a tower so high that all they could see through the large window were dark, moody clouds and, far below, the earth itself. Young and innocent-looking, they were mesmerised by their task, with no one daring to glance away. They were uniformly dressed in a smart, dark blue tunic, rather like girls in a convent school.

Watching them intently to make sure they did not falter or miss a stitch was their supervisor, a stern, forbidding individual, robed in a dark, hooded cloak. He stood over them reading out instructions from a book, which he held in one hand, while he unwound the wool with the other so that there would be no hold-up in the work. He was the self-designated Great Master and they hated him, for he was a bully.

As the needlepoint was completed, the canvas was pushed through slits in the wall of the tower and carefully allowed to descend onto the tattered surface of the earth. Once there, ordinary, unskilled workers would spread it out to cover the land. It was essential that this was done in the correct order, and so an experienced foreman had been appointed. After all, you would not want an erupting volcano spewing out flames and ash next to a permanently frozen expanse of tundra. The foreman's name was Rodrigo and, as you will see, he had had a very specific reason for applying for the job.

Another position of authority was that of the trade union representative of SOW (Sewers of the World). Ingrid sat with her members in the tower, and even she did not ever want to have a face-to-face dispute with the Great Master and, perhaps, be forced go before an industrial tribunal. It would be a total nightmare and she shook at the thought of it. Nevertheless, trouble was brewing on a couple of fronts and, at any time, was liable to spill over. Ingrid's young women were now over-worked, ashen-faced, their eyes aching and their fingers calloused. They were hardly given any respite, even for sleep, and the time for eating was minimal, so that their strength was failing and the work slowing down.

The Great Master was, by that time, even more tetchy and vindictive, but Ingrid knew that the day to speak out had finally arrived. "Come along, ladies. It's time to put your needles down and stretch your backs," she announced somewhat nervously. While he listened to her, a look of total disbelief passed across the Great Master's face. He blustered and swaggered but, like many people of his ilk, he didn't do anything because, actually, he knew he'd met his match. "You have no thought for your workers, Master. Their thimbles are blunt, their fingers sore and red, while you stand there droning out your instructions, your book held limply in your hand. And you think you've done a hard day's work!"

"I unwind the wool!"

"That's exactly what I mean. You just don't do much at all, do you? Believe me, SOW is going to hear about this!" Ingrid could not believe how simple it had all been. "I shall accuse you of treating your workers like slaves. Forced labour is what I call it."

Threats and promises continued to pass between the SOW representative and the Great Master, but in the end everything was more or less settled to the workers' advantage. One little worker, however, sitting in the tower had other things on her mind and it was this that caused the second problem. Whatever Dulcie embroidered had an empty, raw feeling to it, rather like her heart. She was pining away, for she had a lover; it was the foreman, Rodrigo.

No one was allowed to enter or leave the tower and, to reinforce this, there was a little sign on the bottom door that said unequivocally: *Keep Out*. On the other side there was a second little sign that read: *Opening This Door Will Lead to Severe Reprisals.* Both Ingrid and the Great Master could see the sense of these rules, for it kept everyone's mind focused on their work and there would be no unnecessary comings and goings to disturb the rhythm of their labour; it was therefore impossible for Dulcie and Rodrigo to meet up. Ingrid, nevertheless, noticed that Dulcie appeared inattentive at times, but had no idea of the reason for this. In fact, she told Dulcie to pull her socks up.

"Why has your work become so sloppy? It's as though you no longer care. What is wrong with you? I thought you realised how privileged you are to be here. There are seamstresses all over the world who would give their back teeth to be doing what you are doing. Get your act together, Dulcie, or there will be trouble."

"I'm truly sorry, Mistress," replied the girl who

was close to tears and not a little ashamed, for she knew she was working too quickly and that some of her stitches were loose. "I promise that I will mend my ways and focus totally on what I'm doing," she lied through her teeth.

Her need for speed was to prevent the SOW representative and the Great Master from seeing what she was doing on the quiet, when they were not looking over her shoulder. Instead of following instructions properly, she would waste yarn and time embroidering love messages onto the new mantle of the world, trusting that Rodrigo would read them. Being a careful and conscientious worker he certainly did read them, just as he examined everything that was lowered from the tower. He had loved Dulcie for a long time and knew that it was only pride at having won a place in the élite sewing circle that had made her leave him. He would never let her go and had followed her, knowing that sooner or later she would tire of her work because that was her way.

A large tabby cat lived in the tower keeping the vermin at bay, for no one wanted the precious canvas to be gnawed and nibbled. Despite being an expert mouser, the tubby creature led a sedentary, tranquil existence. One day he was lying on the stone, spiral stairway leading to the front door, when he was surprised to hear a key turning in the lock and to see Rodrigo, as quiet as quiet can be, creeping up towards the workroom.

Suddenly, shocked to his feline core, he saw Dulcie

and her lover hurtling down the stairs and fleeing from the tower. Meowing furiously, he tried to give warning of what was happening, but his alarm signals and the flight of the lovers went unheeded.

No one heard or noticed anything at the top of the tower, for another industrial dispute had broken out and the Great Master was so enraged that it seemed he must surely suffer a heart attack.

It was only when peace had again been restored that Dulcie's absence was noted and Ingrid rushed like wildfire down the stairs. So quickly and unseeingly did she move that she failed to see the cat, knocking him against the hard, stone wall and nearly crushing one of his paws. "How dare she do that?" he thought to himself as he licked his paw. "She will most sorely rue the consequences of her clumsiness. I am not one to take such treatment lightly." It was at this point that the cat himself resorted to industrial action, deciding he would go on strike for such an attack against his person.

He sulked, he yowled, he turned his back on Ingrid; he was in a foul mood and it was impossible to make him work. The vermin were going to have a field day. Now there was no one to save the fabric of the world from mice and rats or to inspect it thoroughly when it reached the ground.

Off went Dulcie and her lover in a small, shell-shaped boat, bouncing across the waves of one of the great newly-embroidered seas.

It was a happy journey, for Dulcie felt she had fulfilled most of her duties up in the tower to the best of her ability: given the circumstances, that is. As for Rodrigo he was content, for the moment at least, but he did suspect that sooner or later Dulcie would tire of him. Dulcie had noticed that already the wonderful, newly-embroidered tapestry of the world was looking as though something had been gnawing at it, for the yarn was beginning to unravel and there were holes in the canvas. She could see rubbish gathering in the waters of the sea and that the beautiful, blue stitches were becoming discoloured.

It was obvious that someone had not followed instructions for, while bobbing along in the boat, she suddenly saw on the coastline a huge factory with dirty smoke belching into the air. She so hoped that she had not contributed to this while her mind had been on other things. Did it all mean that sometime soon, after the work was finished, the embroidery team would have to meet again in the tall tower and do never-ending running repairs? When the dust had settled, she might even re-join them, because already Rodrigo was starting to annoy her.

Reunion

"Well, David, it's been a long time, hasn't it? And I've been wondering what I would feel seeing you again."

"And what do you feel?" he asked.

"Well, to be quite honest with you, not a lot!" Words calculated to hurt, which is what she did better than anyone else he had ever known.

He sat looking at her, watching her crossing and uncrossing her long, beautifully shaped legs, the fishnet tights and very high-heeled, black shoes showing them off to their full advantage. The pleasure this was giving him would have been evident to everyone in the room had he been standing up. She was, of course, doing it on purpose, trying to push him as far as she possibly could.

He loved her still, despite the fact that she was a first-class bitch and always had been. Was this, however, really her fault? Or was it something to do with her upbringing, or her environment, or perhaps a chemical imbalance in her brain! Serotonin! Dopamine! Noradrenalin! Too little! Too much! Or was it simply that she was just plain bad?

He used to wonder if she had ever truly loved

anyone but herself. Passing flirtations, sudden obsessions there had been; but love? ...no, he didn't think so!

On the far side of the room, he could see, among the crowd of black-clothed mourners, the nice, uncomplicated little girl he was going to marry – no great love there on his part, but at thirty-five it was time to marry and start a family and he could certainly do worse than Felicity. She would never, of course, arouse in him the same passion, the same tide of emotions that had swept him along when he had had the affair with Marcia, but, nevertheless, she would fit the bill nicely!

He stood up and Marcia came to stand at his side. Sipping her champagne, she seemed to rub herself against him like a cat and he smelt her familiar perfume – something French and very expensive – he had certainly bought her enough bottles!

"So that's her, is it? Oh, she's not for you, David! Far too ordinary! Far too frumpish! I thought I might envy her, but there's nothing to envy, is there? You can't possibly want to marry that! Not if you're in your right mind, you can't!"

"I was thinking just now what a bitch you've always been, Marcia! And here you are again with your jibes and barbed attacks! Never learned how to be pleasant or generous-hearted, have you?"

"But just by looking at her, I can tell she'll never do to you the things that I used to do. No passion there, is there? And, of course, you'll never love her as you love me and love me you do, don't you, David?"

"Love has nothing to do with it. She's a sweet and affectionate girl that any man would be proud to have as his wife."

"Well, if being sweet and affectionate is now your yardstick, good luck to you! But how your standards have fallen, David!"

This was a very smart funeral and, if it had been a wedding, it most certainly would have been top hat and tails! Smart waitresses wearing smart, black dresses and even smarter frilly, white aprons, moved around handing out champagne and canapés on highly-polished silver trays, while the grieving widow, David's godmother, kept her beady eye on Marcia, recognising her as racy and brazen. David made his way to her.

"I didn't realise that you knew Marcia" he said.

"I don't – at least, not well enough to want her here today. I thought she had come with you and thought it not very kind on your part to invite her knowing Felicity would be here."

"An intruder at a funeral!"

"Obviously she wanted to meet up with you again, David! I won't ask her to leave; that would be too embarrassing, but I'd keep an eye on her if I were you. She spells trouble with a capital T."

And how! When he next looked at her she was standing, somewhat unsteadily, where he had left her – still making no effort to socialise, but obviously having helped herself freely to the champagne!

"Don't you think you've had enough champagne?"

"Sorry! What did you say? Oh, you've now

become the monitor of how much I drink, have you?"

"Well, do try to remember that it is a funeral!"

"And a funeral is just what it feels like! What a boring lot of old sods they all are! I really feel quite sorry for poor little Felicity if this is what she's going to be surrounded by! Look at that old girl over there – 90 if she's a day and you could scrape the make-up off with a trowel!"

"For God's sake, keep your voice down, Marcia!"

"Don't you tell me what to do! No one does that!"

"Don't be silly, Marcia! People are beginning to look."

"Well, in that case, I'll give them something to look at!"

With that, she suddenly grabbed a tray of canapés from a hovering waitress and flung it at the nearest group of mourners. A colourful arrangement of salmon, cucumber and tomato now decorated his godmother's hair, while the other women tried to retrieve anchovies and slices of lemon and ham from their smart dresses. A shocked silence, broken only by an involuntary guffaw from one of the men, had now been replaced by cries of consternation, but the entertainment was far from over. Marcia then hurtled towards the table where all the drinks were arranged and seized an open bottle of champagne. Pushing her way through the astonished crowd, she headed in Felicity's direction and, tipping the bottle high in the air, poured the contents over her head.

"What does she look like now, David?" she

screamed, holding the empty champagne bottle up like a trophy. "Still fancy her, do you?" The look on her beautiful face was positively demonic.

Poor little Felicity, bewildered and wide-eyed, burst into tears, whereupon Marcia grabbed her arm and bundled her out through the French windows and into the garden, where snow lay in grubby heaps on the lawn.

Like a flurry of black rooks, almost falling over themselves in their eagerness, the funeral party followed Marcia as surely as the rats had followed the Pied Piper: amused, fascinated, horrified. They would all be dining out on this story for years to come, so it was important not to miss a single detail.

Felicity managed to free herself from Marcia's grip, darting this way and that, trying to elude her pursuer, but being a little stout, she was unable to keep up the momentum. Heads were moving from side to side as though this were Wimbledon, not a gathering to mourn the death of a human being. Then, suddenly, a communal groan arose as though the match favourite had lost an important point, for Marcia was now dragging her victim towards the swimming pool. The pool was without its usual winter cover so that, even on this sombre day, the trappings of wealth might be seen to their greatest advantage. Pieces of ice were floating on the surface and, suddenly, flakes of snow began to fall from the leaden sky.

"Let her go, Marcia! What the hell do you think you're doing?" shouted David.

He lunged towards Felicity to rescue her from Marcia's vice-like grip, but too late! "What I'm doing is this!" With that she pushed Felicity into the freezing water!

The mesmerised spectators wrongly suspected that this was the climax of the drama being played out before their eyes and, even as their breath condensed in the frosty air, they forgot their discomfort and were rooted to the spot by what they were watching.

"Get her out quickly!" yelled someone, "or she'll freeze to death. She can't swim!"

"What d'you mean the silly bitch can't swim?" snarled Marcia and, without even stopping to take her shoes off, she dived into the pool, the ice moving about her like miniature ice-bergs. She grabbed Felicity under the arms and dragged her to the steps of the pool where some of the mourners, finally mobilised, were waiting to receive her.

Marcia, in the meantime, had disappeared under the water.

"Don't be stupid, Marcia! We've had enough of your silliness for one day!" shouted David . . .

He dragged her out of the water, blood from a cut on her forehead running down her face and laid her on the lawn, her face already like a death-mask. Finally, hearts were touched and people began to weep at what they had just witnessed. The story that they would in future years tell over the dinner table had now taken on a different slant! A heart attack was given as the cause of her death; it was such a pity that the one generous, unselfish act of her life should have ended that way. Six months later David and Felicity were married, but it might as well have been a wake as a wedding, for there was no joy there.

Of course, it was a marriage doomed from the start. How could it not have been with the martyred figure of Marcia hovering over them? In fact, so forceful was her presence she might as well have been sitting in her fishnet tights and high-heeled shoes watching television with them.

After the divorce Felicity married a nice, ordinary no-nonsense man and lived happily ever after. As for David ...well, no one has set eyes on him for years; not since he was glimpsed kneeling at Marcia's graveside, tears streaming down his face. What eventually became of him is anybody's guess!

Rivals

"I really don't think that we should be standing quite so close together," she lisped, as she deliberately brushed the sleeve of her white and yellow, frilled gown against the material of his jacket, letting her fingers flutter for just one second against the back of his hand, as though in protest at this daring proximity. She then looked at him coyly over her fan with blue eyes in which he would willingly have drowned, a faint blush rising to her cheeks; Dominique knew all about the art of seduction, the cunning little vixen! "I should so hate people to think cruelly of me!" she simpered modestly. On hearing those words Didier fell completely head over heels in love!

However, there were at least two other hearts, in that sun-filled conservatory, beating with envy at what was going on; a scene from which they had both chosen to turn their heads away, as if it were of no consequence to them. Two love-sick sisters, virginal in body, but certainly not in mind: Mirabelle sipping her tea as if it were the most interesting thing in the whole world and Odette just about to pick up her cup and saucer, wondering where she might sit so that she could observe what was happening, without being seen to do so. How handsome, how manly Didier was, standing there enraptured by Dominique's charms, his hands behind his back clasping his elegant grey, silk top hat. The background of lush palms and exotic flowers against which the favoured pair stood, together with the vivid Japanese vases and bowls that adorned the room, made it seem as if some artist had deliberately chosen the most vibrant colours from his palette to paint the scene.

As Odette stood there, with her hand poised above the tea tray, she looked straight ahead and saw another source of irritation, this one seated in a wicker armchair: their neighbour, the grand Mlle Fournier, leaning over in a cosy gesture of complicity towards another very acceptable young man. Not quite in the same league, of course, as Didier, but nevertheless, what a catch he would make! How pleased Mother would be if one of them managed to net him in! Jean-Jacques, their second cousin; almost impoverished, but also next in line to a title!

Surely Jean-Jacques was not setting his sights on Mlle Fournier? No, no, no! Such a dull, pale-looking creature and far too old for him! Why, she was all of twenty-two if she was a day and what was she thinking about when she chose that dress – brown and salmon pink? Well, the colours just didn't go together, did they? She was so lifeless, forever languishing, barely, it would seem, having the inclination to put one foot in front of the other. It was just so fortunate that she had plenty of servants to do everything for her. The lazy, rich bitch, as the sisters had so very impolitely labelled her!

Mirabelle and Odette, overflowing with vitality and raring to go, knew that on that afternoon they both looked their radiant best, identically dressed in frothy, pale aquamarine gowns. What it was to be young and pretty and how they adored all the parties, the balls, the soirées that they attended – why, it seemed that every week there was something for their delectation!!

They were, where matters of the heart were concerned, the deadliest of rivals, but at that precise moment they were most definitely of one mind, truly united, as they sent their arrows of ill-will and jealousy in the direction of that flighty little tramp Dominique.

"I hate her! I really hate her," whispered Mirabelle, giving Dominique a side-long glance.

"Not as much as I do! Wouldn't it be wonderful if she were to have an unfortunate accident of some sort?"

Mirabelle, in truth rather shocked at her sister's words, nevertheless found the idea rather appealing and, still simmering away with resentment, sat turning various possibilities over in her mind. As for Mlle Fournier – well, she seemed far too wrapped up in her intimate little tête-à-tête to feel the waves of resentment coming towards her.

However, things were not quite as they seemed to be...

Poor Mlle Fournier, she of the broken heart, pining away as she watched the delectable Didier sweet-talking that frightful hussy, in her frightful white dress, with its frightful yellow frills and bows; rather like a fried egg on legs, she thought. Unkind, but then it's hard to be charitable when your heart is breaking and you see your rival snaring the man of your dreams while she had to sit there listening to the awful Jean-Jacques– what a dreadful bore he was!

Why did Didier find Dominique so alluring, she pondered for the umpteenth time? She was pretty, certainly; intelligent, yes; rich, well that went without saying, but… oh dear, there were no buts, were there? It seemed that the gods had truly smiled upon Dominique at birth, showering her with more than her fair share of gifts. She sang like an angel, played the piano like a virtuoso and could charm the birds off the trees! Poor Mlle Fournier!

The object of all this seething passion – what of him? Well Didier, at that moment, was so captivated by his companion that he was completely unaware of anything else; no other thought or emotion touched him, least of all the idea that there were three young ladies sighing and swooning over him, their adoration unrequited!

There was, moreover, yet another heart pierced with love's arrow, one that marched to a different beat, for Cousin Jean-Jacques too was watching him with admiration and even, dare one say, with desire.

The sisters, meanwhile, drinking their tea and eating their cream cakes, sat there keenly observing everything that was going on around them, from beneath lowered eyelids.

"Perhaps I shouldn't have said that I hate her – it's not a nice thing to say, is it?"

"Don't be so silly, Mirabelle! You do hate her, don't you? So why not say so? All's fair in love and war, after all!" answered Odette, staring very hard indeed at her sister.

"You're quite right, as usual! Of course, in love and war all *is* fair …and, yes, I do hate her!" She thought how much she loved Didier, how she would do absolutely anything to have him.

The air of the conservatory, already sultry and moist from the jungle of tropical plants that the gardener had created there, had gradually grown even heavier and more cloying from all the emotion that it now contained.

Indeed, the heartfelt longings, the jealousy, the loathing, the bitterness seemed to seep into the very fabric of the room, so that, even years later, anyone of a psychic disposition might well have been able to sniff out something strange and not very pleasant about the place. A curse had surely been laid upon the conservatory that afternoon …if you believe in such things!

The sisters, now dressed in deepest mourning, sat once more in the conservatory while the rain poured down outside. Mirabelle perched on the end of the chaise longue and Odette sat the wicker armchair. How fortunate that black suited them so well! They both stared down fixedly at the dark-red, Japanese carpet with its wondrously intricate pattern, but its beauty went unseen. It was exactly four weeks to the day since the tea-party, during which time things had happened – bad things. New emotions had overtaken the sisters, ones that they were unaccustomed to feeling. How, for example, could they possibly have thought such unkind things about poor Mlle Fournier? How could they possibly have imagined that she would now, such a short time later, be lying deep under the damp earth in her cold, cold tomb, overwhelmed by some secret sorrow that she had kept silently locked away in her heart?

Even worse, Jean-Jacques, their handsome, debonair second cousin, had also gone to meet his maker, killed in battle on some distant field near the Prussian border. The dreadful news had arrived at the house just a few short days ago, since when they had truly, truly bewailed his loss. In fact, they had both felt that such terrible tidings deserved at least one new, stylish, black hat apiece, complete with ribbons and a veil!

Today, despite all these misfortunes, unexpectedly, miraculously, fortuitously, their grief had taken a different direction, had a different edge to it, for they were now bereft of a dear, dear, beloved friend trampled to death but an hour ago, under the hooves of a runaway horse; a pale horse that had suddenly appeared out of thin air like a phantom! Dominique's luck had finally run out! Now Didier was there for the picking!

So, as they both sat looking at the carpet, heads down, crocodile tears flowing freely, each sister's eyes were bright with excitement, each heart filled with hope and anticipation, each mind in a turmoil, while each one sent a silent prayer of thanks up to whichever lucky star had arranged this very satisfactory dénouement! Poor, poor Dominique!

Now the knives were well and truly out, swords drawn, pistols primed, for the warring sisters were about to take up arms in earnest, one against the other. This time they were on home ground and there would be no quarter given! Then, abruptly, Odette stood up and smiled at her reflection in the mirror in the strangest manner; convinced that most definitely, there would be no doubt whatsoever as to the victor. The spirit who had placed the curse upon the room smiled with her, as a priceless, samurai sword hanging on the wall slowly slid from its beautifully ornate scabbard and, with no human intervention whatsoever, went flying through the air! Poor, poor Mirabelle!

Shadow Love

The narrow, seedy streets were like a dream: the buildings bathed in a scarlet glow, the sky sable. Shadows were darkly delineated on walls and on cobbles; high slender arches and little stairways hid who knew what. From one of the arches a big-eyed cat peeped out, the only witness of what was to follow.

As the bells rang out to welcome in the New Year, it was time to say farewell. Their liaison had run its course. There was absolutely nothing more to say. It was all such a pity because Hywel and Cerys had been together for more than five years.

They stood looking at one another; he in a black derby hat and frock coat – the epitome of an Edwardian gentleman, she in a plain, hobble-style dress with a small matching hat. They dared not touch, dared not exchange a friendly kiss, for it would have meant another beginning that would have been a fatal idea.

It appeared that they both intended to leave, indeed, to run away to the valleys as fast as they could; they'd both, so it seemed, had enough of each other and of the city.

"Well, Cerys, this is the end of a long, interesting

journey. And I'm really sorry."

"I, too, feel deep regret, but it can't be helped. That's life."

The cat, gazing at them, did not agree. What a silly pair they were! The cat could feel the love that they still felt for each other, but they were too stubborn to admit it.

It was all rather over-dramatic, he thought, something from the pages of a romantic novel. The cat was like a Greek chorus, always ready with his opinions and comments on the action. They had, at this point, almost shaken hands. If only they had done so, everything would have changed.

After the farewell scene the action moved on and the cat stood up to watch Hywel walking towards his future. He decided to follow him home. A storm was brewing: rolls of thunder boomed in the distance. It was not a good omen. Drops of rain began to fall and soon both Hywel and the cat were drenched.

Nothing had been what it seemed. Yes, Cerys went back to Wales: to the lush, green hills, to the tranquillity and the simple life of her homeland. All day, all night, she thought of her lover and the longing for him would never leave her.

Hywel, however, did not go home to Wales, nor did he want to. He had things to do, places to be, someone to kill; there was far more scope for his career as a banker in the city, but things had been utterly spoiled for him: no peace day or night.

The cat wasn't stupid and realised that there was something not quite right with Hywel. His proud demeanour, immaculate clothes, befitting someone who worked in finance, and the smart, well-furnished rooms where he lived, belied a darker side. His eyes were furtive, constantly moving, but this had never registered with Cerys. Indeed, the cat, being a perceptive animal, thought he could detect madness in those eyes. Cerys had never moved in with him and her visits to his home had been random, so she didn't realise the torment through which he was living. The cat, knowing how things were, was relieved that she had gone.

Hywel resided on the second floor and it was from the rooms above him that the problem came. He was now shaking, on a mission of murder and revenge, which he could pursue freely, as Cerys was no longer there.

As Hywel opened the street door, the cat slipped inside too. Well, it's not much good being a chorus if you can't see what is going on. Unlocking the door to his rooms, Hywel could hear that the horrific noise had begun again; the tramping of feet across bare floorboards, the barking of the dog, the banging of doors, the never-ending, mind-bending scraping of a violin. Hywel detested that violin, just as he detested anything that impinged on his privacy. Really, he should have been living in the middle of a desert, far from all human contact. That wretched neighbour was doing this solely to annoy him. He was convinced of it.

He had never met his torturer, never seen him, but he had ruined his lovely home for him, spoiled his oasis of calm. The neighbour had been there for only a month and Hywel had tried to speak to him, but there was never any answer when he rang the doorbell, so he decided to take action in the only way possible: murder.

Up the stairs traipsed Hywel, followed closely by the cat.

Again, there was no reply when he rang the bell, but the door was slightly ajar, so in he marched determined to have his say and if that didn't work, well…

The room was darkly furnished: heavy, brown velvet curtains, deep red sofas, oak tables and chairs, and no carpet. Someone had been reading *The Times,* which had been dropped untidily onto the floor. A violin lay on a side table. The coffee pot was still hot as, indeed, was the coffee in a rather nice, gold-leaf cup.

"Come out here, damn you! There's no escape. I'm not stupid, you know! Even your coffee is warm."

That was the moment when the cat knew definitely that Hywel had lost his mind.

An hour later the egg whisk lay alone, forgotten in the kitchen sink; it was glad of the rest for it had been working overtime. It was covered, not surprisingly, with beaten egg, but still there was something not quite right about it, for there were little pieces of red mixed in with it: surely not a tomato or a red pepper. No, more likely, slivers of raw meat! Rare beef perhaps? No, of course not; it was human flesh. The same colour effect could be seen splattered over the wall tiles. That was Hywel's handiwork: the flesh – that of his noisy neighbour.

Actually, it was a far greater scene of destruction than had been necessary to kill one person. Nevertheless, his anger and frustration won through and he had created a bloodbath. Apparently, the barking dog escaped injury, but the violin would never utter another note, its frame and its strings were destroyed completely by someone in a towering rage.

It was now Hywel's turn to make a noise, shouting, bellowing and screaming loudly enough to wake the dead. The cat wanted to sleep; his head was pounding and the emotion of it all had finally got to him.

We all have different perceptions of the same thing.

Hywel had certainly not seen what the cat had witnessed at the scene of the crime. Hywel had experienced a fully-furnished room and a kitchen with truly gruesome decorations. The cat, however, had seen what was really there: an empty room and an immaculately clean kitchen.

Later the police took Hywel again upstairs to witness the mayhem he had supposedly created, but when he looked it wasn't there.

The directors of the bank were very understanding, but his career as a banker was over and he was put out to grass. After his month of anguish and of an imaginary, noisy neighbour he was never to be the same again and remained sequestered and heavily sedated in his rooms with a housekeeper to care for him.

On a high, windy hill in a picturesque Welsh church an age-old rite was taking place. There was Cerys, in a simple, white dress with her hair crowned by a circlet of flowers, marrying a wealthy local farmer. She was very fond of him, but Hywel had been the love of her life.

The cat, paws tucked into his chest, was again sitting in the red glow under his usual arch where he continued to be an eternal observer of life. He watched as two long, black shadows, following the paths the lovers had taken when they parted, slowly moved towards him over the cobbles. The shadow faces stopped suddenly, opposite where he was relaxing, came together and kissed. True love is forever tightly bound, even if only in a shadow world.

Dead Art

The canvas showed a creation of straight, aggressive lines, sharp as needles. There were occasional curved shapes, but it seemed that the artist had not really wanted them there. They were an intrusion in the harsh, abstract scene that he had created. The colours were vibrant, almost overwhelming the spectator with their life and energy. What the painter had tried to portray was the focus of many an argument among both his admirers and his denigrators, opinions as varied, it would seem, as the number of people actually viewing the work at that moment.

Hanging on the gallery wall the canvas was so large that it was more like a mural than a normal painting. Ishmael and Leah loved it, although each saw it through different eyes. Yes, they were enamoured of it and sat on a small sofa sipping their flutes of champagne, mesmerised by its power. It was the first time it had been exhibited publicly so this was a very important event for the gallery and its owners who were hoping to attract a wide audience with wallets overflowing with money. Perhaps Joel Jenkins would turn out to be one of the greatest living surrealist painters of all time, the Salvador Dali of the twenty-first century.

"It's a war!" said Ishmael.

"It's a cocktail party!" said Leah.

"It's neither!" said Joel Jenkins suddenly from behind them. He then wandered away leaving them, again entirely ignorant of its true interpretation. Nevertheless, the painting had been given to the world and anyone's idea was as valid as that of the artist himself. He was now merely its creator.

At that precise moment it seemed that war rather than a cocktail party was the more likely of the two, for in the air there was definite aggression and belligerence coming discreetly from a loud speaker in the wall; Shostakovich at his most bleak and moody, the orchestra soulfully sending forth notes of marching feet and gunfire, drums and trumpets passionately imitating war in all its horror, until finally the bells of victory rang out and the music came to an end.

Leah and Ishmael, denizens of New York's Upper East Side, the epitome of luxurious living, who were frequent visitors to the gallery and two of its most enthusiastic clients, were allowed every privilege. They sat in the same spot the whole evening and, when the formalities were over, were invited to stay as long as they liked. The gallery owner lowered the lights and left them to it, sitting on the sofa, slightly squiffy from all the bubbly consumed. The only full illumination left was above the large canvas so that its colours seemed to shine even more brilliantly. The music had returned once more to Shostakovich, this time less rumbustious, but stranger. The deep sounds of a cello, so hauntingly sad and mysterious, made Leah think of a rocky landscape in some dark, alien world. It was suitable music to accompany death and would soon be called on to fulfil that task.

Now that everyone else had gone, the distinctive scent of marijuana drifted in the air as the couple smoked their cigarettes, puffing the smoke into curling patterns. They knew without any shadow of doubt that the painting would soon be theirs, for they had made the decision. They could imagine it in its new place in their imposing brownstone house.

Leah stood up rather unsteadily and approached the painting. She noticed someone holding a cigarette – perhaps he too was smoking a spliff. Unless, of course, he was eating a cocktail sausage, for looking at these figures with their triangular, featureless faces you could imagine anything. That was one of her reasons for loving the abstract painting so much. She felt that it was definitely a cocktail party, however, perhaps to celebrate a book-launch of an esteemed author. There was what could only be a pile of books lined up on the floor – unless they were odd-shaped abacuses. You simply could not tell.

At first no one spoke to her, but then gradually the atmosphere changed. "Welcome, my dear lady, I don't think we've seen you here before at one of our little gatherings" said a very elite Boston voice in her ear.

"Do have a glass of something!"

"Why am I here?" asked Leah. The voice laughed as though she had spoken the most amusing words in the whole world.

"Why, to celebrate the publication of my new book. But, of course, you knew that, didn't you? Just your little joke."

"Well, actually..." she began.

"I do so hope that you will enjoy reading it. It would be my greatest pleasure to present you with a signed copy."

Leah, however, was looking down at the pile of books, but they were giving out clicking sounds and little counters were moving along wires. Yes, she'd misunderstood everything, because they really were abacuses.

Suddenly a mule with long, bent ears passed in front of her. What on earth was it doing at a cocktail party? She was beginning to feel rather like Alice in Wonderland where nothing made sense.

Swathed trains belonging to glamorous evening gowns draped across the floor. The next thing she knew she had committed a social faux pas and had dug her heel into one of the most elegant of these, causing a slight tear in the material. After a hasty, embarrassing apology she moved across the room. A figure sat on the floor, perhaps the author's child, and she gently patted his triangular, hairless head.

It was so unnerving that all the faces were eyeless and therefore seemed to be completely impersonal; no noses, no mouths to give them an identity. All at once she felt so sleepy that she simply lay down on one of the satin trains, just as a yellow fish with bright, turquoise fins floated by.

Her last thoughts before sleep overcame her was what a brilliant artist Joel Jenkins was. His paintings offered you a whole world of thoughts and feelings; you could imagine that anything was possible. She even considered the possibility that Ishmael had been right after all and that it was aggression that Joel had wanted to show them, for she was conscious of a green-coloured, pencil-thin figure aiming a bow in her direction, but as he didn't seem to carry an arrow it must all be in her imagination. So off she slipped into a peaceful, alcohol-induced slumber.

Then Ishmael entered the cruel, aggressive canvas and the first thing he saw filled him with horror: Leah covered in blood with an arrow through her heart. All around him was violence. Men and women throwing punches at one another and approaching him with menace.

"Go, stranger, said the very elite Boston voice," this is our battle, our war. You are not wanted."

"But this has everything to do with me. You have killed Leah. What harm had she ever done to you?"

"She was mad, mumbling about books and abacuses and cocktail parties. We do not allow madness in our society. It has to be eliminated, for here everything is the epitome of perfection.

"But you allow aggression and hate!"

"But that is part of our nature and therefore is

perfectly acceptable"

A young boy sat on the floor trying to rise, but he was so badly injured that he was doomed. In some distant place Ishmael could again hear troops marching to battle as the music of Shostakovich grew louder and louder. He began to argue his case again, but all at once received a sword thrust through his neck, falling to the ground mortally wounded.

Later in the evening, thinking that the pair would surely have decided whether they wanted to buy his canvas Joel Jenkins entered the exhibition room accompanied by the owner of the gallery. They were both totally shocked to see two extra, bloodied figures on the canvas that had certainly not been there before. On the sofa, in the real world, sat Leah and Ishmael, their spliffs of marijuana still burning weakly and their glasses of champagne lying broken on the floor; they were both dead, but with no obvious sign of injury to either of them. Later, death from natural causes would be deemed the reason for their demise. It was such a strange thing to have happened.

Joel Jenkins smiled weirdly for they had finally understood the work that he had so anxiously wanted them to buy. It was not a cocktail party or even war that he had wanted to portray, but that darkest of all subjects: death itself. Ishmael had certainly been nearer the mark than Leah.

The figures added to his canvas would remain there and the painting would be entitled Death in Progress.

There would be no question whatsoever of any alterations being made. No one believed him when he denied having created the dead figures, their blood still wet to the touch; everyone thought it most odd that he should want to commemorate his two best clients in such a macabre fashion ...and the cello suddenly started to play again, lamenting their death.

The Wise Woman

Wolfgrim crept stealthily through the forest where dark trunks bore the weight of branches so thick and lush that they almost shut out the light. His heart was racing for he was heading towards the wise woman's little house. She enchanted him, and he simply could not stay away from her. It was Autumn and the dead brown and orange leaves crunched under his feet but, even so, the moribund foliage did not affect the dense covering over his head and he had to scrunch up his eyes through the gloom to make out Susannah's small, grey house like a miniature castle.

"I shall soon be with you, my love," he announced aloud to the empty air."

Susannah was waiting for him. For the moment he was the centre of her universe, but she was a fickle wise-woman and only the spirits of the after-world knew how long this feeling would last! Any man would fall in love with her. Just look at her and you could see why!

There she was, sitting on an ornately carved, stone chair, almost like a throne, with a red cushion under her, her shapely arms resting on a white, marble table. Her skin was pale and in sharp contrast to her brilliant, red hair, which was tied back at the neck.

Her dress was like gossamer whose colour matched that of the orange leaves over which Wolfgrim was treading.

The wise woman's hand lovingly touched a fallen chalice that lay in front of her. Blood escaped from it, dripping drop by slow drop over the edge of the table. She dipped a finger into the scarlet liquid and put it to her lips sucking it with such joy on her beautiful face that it must surely have tasted like nectar. It had been the life blood of a creature sacrificed in the manufacture of one of her potions.

She heard a low growling coming from her darlings who sat in front of her, so she knew that Wolfgrim would appear at any moment. The black panther, the leopard and the lion gazed at her, mesmerised and drunk with adoration. Her favourite, the tiger, stared at her as though drinking in her beauty. His chin rested on her table, but her sorcery for some unaccountable reason had failed... The paw he had placed before her was like a frog's foot, but she wouldn't worry about that now ...she could always repair him at some other time. The animals were restless, but their drugged state ensured that they would not become troublesome. A small group of pigs with their piglets huddled in a corner of the room, snuffling and snorting gently.

"Be quiet, my darlings. It is only Wolfgrim so you have nothing to fear."

The pigs did not, however, seem too assured by her words and began to nudge each other restlessly.

A copper tripod rested on a shelf behind her; the precious vessel in which she always mixed her magic potions. Without it, all these creatures would have remained in human form which would not have pleased her at all. Without exception each one of them had become a nuisance to her and had had to be transformed. A small, orange snake slithered silently across the table, disappeared through the arched window and slowly climbed one of the trees to watch what was going to transpire.

Then Susannah heard her loved one's voice.

"Susannah, my sweetheart, please allow me to enter."

He entered through the door as easily as though it were spider's web. Her heart jumped – he was so handsome. In fact, none of her animals in their human form had come anywhere near him for physical attraction. She knew that he must be thirsty after his long walk, although she truly didn't know where he'd come from or even where he lived. It was a mystery, for he always avoided being too specific when she questioned him. She put a wooden bowl into one of two large terracotta pots wreathed about with ivy that stood at the side of the table. The cooling water they contained was like a gift from the gods and, as she held the bowl towards him, he gratefully lowered his face to accept a drink as one of her animals might have done.

As he dutifully drank, Wolfgrim raised his eyes and

looked closely into her face. Underneath her exquisite beauty he could see burgeoning wrinkles, blue smudges under her eyes and touches of silver amid her red hair. He knew what this signified, but he was so blinded with love that he simply did not care. What could he expect, because she was after all a wise-woman, a sorceress, a witch who could change her appearance at will? In the meantime, the orange snake had come down from the tree and was now coiled up on the sill of the arched window to have a better view.

Discretion is always the better part of valour and it was then that Susannah made her big mistake. She thought that, with his thirst gratefully assuaged, this was the right moment to pry into his origin; a sorceress she might be but she had never had a satisfying answer to her intriguing question. Her spells and potions for some mysterious reason had, so far, failed to help her in this.

The animals intuited that she was going to grill him, which gave them an anxious feeling. They wanted to turn their heads away and close their ears to it all. Should the wise woman be so intrusive? It was after all Wolfgrim's own business where he came from, and what did it really matter anyway? If only she'd followed their silent advice, events would have taken a different turn for them all. Wolfgrim would have kept his temper and their mistress would not have been forced to change her abode to somewhere considerably less pleasant. The only satisfying outcome of the whole affair was that the animals would be liberated from their accursed imprisonment.

"I want you to tell me once and for all where you come from, Wolfgrim. You will tell me, won't you?" she said, voluptuously stroking his arm.

At that moment the atmosphere changed completely, the rich oranges and terracotta colours of the room whitened and it seemed to the snake that icicles now hung from the windows, freezing all the poor transfigured creatures ensnared in Susannah's sorcery. No longer did they move or snuffle or snort or grunt. It was as though they had frozen in time.

"I think I misunderstood your question!" said Wolfgrim, his voice as sharp as shards of broken glass. "I don't have to make myself fully known to you, nor indeed to beings far more powerful than you. I'm disappointed in you, for I thought you loved and trusted me, but I shall answer your question in no uncertain manner."

The wise woman looked at him in amazement as he disappeared in front of her eyes. She had thought that only she could accomplish such trickery: certainly not her lovely Wolfgrim. All at once colour returned to the room and the icy coldness went back to wherever it had come from.

The next moment she realised that she was completely powerless. The room had suddenly become oppressively hot and her animals panted and drooled from thirst. Through the window it seemed that the dark, cooling trees had gone, only to be replaced by a sun that was relentlessly throwing out such heat that she had never experienced before. The orange snake, now blackened, lay inert on the window sill: if it had been touched it would have disintegrated into ash.

Susannah passed her hand across her face to remove beads of perspiration, but when she looked again in front of her, there floating in the air just an inch or two above the floor was a living nightmare.

Wolfgrim, that primordial goat-headed devil with his huge, curved horns and hairy, bearded face was sitting cross-legged looking at her. His gleaming, red eyes surveyed her, and she could feel evil all around her, indeed in the very depths of her soul.

Her poor animals whined and groaned and moaned in torment and, as for herself, she wanted to die, for there would be no mercy from such a being as this one.

His huge wings were folded back and now she knew his origin full well. "You and I, wise woman, have a conversation pending; one that will teach you a lesson. Do not ever again presume to ask questions from one of my ilk. We do not care to be interrogated."

His deep, vibrating voice seemed to come from the pit of Hell and most probably did.

Susannah gasped from lack of air and from sheer, naked terror, but for some reason she thought mainly of her animals.

She regretted what she had done to them for, after all, they had been mere mortals who had unthinkingly offended her. Had she perhaps been too cruel towards them, too sensitive to slights that had probably not been intentional?

"Please, Wolfgrim, save my animals. Allow me to transform them again into humankind." She held her breath praying that this terrible devil-figure would agree.

The voice from the underworld spoke.

"I shall agree to this, but only if you accompany me to Hell and swear to serve me as a slave."

Hardly giving this suggestion a moment's thought she agreed, her now wrinkled body and grey hair shaking in terror.

She went around to the lion, to the panther, to the leopard and finally to her beloved tiger, kissing each head as she did so; she hugged the pigs and the piglets; she placed her hand carefully on the charred snake and all was made right again.

In the flash of an eye a fine array of young men were released from her sorcery and free to return home. They would never, of course forget her: she who had been their jailer and was now their saviour.

Thus the poor sorceress went to spend eternity in the underworld with Wolfgrim, but nevertheless, she felt that she had made the best she possibly could of the bargain.

A Kiss from Alice

It had been a very warm, almost rainless summer but, even so, Alice's mother rarely opened the windows. Thus, the house was musty and stale. Air fresheners would have been a luxury for, since father's passing, they had lived a hand to mouth existence amid the shabby trappings of their surroundings.

They had recently risen slightly up the social scale when Alice, that strange, eccentric, little creature, had somehow miraculously acquired a man friend. Larry, a small, greying figure, drove an old banger of a car, but as mother and Alice had always relied on public transport or on shank's pony, this was a distinct improvement. Sullen, moody Larry, for some unaccountable reason, had latched onto Alice when he had met her in the paper shop. As soon as he had stepped onto the scene, mother made sure he didn't escape. He was plied with all sorts of delicious home-cooked meals – well, as delicious as the stretched household accounts would allow – and it was always he who was given the privilege of choosing what they watched on television.

The hands of the old, wooden clock on the

sideboard moved ominously towards the dreaded hour, time speeding up and relentlessly eating away the minutes. Alice's heart was pounding and her stomach churning; it was going to be a difficult afternoon. She was weak from lack of food, which the coming procedure forbade her to consume. Her companion on the journey to the hospital would be of little comfort to her and would offer no words of kindness and encouragement.

The phone rang out imperiously, demanding her immediate attention.

"Hurry up, Alice, it's Larry. Don't keep him waiting." Any upset and mother always imagined what life would be if they had to give up their transport; it would be simply too degrading to wait again at the bus stop while all the neighbours passed by in their cars, some not much better than Larry's old jalopy, but at least ensuring independence of movement.

Larry was not going to pick her up for another half hour, so what was the problem?

"Where are you?" he said abruptly.

"Why, I'm here at home. Where else should I be?" Mother frowned at her, for this reply seemed almost insolent.

"Well done, Alice. It's now 4:15 and you're supposed to be standing on the corner."

"No, Larry, you said 5:00."

"I said what? Wrong again, Alice. You said you wanted to leave at 4:15 so as not to arrive late."

"But ...!"

"Don't argue with me, or you'll find yourself walking to the hospital. Just get out here in double-quick time."

He ended the call abruptly, not giving her time to reply. She was now feeling even more tense, and the tears were beginning to well. There had certainly been no mistake over the time, but she couldn't fight back because she was completely at his mercy. A whispered mutter of *bastard* was her only retaliation. She dared not give him up or mother would kill her, but he was always so volatile and unpredictable that she never knew where she was with him. She thought it was undoubtedly true when people said that it was better to be alone than badly accompanied.

With her fair, greasy hair arranged straight down her back and her legs hidden in white and red popsocks you could well understand that she was not attractive to men and was more than lucky to have Larry – the mean-spirited little sod! She got into the car and the displeasure coming from him was like a living entity, a touch as cold as ice to the fingers. Dutifully, as ordered by mother, she went to kiss him, but he just turned his face away as he always did when something upset him. If anyone ever disagreed with him or there was a perceived slight, this was his habitual reaction. At this point she thought that a tranquilliser might be the answer to the increasing tension, but because of the procedure it was better to have restraint and just put up with the misery.

As they approached the towering buildings of the

drab city Larry was once again in full verbal flow: a one-sided conversation that needed no response from Alice, for it was a soliloquy of moaning and groaning about the world in general. Everyone with power, big or small, was deemed corrupt: the government was rubbish, the health service was rubbish, in fact, it seemed that the whole of existence was rubbish. Not a good word was said about anyone or anything and Alice's inside twisted and turned at the meanness of it all – no soul, no heart, no feeling!

The clapped-out banger ground to a noisy halt in the hospital car-park.

"Well, let's see what the NHS can do for you, Alice, shall we? Perhaps while they're at it they could do something to improve your appearance."

"But, Larry... "

"There are no buts ...if it weren't for your mother's cooking, I think I'd probably prefer watching a good porn film to being with you."

This really was the ultimate hurt. He'd excelled himself this time. How could he say that? Especially on a day like this! In the meantime, she'd have to bite her tongue, grin and bear it, for she needed him, or rather, she needed his car to get her home. To be stranded in the middle of the city would be a complete nightmare. She certainly couldn't afford a taxi and the buses were so hit and miss that they would be useless to her, especially after her procedure. He had not turned off the engine, and without even looking at her gave a dismissive gesture with his hand.

"Go on, then! Toddle off! I've things to do, like having a few beers. I'll be back for you at 7:30 so make sure they've finished with you by then. And I'll be here in this exact spot, so get that firmly into your head."

Poor Alice, not in the least surprised by this abandonment, had to make her way alone through the doors of the hospital, make her presence known at the reception desk, change her clothes and just pray that they would not keep her waiting: no one to hold her hand, no one to give her an encouraging hug.

She lay in the dark and felt herself drifting off into unconsciousness, the machines winking at her. Her prime emotion at that moment was not fear of the procedure, nor of arriving late at the car-park – no, it was one of raw, naked anger, of the deepest hatred she had ever experienced.

Alice, still woozy from the anaesthetic, held onto the wall as she made her way round to the cafeteria. The nurses had tried to make her remain lying down until she had fully recovered from the sedation, but she knew that she had to be somewhere else. No, it was not the car-park that called her, but the cafeteria for she was ravenous with hunger after so much fasting.

Bleary-eyed and weak, she at last told herself that this was her life, the only one allotted to her as far as she could tell. If there were to be another, she just hoped that her mother and any men friends would be of a different ilk.

If only she could concentrate...

Had the anaesthetic affected her brain? She was certainly experiencing a different mind-set and a more positive attitude.

After a deliciously frothy coffee and a croissant in the lovely modern, windowless cafeteria, with its bright colours and subdued lighting as welcoming as the womb, things felt very different. No old furniture here, no shabby, wooden clock dictating to her with its moving hands, no pressure to hurry, no compulsion to obey. It was all perfect. She had glanced at her watch – 7:45 – damn him, let Larry wait. If he didn't, so what? It wasn't the end of the world.

All at once she felt a pair of hands pressing down on her shoulders and she glimpsed white sleeves decorated with red hearts. The finger nails were scarlet. She heard in her ear a woman's voice, soft and seductive and saw the fairy-book crown that adorned her head. This was all so confusing thought Alice!

"Off with his head, Alice, off with his head! Don't spend any more time being unhappy. Off with his head!"

She looked down in front of her. Yes, there it was – perfection – the sharp knife, still covered in crumbs from her croissant. She picked it up, looked at it lovingly, and walked out unsteadily, through hospital entrance; not however, without a nurse stopping to ask if she was all right.

"I couldn't be better, thank you. Life is perfect. All is perfection."

She tottered into the car-park, finding the sudden

rush of fresh air invigorating as the sun slowly made its exit from the sky. Yes, there was the old car and there was Larry, sour-faced and angry.

"What the hell have you been doing?"

"Waiting to see you, Larry. Waiting so anxiously to see you!"

He glanced at her rather curiously and then, as usual, turned his face away. She put her head and shoulders in the car and then launched herself towards him, the knife held firmly in her hand. He really shouldn't have been looking the other way, because that gave her the split-second advantage that she needed and before you could say Jack Robinson, or indeed, *off with his head,* she had one arm around his neck, cutting his throat from ear to ear with the other. To have removed his head as the strange voice had suggested would have been a physical impossibility for she lacked the strength. As he died she whispered into his ear. "I want to kiss you, Larry," she giggled. "I think you deserve to leave with the kiss of death upon your lips."

Even though Larry was now out of commission, Alice didn't need to call a taxi or to catch a bus, for she never went home again, but remained forever after in the city: first in the police station, then in the court room and finally, and certainly more permanently, in the prison. On visiting days, she would lie in her gloomy cell smiling as she dreamed of her mother standing in the pouring rain waiting for the bus.

Congratulations

"Congratulations, Pete," said the Lord God. "I've chosen you to be my representative in Rome and on the earth."

"But why me? I've never even been to Rome."

"You know that, and I know that, so it won't worry anyone else, will it?"

"I'd much rather go to Egypt, if you don't mind. A nice, big river to fish in, just as I did on Earth".

"Well, you can't, because it doesn't fit in with my plans. I don't want you standing on top of a pyramid with a halo on your head with lots of camels making those funny facial expressions and grunting your praises. It's just not how I've envisaged things. Anyway, you're going to be buried in Rome in a huge building bearing your name."

"But I can't be in two places at the same time. Either I'm manning the gates here or I'm being your agent, lying in a big, echoing edifice.

"You'd be very, very surprised at all the things that can happen at the same time. But I shall, however, only allow that sort of information to seep out gradually. It's called science. Really all very basic stuff, but people have to be a taught the facts little by little."

When seen for the first time the Pearly Gates seemed frightening; they were so forbidding and strong that no one could possibly pass through them. More congratulations, however, came Pete's way for he was given a stout set of keys that would solve this. He was an enormously strong-looking man, like a human rock – even stronger than the Lord God who was decidedly floppy and flabby as the result of too many hours lounging on the judgement seat.

All at once a nasty laugh came from the front of the gates. "And why are you smirking and looking so self-satisfied?" asked the Lord God of a small, ugly man with rope burns on his neck. "Wouldn't you have liked to be my representative? Come on, Jude, admit it!"

"No way. I'm too involved in other interests. I have no ambition whatever in being worshipped and fawned upon."

"But we all like a bit of adoration. I know I certainly do. And very soon there are going to be loads and loads of temples and churches and chapels and chantries just for that very purpose."

"And what about you, Tom?" asked Jude "What do you think of all this?"

"Well, I personally think it's all a load of bollocks and don't believe any of it."

"If you don't change your attitude quickly, Pete here won't allow you through the gates and then where will you be?" asked the Lord God.

"Down with the very, very bad people, I suppose. But, actually, how bad do you have to be to go there? Why is Jude still hanging around here, if you'll forgive the pun?"

The Lord God replied, "Believe me, there will be far worse sins committed than Jude's little, money-grubbing enterprise. Hell will be so crowded that there won't be any room for him."

Jude piped up defiantly, "I gave that particular source of revenue back to where it came from, so don't blame me. Anyway, I don't really know where the idea for that strange kiss came from in the first place."

"It was to serve a purpose," muttered the Lord God who was tired of standing around outside the Pearly Gates and keen to return to his judicial duties.

Suddenly there came the sound of beating drums and the gates appeared to lose their strength, becoming indistinct and insubstantial as though the whole of humanity could pass through them. A special squadron of supporters had arrived who could just waft through them with no trouble at all. This was the fishermen crowd still carrying their nets as though they had just stepped out of their boats. Their well-developed muscles gleamed and rippled with health, their faces deeply bronzed by the sun.

With them came Mat, the tax collector, never their most popular companion. Being a mere white-collar worker, he looked somewhat weak and watery standing among them, for he had never needed to develop his body with hard, manual labour. After all, to carry a few tax papers around doesn't require much strength. However, he and the others could come and go as they pleased for they had been the chosen ones. They didn't even require voice identification or electronic finger-printing to access heaven, which is just as well as most of them would have been totally confused, not being the brightest stars in the firmament.

Poor Mat looked even more lack-lustre than usual.

"What's the matter with you then?" asked Jude.

"I'm suffering, truly suffering. I think some of your loaves and fishes were rather past their sell-by date. But I want to know, Lord God, why we have to suffer from anything."

The Lord God turned bright red. "It is my right to plead the fifth amendment!" he shouted, as he rushed at full speed through the gates with a look of deep guilt on his face. It was the same response that they always received when this question was asked.

The answer to this imponderable question was never to be solved, nor the reason for the Lord God's intransigence to respond, for the end was nigh. A loud trumpet sounded, its echo filling the skies. All those present turned and bowed their heads as they watched enter among them a youngish man, thin as a rake with deep purple shadows under his eyes as though he hadn't slept for weeks. He came through the gates and was greeted by the Lord God.

"Hi there, son!" said the Lord God. "Where have

you been all this time? I really could do with your help to cure the ravages of the human mind and to purify the souls of those in my care. But you, J.C. seem reluctant to be much bothered by these matters any more. I think it would only be polite of you first to congratulate Pete on his promotion, don't you?" Silence, complete disinterest was the only feedback.

His son yawned loudly, but suddenly raised his half-closed eyes that were now full of enthusiasm, for he had heard a knocking from under the floor. The voice that accompanied this was full of deepest guile, but also alluring at the same time. "Yes, I'm coming," said the Lord God's son as he kneeled to put his ear next to the marble floor. The floor trembled and was pierced by a pitchfork that everyone could see appearing underneath the judgement seat.

"Hurry," said the velvet voice that was not to be denied. "You know that you're bored up there. You need the pleasures of the flesh, the joys of being free to do as you want. You need my kingdom."

So, the obedient son who had always followed his father's orders betrayed him and left through the Pearly Gates for the last time, bent on a life of sheer selfishness and decadence. With him went Pete who rather fancied what he'd heard coming from under the floor and for whom all this seemed a much easier option than being a gate-keeper and bearing the responsibilities of that great edifice in Rome. One by one the fishermen and the tax collector too followed their example, until there was no one left in the Lord God's kingdom, so that the

Pearly Gates gradually rusted and became lost forever under a vast covering of ivy.

The Billionaire's Yacht

"I'm reasonably fond of you," said Lord Satan to Pietro.

"And why shouldn't you be? I do everything you ask of me. Never have I disobeyed you. Not since I was born nine years ago."

"I can't, however, say the same about your parents. Giorgio is an ungrateful sod. There he is ensconced in that fabulous yacht with not a financial worry to his name and still he sulks and thinks that the world, including me for that matter, owe him more than he will ever need."

"And, Lord Satan, don't forget Felicia, my beloved mother. You should have put her out to grass a long time ago!"

Suddenly Pietro felt his throat grabbed in Satan's black talons. "Don't you ever again attempt to give me advice. It will be my decision and mine alone what happens to Felicia, to Giorgio and, indeed, to you, and don't you forget it …ever!"

Little boats were coming up the estuary. The unmistakable smell of the sea and the screeching of the seagulls filled the air when the yacht appeared, a sailing miracle that is more wondrous than any man-made structure standing on the shore, at least on this shore. Pirates in their galleons would not have recognised it as something that could transport them across the ocean. It is an object that, until recently, one would have imagined coming from some alien corner of space – incredibly imaginative, its beautiful lines a thing of dreams, of fantasy.

Yet mortal men walk on its decks and propel it over the waters of the earth. I know that this sailing wonder belongs to a billionaire – no great stretch of the imagination there, you may say. However, what you know and what I know have nothing in common ...but more of that later. The envy that it engenders must make those who are of a bitter, mean-minded disposition feel slightly nauseous with disbelief that such wealth exists. To build a creation like this, to maintain it, to man it, to load it every day when it's in port, with blooms that would do credit to the Royal Flower Show and to stow, aboard it, fantastically expensive wines and to fly in, from exotic places, food that makes taste buds ooze with pleasure, is beyond most people's wildest dreams.

I, Felicia, sit on top of a hill in my ivy-leafed tower watching this eye-catching miracle approach, wondering where Giorgio is, for it's his yacht. I know him well – my sometime mentor, lover and provider of life's little goodies, was also the father of my son and, indeed, still is.

He is coming up this English estuary, instead of floating on the waters of the Caribbean, to make me suffer further for what I did. He has incarcerated me in this tower and intends that the rest of my life should be spent here. He will make sure that the yacht's passage is as painstakingly slow as possible so that my memories will linger as long as possible. Not that I need any help to remember what I did.

For the moment this event is taking my mind off one of the most intriguing aspects of human existence: those ten little creations that are all mine, unique to me, completely different from anyone else's. I spend hour upon hour studying them; in fact, I have a magnifying glass so that I miss nothing of their intricacies, so that I can see them in all their glory.

I am, of course, referring to my fingers prints, without which I would be completely lost and bored. Just look at their whorls, loops, ridges and arches. I swear I can see the waves of the sea and the valleys of the earth all gathered on my fingers tips – or is my imagination in overdrive?

It's a misty day and thus the yacht's foghorn gives warning of its approach. However, I call it noise punishment, polluting the air to cause me as much annoyance as possible. I have done so much with these fingers of mine, things I couldn't possibly tell you ...but you know the sort of things I mean. Although you've probably done much worse, much more disgusting things, because that's human nature. I have even let my fingers move gently over the wheel of the yacht, been in full control of my billionaire's plaything of the sea, before things went so awfully awry. Oh, Giorgio, you shouldn't have done it, but I made you pay dearly, didn't I?

Believing him to be a danger to life and limb, you tried to kill our son, but it wasn't your right to do so, for you weren't the one who suffered the torments and agonies of childbirth. Did you really think that you would remove him so easily from the world by merely holding him under the water of the yacht's glorious swimming pool? I believe that you were eaten up with jealousy that Lord Satan had chosen me to commit the crime. Night and day, I enjoy my magical fingerprints, for I have decorated the walls of my tower with hand-prints and fingerprints, rather like cavemen used to do in their ancient, stony dwellings. The prints are all red, of course, without fail. Why, I've even crawled down the winding steps of the tower on my knees, so that I can have red decorations underfoot.

Yes, there must be a myriad of red prints on the wall and the floors of this tower, just like there were three years ago on the walls of the yacht, but that was blood not paint. The blood of my son – you'd be surprised how much blood gushes from a small boy's body, but I was, after all, just carrying out the orders of Lord Satan. He wanted a death and a death I gave him.

When I first held my son in my arms he was my sweet baby, but not for long. His true character soon showed itself: staring unblinkingly at me, biting and gnawing at me mercilessly and painfully when I gave him my milk, pummelling me with his small, cruel fists whenever he had the opportunity. He was a bad one from the beginning. Pietro was the name we had given him, a son of Satan rather than ours.

Pietro hated me, hated his father and the three of us hated each other. One unforgettable day, on board the yacht, red prints from his fingers had slid down the wall, scraping and clawing at the paint, while he died from the wounds I had plunged into him with my knife, but I couldn't let him live, could I ...a son who talked to demons and who cast spells on those around him? Because of his devil-driven mischief, the beautiful yacht was often in danger of sinking as it swayed and pitched, the waves and winds threatening to send it to the bottom of the seas.

Pietro is the only son, as far as I know, that Giorgio has ever produced, and for this reason alone there existed a very tenuous sort of paternal love. Nevertheless, Giorgio, too recognised evil when he saw it and blamed me for producing what he referred to as the spawn of the devil. However, it takes two to tango; whose genes were to blame for this imperfection would never be known.

Three years ago, Lord Satan told Pietro that he would die, but not to worry because he would not disappear permanently.

This has proved to be true, because Pietro is now with me in this tower, listening to the fog horn and to the gentle rhythm of the yacht's engine. He's in the whorls and the swirls and the spirals of my fingertips; I can see him quite plainly.

Satan has spoken to me very openly and told me that I am insane, but that I will just have to accept it.

"Yes, Lord Satan, I do accept it," I have said to him." I accept whatever you tell me."

As far as I know I am in this tower for ever, condemned here by Giorgio. By most people's standards it is a place of luxury, but I want to return to the yacht. Giorgio has a mistress on board, but one who will not be a mother, for he would never allow that to happen again... heaven only knows what she might produce.

Lord Satan appeared to me last night and told me what I must do. "Gnaw your fingertips until they bleed, rub them with sandpaper until they are smooth. Then we will be truly rid of Pietro, which is what we all want. He could one day, possibly, become my rival, which I cannot allow. Far better that he should sink forever into the skin of a mad woman like you, don't you agree?"

"Yes, Lord Satan, I agree."

Sleepwalker

Barbara sat in the middle of the lawn and, screwing up her eyes, looked at the amazing, silvery, full moon hanging indifferently in the sky. She held her hand up and touched its cold surface. It was uneven. She ran her fingers over its bumps, lumps and wrinkles, feeling its powdery covering of sand and dust. She longed to walk among its valleys and hills, to watch the distant earth turning on its axis.

Half awake, half asleep she felt a soft hand gently stroking the back of her neck. She loved the feeling. She wanted it to continue forever. Bingham sat down beside her on the grass. His warm breath stirred her dark curls. Her dreamy hope was that he truly loved her.

He did not. He did not love her, even one little bit. He loved Claudia. There was no one to compare with Claudia. No one could hold a candle to her. The flame of love burned only for her.

Bingham touched Barbara's hand.

"Back to bed, Barbara," he whispered. "It's too cold out here." Barbara wished the moon a fond goodnight. She promised to return another time to feel its soul, to feed upon its spirit. She allowed Bingham to lead her into the house. He pulled the eiderdown over her and kissed her forehead. She fell into a deep sleep.

In the morning, the sun made a fiery, intrusive entrance through the bedroom window. That was its nature. It was hot, golden and interested in everything. It was the world's signal to start the day.

Barbara knew that she had walked in the moonlight, for her feet were dirty. The eiderdown was clearly an act of kindness shown to her by Bingham. It was not a usual occurrence. If only he always treated her as he had seemed to do last night. Had she perhaps dreamed it?

It was Claudia, his lover, who freely received what was hers. Barbara hated her. She felt unbearable anger towards her. She was jealous of her.

"You know what you have to do, don't you, Claudia?" said Bingham.

"Yes, I do," replied Claudia.

Murder would have been the more precise reply. Then there would have been no room for doubt. Nevertheless, both Bingham and Claudia understood perfectly. After all murder is one of those things that you don't really mess about with. Do you? You must have a workable plan. As you will see later, Claudia's heart was just not in it. Religious doubts! They needed a rainy day. What was required was a slippery, dark, rainy day, with everyone staying inside for shelter. With a text message, Barbara would be lured to the main road. With a push, Claudia would then send her skidding underneath a lorry. Its wheels would crush her. The dirty deed would only take a split second and they would be free. Then a life of happiness would follow for the lovebirds. After the police enquiry and a post-mortem, that is!

The plan was flawed. Well, what a silly plan it was, like kids playing at cops and robbers. Barbara lost her mobile. This was a foreseen circumstance and should have been taken into account. She was always losing her mobile. Claudia pretended to have sprained her ankle.

Barbara stood at the long window. Outside a flock of small, white birds passed in front of her eyes, which signified healing. However, murder was on her mind. The murder of Claudia! Poison was to be the answer to ending her Calvary.

The two tea cups moved in their saucers as Barbara rushed past them to open the door. The spoons clinked.

"Come in, Claudia! I'm so pleased you accepted my invitation," gushed Barbara.

"How could I not? Such kindness!" replied Claudia, insincerely.

Barbara patted her dress pocket reassuringly. A phial of poison lay within. Soon it was mixed with the scented tea in one of the pretty, flower-patterned cups.

Claudia, suspicious, knew it was war. She did not eat a sandwich or a cake.

She did not take a single sip of tea.

"I apologise, Barbara, but I don't feel well. I must

go home to bed." She stood up to leave. As she left, the cat entered the room, feeling very thirsty. *"I'll have a drink of tea",* it thought.

The cat died.

Claudia did not die.

Dammit!

Claudia, in her spare time a wiccan witch, was sworn to harm no one. This was a problem. Otherwise she was free to do as she wished.

Sitting at the kitchen table she studied the Book of Shadows, her cookbook of spells. Magic was her ally. She had the support of her coven. She was, therefore, bound to triumph. How could she fail? Barbara's days should be numbered. Murder, however, was out. Find Barbara a lover. That might be a good idea, but surely no one would want her. Spread around the room were the tools of her faith: a broomstick, a cauldron, candles, incense, statues of the Moon Goddess and of the Sun God, those dual protectors of the earth. Around her neck hung a pentagon on a chain.

Bingham watched her. He suspected that she would never do the dreaded deed. Her faith told her that if she did harm she would be paid back threefold.

"You believe all this magic mumbo jumbo, Claudia, so do something constructive for a change."

"What can I do? I can't harm her. She tried to poison me, but I still can't hurt her. Thanks to the Moon Goddess she lost her mobile, thus saving both herself and me. Wicca spells are only cast to achieve good."

Bingham was beyond frustrated by her. Was it really so hard to encourage the love of his life to kill off her rival?

It seemed it was. However, as you will find out, there was one solution.

Barbara lay slumbering in bed. Soon she roused. She made her way confidently down the stairs, eyes glazed. She unlatched the door and stepped once more into the cold light shed by the moon. She gazed again at its face. She loved the dark patches on its surface. It was like a person. Look at it and all sorts of features appeared. You needed a little imagination to see this miracle. Tonight, she did not touch its face. Tonight, she left it to shine in peace.

Animal noises could be heard in the bushes ...a badger perhaps, mice or even a fox! In the trees, birds were snuggled up together, liking the company.

Barbara was asleep. She was also awake. She was again sitting on the grass. She sensed a presence. She could smell Bingham's cigar. She saw its glow in the darkness. He then knelt down by her. He lay on top of her, body to body. Barbara was so happy. There was nothing sexual about it. It was pure love, she thought.

The dark hours were about to change into ugliness. Bingham was grimacing unpleasantly. He placed his hands tightly around Barbara's neck. "Beautiful moon," she pleaded, "don't let me die. Please let me live so I can talk to you while I wander in the night."

He squeezed and twisted until she was dead. "I'm

so sorry, my darling, but really, in truth, I didn't like you."

Claudia looked upon the scene from a lighted window in the house. She had won. She herself was innocent, because she had not raised a finger to hurt Barbara. Her conscience was intact. She would not be punished threefold. Bingham was hers. Barbara's light had been extinguished for good.

She came down to the garden and stood at Bingham's side. They both looked up at the moon. Its face was ugly: its silver had turned blood red. Yellow-edged, moody clouds passed in front of it. In the bushes and trees nothing moved, nothing made a sound.

Claudia was frightened and Bingham was shaking with terror.

He had killed the sleepwalker.

He had angered the moon.

He had transfigured the night.

Stormy Weather

To be in love was the most wonderful feeling in the world for, however bad the weather was, in one's heart the sun was always shining.

As Fleur and Seth walked along the station platform the rain was still coming down so, arm in arm, they cosily shared a red umbrella. They looked along the length of the train and could see, rising in the distance, the tall houses of Paris.

They were delirious with happiness, for they were on their way to Istanbul, A porter was following them with their well-worn luggage decorated with old train and hotel labels. Seth was a dealer in precious gems and travelled all over Europe, but this time Fleur was with him. It would be her first visit to Istanbul, that wondrous city where two continents face each other across the Bosphorus.

The clouds were darkening, and it seemed that a storm was threatening, for they could hear the gentle rumbling of thunder somewhere in the distance.

Fleur and Seth were smartly dressed travellers; Seth in his cream raincoat and homburg hat, Fleur wearing a red dress and black jacket, set off by a red cloche hat. In her hand she carried a black clutch bag. A handsome pair was how people-watchers would have described them: Fleur with her blonde hair coiled into a chignon and chisel-featured Seth even better looking than Ivor Novello: in other words, a real matinée idol. Elegance was the keynote of the day, for it was the Orient Simplon Express that was to carry them to Istanbul.

The lights were on inside the train and, as they passed the carriages, they glimpsed through the windows a plethora of colourful day-dresses and men in dark suits. Walking along, they also saw people drinking in the station's refreshment room, the delicious smell of coffee beans hitting them as the door opened and closed. Rain gurgled and dripped from the guttering above, making little whirlpools in the puddles beneath.

Then a sudden lightning flash split the sky and the thunder roared; this seemed like a rehearsal for something bad ...everyone knew that stormy weather was forecast, not only meteorologically, but also across the political front. War was hovering on the horizon. They all feared that soon it would be the thunder of guns and the lightning crack of rifles that filled the air.

Under the drenching, a slatted wooden bench with wrought iron decorative arms stood unattended and empty. A newspaper had been left on the seat, which was in danger of disintegrating into a sodden mess that would not survive being moved and in front of the bench was a battered, brown suitcase that had long ago seen better days: obviously not destined for the Orient Express, although you could never tell.

When Fleur saw this sad little trio of abandonment – the bench, the newspaper and the suitcase – her heart fell, and her stomach turned; there was something vaguely disturbing about the scene, but she could not grasp what it was.

In a flash, however, this was forgotten. She felt Seth's hand squeeze hers as they both held tightly onto the umbrella; a sudden blast of wind catching it would have carried it into the air had it not been restrained.

A guard standing on the train steps watched and envied them. Such happiness, he thought, was to be savoured and appreciated because it is often something so fleeting that it is hard to capture again. Thus, he stood in his smart uniform with braided, cuffed sleeves, immaculate white gloves and a small bow tie, all topped off by the kepi he wore on his head. When Seth saw him he noted his small, dark moustache and the swathe of dark hair across one side of his forehead, the very image of that awful little man in Berlin who seemed to be flitting in and out of people's thoughts and dreams, making them less sure of the future. The lightning zigzagged again across the sky like a heart breaking in two, and the guard thought of his dead wife whom he had loved deeply.

They reached their carriage and waited for the porter with the trolley. Near at hand was their steward ready to welcome them on board and escort them to their compartment; like all the staff he was immaculately dressed and well-mannered. By this time steam was billowing fiercely from the engine and the smell of burning coal and oil assaulted their nostrils as the driver prepared for the journey.

Seth was the first to board because he wanted to help Fleur onto the train. She put up her hand to grasp his ...and then she knew no more of the journey to Istanbul nor, indeed, of Seth. The earth seemed to move as the thunder and lightning reached their peak, and the rain came down in a torrent. Clashing, flashing, reverberation and unrelenting moisture assailed her senses.

Fleur had clearly seen Seth's outstretched hand reaching towards her, but before she could take it she was torn away, pulled backwards and was lost and blind in a thick haze of steam. She could see absolutely nothing of the Orient Express and was conscious of being turned around in the opposite direction by some unknown force.

As she walked through the steam she found herself still on the platform and it was still raining. However, she remembered neither Seth, nor the red umbrella, nor the Orient Express so she was, therefore, not annoyed that he had left her unprotected from the elements and that within half a minute she was soaked through. Feeling like a drowned rat and beginning to shake with apprehension, she just longed for a hot bath and a good night's sleep.

As she walked down towards the slatted wooden

bench and the station refreshment room, a familiar sight greeted her: one that she did not relish. Zacharias, sheltered by his grey umbrella, was waiting for her, seated on the bench with his newspaper, safe and dry, tucked into the breast of his raincoat. He had not long arrived from Venice and was incandescent with rage that she had not been there to meet him. When he stood up she could see that, not unusually for him, he had been drinking – neat whisky, for sure, from the refreshment room – for he staggered slightly and slurred his loving greeting to her.

"Where the hell have you been, then? You look as though you have been dragged through a hedge backwards."

"I'm sorry, but I truly couldn't help it. The car is so old it just doesn't like the wet weather."

"Don't start on about that again. You know what, Fleur, you're becoming a real nag and I don't like nags. Nags have to be punished, so we'll talk about this when we get home, shall we?"

Although he had plenty of money, Zacharias had a tight fist and would not splash out on what he considered unnecessary luxuries – hence his rather shabby appearance and his even shabbier, brown suitcase. His tight fist also contributed to Fleur's bruises, all applied to places unseen by others. He brought not one whit of happiness, of kindness, or consideration to her life: it was a loveless, cold, vicious relationship.

Meanwhile Seth, still at the station, was hanging out of

one of the train windows. He knew she would be late for she always was, forever leaving things to the last minute. She enjoyed making an entrance so that everyone could tell her how beautiful she looked.

A sudden commotion somewhere on the platform made him turn his head, and there she was, that exotic creature, swanning along in her ridiculously high heels, as always dressed to kill, with a retinue of porters and guards all in tow. Her wonderfully tasteful, deep-blue luggage would doubtless be new. Each time she travelled on the Orient Express she purchased a new set, the colour always carefully coordinated with her clothes bought from whoever was her favourite designer of the moment, be it Schiaparelli or Coco Chanel. She approached wafting the alluring fragrance of Bellodgia in her wake. She was in tune with the rain, carrying as an accessory an elegant umbrella, still unrolled however, because she had been protected from the elements by her coterie of new admirers.

Seth was sexually consumed by her, but recognised that basically she was not a pleasant woman. She was egotistical, self-serving, someone from whom there would be no tender love. She was sarcastic, sharp-tongued, someone from whom there would be no gentle, shared laughter. Her name was Mireya.

When she entered the compartment he immediately grabbed her, but she summarily pushed him away. "Can't you ever wait, Seth?"

"Not for you, girlie!"

"Don't call me that, please. I am not your girlie, as

you so eloquently put it. It sounds so common. And stop using that silly cockney accent. It annoys me beyond belief."

So, there were Seth and Fleur, two unhappy souls in an inhospitable world. Each in their own individual realms of existence, they intuited that somewhere else, in another dimension, things were different; that true, selfless love was possible and, far away from the stormy weather, there was a place with sunshine, warmth and rainbows.

Time dragged slowly as the skies continued to darken for Fleur. If she had but known it, however, she only had to raise her hand and a hair's breadth away, invisible and untouchable, was Seth in his own universe. She would have been able to watch him fall onto the sodden mud of a foreign field, slaughtered by the soldiers of a tyrannical one-time house-painter. She would have mourned for him with all her soul. Mireya simply shrugged off his death as an unfortunate accident, before resuming her shallow, butterfly-life protected, as ever, from reality by her lack of feeling. Eventually the storm clouds moved away, and Europe slowly began to recover from the buffeting it had received, but Fleur and Seth were separated, it would seem forever, until the day their worlds would collide again, and they would be united for another few years in the great circle of time.

The Abandonment

Revenge is wonderful, and Miriam was nobody's fool. Therefore, she had purchased a plane ticket to Tijuana as a birthday present for Carrie, her very best friend in all the world.

At the moment Miriam was doing her Lady of the Camellias bit, because she'd been abandoned, dumped, left on the rubbish pile. She felt like a stray dog – a well-heeled dog, but, nevertheless, one that no one wanted. Basically, we all take rejection badly and Miriam was no exception. Well, she could wilt with the best of them – nothing like a good wallow in one's own misery to make one feel better. She would just have to be careful not to overdo it or her friends would become fed up with her – after all, one can only stand so much unhappiness and then it all gets rather tedious.

Nevertheless, while it was hot off the press she was going to milk it for all it was worth (there's a mixed metaphor for you – so much for her very expensive education). She would wear darker clothes, put on paler make-up, leave off the lippie – it would all add to the drama of the situation, (perhaps she had missed her true vocation by not treading the boards – but mother would never have approved!)

She had seen Dominic's abandonment coming and had prepared for it accordingly. Her darling friend of so many years' standing, that bitch Carrie, was as thick as two short planks, but unfortunately beat Miriam hands down in the beauty stakes; she was prettier, had a better figure and possessed a lovely, sexy voice that in no way could be imitated. Carrie would not, however, be happy for long. Unfortunately for her, she had always thought of Miriam as an expert on everything: a sort of modern-day oracle, especially when it was a question of cosmetic surgery.

Carrie had always been far too pretty for Miriam's peace of mind, but Carrie didn't think that absolute perfection had been achieved, so when she asked Miriam to recommend a good plastic surgeon the temptation to give the name of probably the worst one in the whole world could not be resisted. She knew that very soon Carrie would be over the Mexican border and into Tijuana and, if things worked out as they should, would come back with an extremely botched cosmetic job. She'd probably been persuaded to have other parts of her anatomy sorted out – the more the merrier Miriam thought!

That very evocative, very mysterious word *love* was to be found nowhere in Miriam's lexicon. To be honest she wasn't sure that she understood too well what it meant. She knew that one of her children, in a petulant, hormone-driven mood, had told her that the only person she loved was herself, which she had thought was quite unkind, but didn't dwell too much on it. Did she love Dominic? She didn't think so – in fact, hate might have been nearer the mark. Had she ever loved him? Probably not! There was one aspect of marriage on which she didn't like to dwell –she just didn't understand what people saw in it: a pretty weird business she thought. Why couldn't God, or whoever was in charge of these arrangements, have found an easier and more pleasant way to procreate the species? Sometimes she wondered why he had bothered at all – her children would be prime examples of procreation gone wrong. It doesn't sound very motherly but *little devils* was the description that passed most often through her mind! They still thought that the sun shone out of Dominic's whatsit, but she wondered what they would think of this latest fracas: their mother abandoned and left helpless, to fend for herself!

Actually, in some ways, she was quite pleased he had gone – the trouble with people who work at home was that they were there all the time: there was never any respite; a continuous awareness of someone else's likes and dislikes; never fully able to please oneself. Her idea of heaven, and one in which she intended fully to indulge herself from this time forward, was whole days spent reading a juicy Jackie Collins, (why did sex always seem so much more appealing in fiction than it was in reality?) with Wilfred, the pug dog, lying on her lap, and a huge packet of scrumptious, teeth-ruining, fat-forming Maltesers; in fact, several packets – the best way possible to get spots – but who cared?

Well, actually, she did because, from now onwards, she was hell-bent on finding herself a new man – no real commitment, you understand – no sex (well, you've heard her views on that one) – only promises left dangling in the air, as one might say. She rather fancied the idea of a married man – exciting little rendezvous in discreet, expensive restaurants, secret meetings in lovely bijoux hotels, even weekends abroad – though that might involve more than she was prepared to give.

However, it would be a wonderful excuse for buying lots of lovely, frothy underwear and, she supposed, if the worse came to the worst, she could always lie back and think of England (heaven knows, she'd had enough practice!). She would, of course, expect ridiculously expensive little gifts such as a diamond ring or two – she was not the love-in-a-garret type!

Eventually Carrie returned from Tijuana in an awful state – her former beauty not completely destroyed, but certainly far from the near-perfection it had once been. Something desperate had happened to her lips and to her nose, her skin so tight that it seemed she would be unable to smile ever again ...and what joy that was for Miriam! Nevertheless, the shocking, stunning discovery was that Dominic was still with her, apparently still loved her. Good grief, was this what true-love meant, had she in some way missed the boat, misunderstood the nature of that strange emotion?

Every time she looked in a mirror, Carrie saw this ugly face looking back at her and was not best pleased, but Miriam had been lulled into a false sense of her own superior intelligence, for Carrie had a dark side, hidden under her cloak of naivety.

So she decided to pay Miriam a little visit, share a drink or two or more with her. Miriam had always been very fond of dry martinis – undoubtedly her favourite tipple – lots of lovely gin with only the smallest possible smidgen of vermouth. Carrie had not stood on ceremony and, as soon as the door closed behind her, went immediately to the crux of the matter.

"You did it on purpose, Miriam. You knew perfectly well that you were sentencing me to a life of ugliness. How would you like to feel the need to put a paper bag over your face every time you have to face the world?" Miriam giggled; her penchant for dry martinis had its limitations and she was now finding the world a very amusing place to be, although it seemed to have a tendency to revolve.

"You're a bitch, Carrie. Best friends don't steal each other's husbands. Dominic was mine and you had no business setting your eyes upon him," she slurred. She then shrieked with laughter, pointing her finger at Carrie's face. "Have you looked in the mirror lately?"

"But it was Dominic who abandoned you – it was his choice, not mine. All I wanted was a little bit of romance and would have preferred to have kept it all secret."

"You sneaky cow!"

"What a lady you are, Miriam, with your cows and your bitches!"

By this time the gin was flowing freely down Miriam's throat. "Hell-cat, crow-face," she screamed defiantly. Soon she was lying in a deep alcoholic coma, snoring loudly, as Carrie opened her handbag to remove from its interior a sharp, medium-sized kitchen knife with which she bloodily destroyed Miriam's face. She should have left the house there and then, but unwisely stayed around so she could glory in her own handiwork.

Not surprisingly Miriam eventually surfaced from her slumber, and was now screaming in pain, but Carrie wanted to wait until she was sober enough to be able to take in what she was going to be shown in her pretty, blue velvet-backed hand-mirror with its surround of coloured stones. Her face was shredded, but Carrie felt no horror or remorse at what she had done. It served the bitch right.

Carrie, nevertheless, had misjudged her victim. In a flash her own kitchen knife was turned upon her and she knew that she was dying ...but not without taking another victim with her.

Wilfred had been watching all these goings-on, barking his little head off, but not for much longer. Carrie, who despite her svelte figure, was quite a heavy girl, fell upon him as she gasped away her few remaining breaths, keeping him under her until she could agonisingly pull the knife out of her body and scrape it across the little pug's stomach. Revenge and hatred had been her last thoughts, as she suspected that Miriam had loved the dog more than she had ever loved any human being.

Thus, the stage was set for the penultimate scene – a dead mistress, a dead dog and a fatally injured wife with a fair amount of blood scattered around. In some distant, foggy place Miriam heard the front door opening and Dominic's keys dropping onto the hall table. It was not a pretty sight that met his eyes and he didn't know what to do – a bit of a conundrum to say the least. It might have been a good idea to ring for the police or for an ambulance, but Dominic's brain had ceased to function, his only thought being to empty the room, his favourite in the house, of all this horror – in other words to have a bit of a clean-up.

He stood gazing out at the garden, wondering what the hell he was going to do with the three gory victims of a gruesome crime. The toss of a coin – that was the answer so that the responsibility was not his, but that of chance. Actually, he didn't realise that Miriam was still, rather groggily, in the land of the living. Heads for the river, tails for the attic. Tails it was; so up to the attic he dragged the two women where he made them nice and cosy amongst the furry insulation cladding where they would soon decompose. What a horrible way for poor Miriam to die: tortured by furry cladding tickling her face.

As for Wilfred, Dominic decided he would pop him into the fridge as a temporary measure; he was a sufficiently small pug-like creature to be able to fit in there quite snugly. He'd been a good dog: nice but noisy.

 It was the next morning when the cleaning lady inadvertently let the cat out of the bag and thus started the final scene of the drama. She had thought it strange that there was blood on the carpet, which someone had obviously tried to remove, but she took out her feather duster and just got on with her work. Why Dominic had forgotten about Wilfred was anyone's guess, but when the unfortunate lady opened the fridge door to take out some milk for her mid-morning coffee, there she discovered the ruined pug lying on the second shelf from the top.

His eyes were still open to reflect the terror he had felt at his end. A horribly deep wound had been carved into his stomach. It would surely have made far more sense to have placed him in a freezer drawer. Wilfred and the blooded carpet made her suspect all was not well, so she rang the police. She didn't realise that Dominic was still upstairs in bed where the evening before he had consumed a whole bottle of Glenfiddich twelve-year-old malt whisky, hoping that the gruesome event had simply not happened.

Now, Dominic is in prison: his cache of bodies discovered, his mind in denial. He is, of course, the only suspect of the crime, but if we are to have any faith at all in the judicial system, his innocence will soon be proven, once the forensic investigators have done their work. There will thus be a happy ending to the story!

The Bartered Bride

She was always looking away, always looking for something or someone, always looking for an excuse not to look at him! There was a slyness about her, like a green-eyed cat with a secret.

Poor Edward, erstwhile widower, now newly wed, sat alone in the dining room as the evening gloom descended. The remains of his dinner lay virtually untouched; only the port had been consumed. He was so deep in thought and so riven with misery that he didn't realise how cold he was feeling. He just stared at the unlit fire, heaped with logs, as though it had no connection with him. Even if he had been aware of the chill, he would have felt little inclination to do anything about it; as for lighting the gas mantles, well, that too was of no interest whatsoever to him.

His hands, inert and lifeless, rested on his knees in such a pose that one could see he had no illusions left; his shoulders were slumped, his chin tucked into his chest; he was truly the epitome of hopelessness. It had all been such a terrible mistake for a man of his advancing years. He should have learned by his age, that it was always better to love lightly. Had he been of a less sensitive nature he would have risen above his tragedy, but this was simply not an option for him. It had been rather like an auction acquiring Lavinia.

Lord Cabot, impoverished, had four daughters of marriageable age, but Edward, rich and a man of property, wanted only her. He knew full well, of course, that it was a purely business arrangement: a marriage of convenience. However, Lavinia, as an obedient daughter, had expressed her willingness to marry him, but that was as far as her part in the affair seemed to carry her. Otherwise, she appeared totally uninvolved, completely disinterested in all the preparations for the wedding.

Now matters had worsened for, as his wife, Lavinia had gradually become more and more morose and sulky: so much so, that it was now an embarrassment, especially in front of the servants. She seated at one end of the table, he at the other, dinner would pass in complete silence with only the sound of china and cutlery being moved by the butler, to relieve it. She made no attempt to hide her ill humour, and so it was well known below stairs how things stood. She was now almost defiant in her unpleasant manner and had begun to mutter under her breath when things didn't quite suit her. Her father would have been shocked if he'd known of her behaviour, for all his daughters had been strictly brought up, not given any leeway where manners and compliance were concerned.

Before dinner that evening, as Edward stood in

front of the cheerful fire in the drawing room trying to engage her in conversation, she had suddenly looked up from her desk, slammed the book she was reading face down, almost breaking its spine in the process. Then she had rushed through the red, velvet curtains into the anteroom, stopped suddenly and, with her head to one side, looked at her reflection quizzically in the large mirror. He watched her as her face seemed to touch the glass; two pairs of green eyes staring deeply at each other, as though she needed to see not only her outward form, but also her innermost thoughts.

"Nobody likes me, do they, Edward?" she said suddenly, turning to look at him. He went and placed his hands upon her shoulders and they looked at each other in the mirror. The thought, not for the first time, passed through her mind that, with his rather strange moustache, he looked not unlike a kindly, old walrus. She then turned her eyes downwards so that this fleeting moment of intimacy should end.

The sun was shining palely, with just enough strength for Lavinia's shadow to fall upon the broad, stone steps that held her gaze as she descended. The cold, blustery wind made her wrap her cloak more tightly around her body and make sure the hood was secure. She hated this place, which she had visited so often in the last few years, but now her hatred had intensified with a vengeance. She hated the tall, evergreen hedges that enclosed the steps, hated the bare, lifeless trees of autumn that could be seen peeping over the hedges, silhouetted against a threatening sky and most of all hated the tall, narrow, turquoise house at the top of the steps.

She had, for some reason, never been inside the house. It frightened her, with its arched, wooden doors that were forever slightly ajar. From them, a flurry of torn, white, blank paper was eternally being whirled in the air by the wind, only to fall eventually onto the steps where it joined the brown, dry, crumbling leaves that were always there.

What frightened Lavinia most were the six arched windows above the arched door; from each one a demon peeped out, gazing at her intently, while white curtains billowed, blown by the wind; she thought she knew what this meant, but didn't like to think about it too deeply.

On all sides she was boxed in by the hedges, by the house and by another hedge in front of her, which almost completely hid a very narrow, wrought iron gate, her only means of escape. If only she were courageous enough to open it! She couldn't do that, however, and so was forever imprisoned on the steps, until daylight shone through her bedroom windows and awoke her from her dream.

One of the first things that Lavinia remembered when the maid came to open the curtains was the feel of Edward's hands on her shoulders. Why this should be, she had no idea, for she certainly didn't love him. An ageing man like him? He wasn't at all what she would have chosen for herself, but then when had she ever had her own way over anything? Her father had been the dominant, overbearing figure in the home that she had not long left. Now there was Edward, someone whom she didn't really know, taking his place. She realised only too well that he didn't approve of her behaviour, but she was unhappy and certainly didn't feel like the mistress of her magnificent, new home. So how, other than with a touch of sulking and defiance, was she supposed to react?

"Why won't you ever talk to me, Lavinia? I'm not some sort of ogre. Why don't you ever want to look me in the eyes? You are always so careful to avoid my gaze. You're not a prisoner here, you know; you're the mistress of the house, free to express your opinions, free to do and command as you please."

Lavinia looked at him from the other end of their breakfast table and, as her hand began to tremble, she slowly put down her cup of coffee. Startled, she opened her green eyes wide and, for almost the first time ever, allowed herself to heed his words and to search his face as she did so. "But I've never been free, Edward. I don't know what freedom is. All I know is that I have been bought and sold for cash like a commodity on the stock market: always, since a child, hemmed in by what other people want."

She was coiled up inside like a spring, tightly enclosed within herself, just as she was within the cloak in her dream. The demons of her past, from which she couldn't escape, were always with her: the bullying from her sisters, the furtive slaps from the housekeeper, the harshness from her father. It did, indeed, seem that no-one had ever liked her; there was obviously something about her that invited this sort of reaction from other people. So, what about Edward? It must obviously follow that he too should dislike her.

"Don't be such a silly girl. I love you and it makes me unhappy to see your discontent, your unhappiness."

She continued to stare at him: Edward unhappy …and all because of her! Who would have thought such thing? She had been so tightly bound in her own misery, that she had never imagined that she could be the cause of someone else's unhappiness. Was she really so important that she actually made a difference to Edward's life? She smiled at him for the first time ever, and a shadow lifted from his heart. This revelation had opened her mind to a world of possibilities never before considered and rising from her chair, she went to the other end of the table. Putting her face next to his she kissed him gently on the lips, while he put his arms around her and rested his head against her breast.

Lavinia again walked down the steps, this time her cloak swung loosely behind her, the hood down. It was a glorious day, the sun shining so brightly that her shadow was dark and sharply defined on the steps. The hedges had been drastically pruned so that she could see over them. The trees were now in full leaf. The demons had disappeared from the arched windows and the doors were firmly shut. Some unknown hand had swept the torn paper and brown leaves of autumn into a neat, orderly pile.

When she came to the bottom of the steps her heart began to flutter as she saw once more the narrow, wrought-iron gate. She hesitated for a long moment, then firmly pulled it open. She just about managed to squeeze through, although a large ivy-covered tree prevented her from seeing too clearly what was in front of her, what she was walking into …and it was Death himself who was waiting for her. With his skull peeping out from his black hood and his enormous gum-less teeth seeming to smile at her, he had come to claim her for his own.

So poor confused Lavinia died of a heart attack in her sleep – peacefully, with no pain: Edward, his newly awoken happiness, and perhaps hers too, suddenly at an end, was completely heartbroken, lonely and cast down. He remained so for one whole year, but the profligate Lord Cabot came calling again as soon as he deemed that a decent interval had passed since Lavinia's death. He was not one to let sensitivity stand in his way.

Thus, once more, began the cattle market. He had three remaining daughters available, but Edward didn't mind which one he married; there was no obvious winner in his eyes. Lord Cabot, however, had calculated carefully the worth of each girl and decided that Victoria was the obvious choice. He didn't appreciate Edward's indifference to it all, his love for

Lavinia still burning brightly. There was no richer landowner in the county than Edward, and Lord Cabot would, therefore, offer him the best of his collection, hoping that he would not look to other powerful families for a wife.

Before many days had passed, he and Edward, plus two very astute lawyers, were huddled together before the fire in the drawing room, haggling and arguing over the terms of the alliance, while the bride-wealth of his cowed, shy, youngest daughter, Victoria, who had her own demons with which to contend, was negotiated: another lamb to the slaughter, another potentially doomed marriage, another bartered bride.

The Doormat

It's payback time, the worm is finally turning. The doormat, at this stage showing its age and well past its sell-by date, is at last moving to a more congenial place where it will no longer be trodden upon. Yes, it's payback time for my darling as she languishes upon the chaise longue – I mean, who these days has a chaise longue, though I've no doubt they do very well at auctions in *Flog It*, or *The Antiques Road Show* and the like? Left to me it would all be minimalist, nice clean lines, nobody's old hand-me-downs but, as usual, my tastes have been ignored and we are surrounded by dark, highly-waxed furniture and a plethora of red velvet.

However, the doormat is not the only weathered object in the room, for my darling has spent far too much time in the full glare of the sun, far too much money cultivating a fashionable tan, which is why we usually sit with the curtains slightly closed so that the leathery skin is not too obvious. If she had been less keen on dieting and less derogatory about her pale, plump friends she would not now look quite so …well …haggard for want of another word!

"What did you say, my darling? Your toes hurt! Just let me kneel and I will massage them for you… There, that's better, isn't it? Can't have those beautiful footsie-wootsies hurting, can we?"

I look into those still-beautiful, blue eyes that gaze down at me from the ravaged, lined face and think to myself; *you treacherous old bitch, you evil woman, you really are a true daughter of Eve*, for I have been as bewitched as Adam was – and look where that got us all!

The only problem is that I still love her to distraction, despite her infidelities, despite her scornful treatment towards yours truly, despite all her other really unforgivable peccadilloes, some of them spectacularly against the law of the land! The tax man would turn in his grave if he only knew.

Of course, a nice little line in blackmail, a few threats hanging over her would always be an easy option – rather too easy, however, because any man worth his salt likes a bit of a challenge and, as I'm about to turn over a new leaf, that includes me! A man of action – that's what I'm going to become!

To be honest with you, at the moment, I'm rather an emotional mess, which is what obsessive love does to you. I've thought of killing her, of killing myself, of killing anyone she looks at twice but, somehow, I never get around to it! Pathetic, isn't it, to be so wishy-washy, so ineffectual?

So how am I going to assert myself? Well, I'm going to move because a change of venue is always a good idea. How I will put this to her I'm not quite sure, because there will be hell to pay when I tell her, if I tell her …oh God!

"You what! You slimy little slug – I bet it wasn't your idea! Not moving into a love nest, are you? Not found a girl friend, have you? Of course you haven't, because no one would want you! And, anyway, you can't possibly leave me …you're too besotted with me, you wimp!"

"I'm leaving you, Veronica, you better believe it! I've had enough of you and your petulant ways …and of this truly awful house – both you and the house permanently like an ice box! The place is falling to pieces – look at the mould on the walls, look at the rotting window frames, look at the bulging ceilings; heaven only know what's up there!" I point dramatically at the offending defects. "And one day someone is going to die if something isn't done about the electricity circuit!"

"Haven't you forgotten, Johnny, that this is my house, bought with my money? You can't afford anywhere of your own – so forget that one!"

Sounds like dialogue from some cheap Hollywood movie, doesn't it? …the sort of script the cast must have a good giggle over!

Anyway, to cut a long story short, after a great deal more conversation in a similar vein I did, indeed, move. Not into something luxurious, not with my small pension – the only money that I can truly call my own. No, my little, rented flat is nothing to write home about, especially if you take into account the continuous noise of heavy traffic beneath my window; second only, I would think, to living in the flight path of Heathrow Airport.

The only object that I own, in fact, is a rather nice Indian carpet that I bought in a sale in Birmingham when I was still married to my first wife, before I divorced her – so I suppose I really own only half of it! The two rooms are, of course, much too small to accommodate it, so it is doubled over under my very nice, queen-size bed, which is my favourite place of retreat, especially as the heating in the flat is on the way out, but the landlord's wife, feeling rather sorry for me has, as some sort of compensation, I suppose, provided me with a very comfortable electric blanket. The furniture is at a minimum, so I finally achieved the minimalist look, but not quite in the way I had imagined.

My darling, in the meantime, is still ensconced, not alone I would think, in the ageing house – perhaps one day it will literally crumble around her – I can only hope so, though I would grieve for her dreadfully and cannot imagine a world without her.

I'm afraid and rather ashamed to say that I have become something of a stalker because I know my darling Veronica's routine only too well; therefore, I accidentally on purpose do bump into her from time to time, usually in The Ivy Leaf Coffee House (where they do a very nice cappuccino with masses of cream on top, finished off with a sprinkling of cinnamon). We occasionally share a table, when I desperately try to make her love me again as she must have done once upon a time. Of course, the conversation eventually and inevitably always ends in the same way.

"Well, Johnny, my little 'fraidy-cat, living alone obviously doesn't agree with you, does it? You should have stayed where you were with your Veronica, shouldn't you? I have to say I never thought you had it in you to leave! You're sure it's not a touch of senility? Personally, I think that's what it must be – you've been showing signs of it for the last few months. You know, if I were you I'd go and have a little chat with the doctor before it's too late – perhaps a few pills might help you, don't you think?"

Surely she isn't suffering feelings of rejection – now that would be a triumph for me! "Bloody woman, that's right, rile me, do your best to make me suffer as you've always done. But I won't be trodden on again by you, my darling heart, my sweetie pie, my one and only love – you haggard-faced old bat!"

Tempers by this time have risen to a peak. As for the rest of the coffee drinkers; well, they are by now either sitting in an embarrassed silence resolutely sipping away or are staring open-mouthed at the floor show, their coffee, croissants and cupcakes completely forgotten.

I have finally realised, rather late in the day, I'm afraid, that I will never get her back and that I made completely the wrong move by leaving because, of course, she can now claim that I deserted her. I suppose this is now just grounds for divorce, which is the last thing I want, because while she bears my name she is still a part of me.

When you read what is to follow please don't wonder how I did it or about my modus operandi, because it was all rather unpleasant and I don't really want to dwell too deeply upon it. To think that I was capable of such cruelty towards another human being, especially towards someone who had been my whole life, simply appals me, so I shall just leave you guessing.

The small television in my bedroom is my one form of entertainment; to read a book is now completely beyond my powers of concentration. I'm not enjoying sleeping in here as much as I did, as I have to keep the window ajar now, which creates a hell of a draught – hence my runny nose and permanent cough. However, at least the smell from the traffic is better than the growing stench coming from beneath my bed, more specifically from the rolled up Indian carpet where my darling lies rotting away. The heat emitted from the electric blanket, has, I'm afraid, precipitated this process more quickly than I would have liked. Poor Veronica would be so upset to know that her delicious, expensive perfumes – Oscar de la Renta, Diorissima, etcetera – have been replaced by the scent of putrefaction.

So, as you can see, in the end I got the upper hand, became a man of action, no longer a doormat; while ironically Veronica snuggles up in an Indian carpet where micro-organisms and enzymes are making a fine mess of her.

The Goddess and the Gambler

The Goddess of Chance walked among her minions. She radiated light. A dark-orange robe, folded and pleated, moved gently around her body. Above her sweet, wide-eyed, innocent face, her scarlet hair snaked up towards the stars. In one hand she carried playing cards splayed out like a fan: the four aces. In the other was a pair of scales. On a shining, golden chain around her throat hung chips and dice, two double-headed coins and a few white roulette balls like beads on a necklace.

She looked downwards over the city streets with their twinkling lights and over the illuminated bridges that spanned the river, listening to the hum of traffic, the horns of river boats and ships. She was accompanied by her entourage who stood motionless, like white marble statues, each occupying a niche in a great archway that formed a processional way; only their eyes moved, following her, for they could not lose sight of her. It was dangerous to do so, for she was too changeable, too capricious and, had they been able, they would have tethered her with a tight rein.

Tyche, for that was her name, stood together with

the ghost-like statues and the archway, floating above London's Shard. From there she could see absolutely everything and everyone: examine hearts, minds and actions: weigh decisions with her scales: change fortunes with the toss of a coin: encourage mortals to live bravely and take a chance.

She was a fickle goddess, indecisive, constantly changing her mind, her thoughts random and indeterminate. Mistress of unforeseen consequences, high priestess of all possible lotteries, she was also the suicide queen, wielding power over probability, possibility, luck, chance, greed; these were her forte. No one could see her or her minions, for everything surrounding her was invisible, thus preventing panic among the citizenry of the great city, thus avoiding traffic pile-ups and serious delays.

Goddesses always kept their distance from the hoi polloi.

She decided to address her slaves as they drove, worked and walked below her.

"You are mine, all of you, none of you can escape my influence. I am omnipotent, omnipresent, the most powerful of all deities. Every one of you is subject to my whims. I spread uncertainty, and hope, over the whole world. Do not ever make plans and believe they will come to fruition, for I am Tyche, the Goddess of Chance and can spoil your lives in the wink of an eye."

Her words went unheard, of course, lost in the wind, lost among the city noises.

The goddess watched Obadiah every day from her eyrie above the Shard and each time loved him more. He was so handsome: dark, swarthy, slightly sinister, slightly loutish. He was a gambler, and anything involving a bet, big or small, he participated in. Had he but known it, he owed all his success, money and opulent life style to her. He was also a womaniser, his wife only too aware of his infidelities, but she loved him and forgave him. She was his slave, just as Obadiah, without knowing it, was Tyche's slave.

The marble-pale beings that lined her processional route, were shocked by her behaviour for she had broken the sacred rule that deities and mortals should always remain emotionally detached. Their pallid skin had turned even more ghostlike with disappointment, for she had let them down, lowered the standards of her divine calling. They could hardly bear to look at her, their faces now turned away from her in embarrassment, eyes closed pretending to slumber. Some stood ramrod straight and stared her out, looking at her so intently that their eyes failed to focus as though she were not there at all. One figure could only endure her presence by timorously peeping out through a chink in the curtain that he had draped over his niche in the archway.

The goddess surveyed Obadiah, watching as he swanned around, his fur-collared coat rakishly flung over his shoulders, revving up his garish, green sports car – if she had been less love-struck she would have realised how tacky he looked, but love is blind even for a goddess. Nevertheless, she could see that the darling little imp was becoming too big for his boots. Suffering one of her more temperamental moods, Tyche decided to change all that. He walked into the casino to buy a large amount of chips and walked into his fiscal advisor's office to talk about stocks and shares.

When he walked out of both places he had set the stage for a future of virtual penury because, overplaying his hand with chance, he had made the wrong decisions. He was wounded with a deep sense of failure for seemingly lady luck had for the first time ever abandoned him, his run of success had dried up: so he tossed the lucky coin he always carried in his jacket pocket into the river. As time progressed the situation worsened and he had to sell his house, his fine car, his collection of vintage wines; his wife's ridiculously expensive jewellery too, met the same fate. "What have you done?" she asked Obadiah. "Why couldn't you have been less daring, shown more prudence. You sometimes seem to think that you are more than mortal." Far above her, in some distant place, the Goddess nodded her head in agreement.

"It's my nature," replied Obadiah. "It's always seemed that someone has been looking after me, dealing me lucky hands and guiding me to make the right choices."

The goddess again nodded.

Obadiah, with tears in his eyes, then went to seek out a good, stout rope. On a beautiful, warm, sultry evening, he walked along the water's edge with suicide in mind, determined to hang himself under a bridge, with the Thames flowing beneath him. The goddess watched him and wept, but she had decided that he must, at this crucial point, have control over his own destiny; she would allow him to commit this heinous crime for she had interfered too much already.

However, as Obadiah swung on his gibbet the thick rope suddenly, magically, miraculously unravelled and he fell to the ground. His eyes opened and he saw the wonders of the universe sparkling above him. He felt gratitude for his deliverance, but the goddess knew that she had taken a step too far and should not have interfered with his fate; on the other, hand, if she couldn't, who could? She wouldn't, however, wait for more scorn and disapprobation to fall upon her from her entourage. Had it been kind to treat mortals as arbitrarily as she had done? Had the time come to hand in her scales to someone more suitable to the rôle; to someone who would not let personal emotions interfere with her calling?

So looking down upon the Shard, she allowed the playing cards to float away over the twinkling lights of the city. She tore the necklace from around her throat, the chips, the dice, the roulette balls and the double-headed coins tumbling like acorns on to the streets below to be crushed to pieces by the traffic. She carefully placed her golden scales, the symbol of her office, in front of her simple, stone throne, leaving them within easy reach of her successor. Thus, her rule came to an end and, for the duration of the blinking of an eye, everything in the world was totally predictable as though the earth had ceased on its axis; no chances could be taken, no decisions could be made; it was all so dull and unbelievably boring. That is until one of the marble figures stepped down from her niche, underwent a metamorphosis, ceremoniously picked up the scales and seated herself upon the stone throne, while her entourage relaxed and smiled. With a silver, winged helmet covering her dark, curly hair, she looked superb in a robe covered in small wings and birds' feathers; she was obviously going to be a more energetic goddess, more well-travelled, not remaining forever perched above the Shard. With the new goddess in place, mortals were once again able to take a stab at chance and play the hand of fortune.

Tyche meanwhile, now a mere mortal and looking rather ordinary, walked among the streets and parks of London until she found Obadiah and, as time passed, drew him away from his wife with her wiles. While they kissed she would look up above the Shard and, in her mind, saw the sacred processional way, praying that the new goddess would bless them with happiness.

Obadiah's deserted wife was certainly blessed, for she was rewarded with a large fortune in a lottery draw, while Obadiah and Tyche struggled to make ends meet, which was probably only right in the circumstances. It seemed that the new Goddess of Chance had, on this occasion at least, adjusted her scales to synchronise with those of great Lady Justice.

The Second Coming

The second coming was imminent and expectations were rife; at least, among members of the Ferguson family where emotions ranged from serious doubt right across the board to the height of absolute faith. He was going to be with them again, flying through the clouds to save them: all the way from Miami!

"Come on, Patrick!" yelled mother." If you want our golden boy to buy you a car, the least you can do is to be at Heathrow to greet him." The others, as well, had a mental shopping list for their so-called cousin Frankie – surely, the prodigal visitor would not let them down. Deirdre Ferguson's children had never quite worked out their exact relationship to him, for they were a very extended family: paths going this way and that.

Nevertheless, letting them down was just what Frankie did immediately upon his arrival, for what a gangster-style disgrace he looked – white tie, black and white shoes – you know the sort of thing. Worse still, he had come empty-handed – his bank balance apparently sadly reduced or perhaps, more truthfully, his sense of generosity exhausted. He was an overwhelming disappointment to the whole Ferguson clan. As well as no car for Patrick, Big Tiger would go without his rifle, Kevin would dream in vain of his motorbike, Tracey could forget about her shopping trip to the West End and, certainly, there would be no money forthcoming for Sharon's horse and full livery.

Meanwhile, in another part of London, seedy Joshua Goldberg, a barrister-at-law, but with fingers in many other pies, was also awaiting the return, but he was out for the kill. He was sitting in his office, that epitome of bad taste: large, gilt chairs with red velvet seats: swirling, heavy, red velvet curtains with elaborate, gold-coloured tie-backs: a black, faux-marble desk with too many curls and curlicues: statues, busts and overpowering gilt-framed paintings. In a nut shell, Versailles comes to Hackney! Putting the phone down, having just summoned Frankie to his office, he adjusted his turquoise bow-tie with its white spots, and fiddled with the large, gold bracelet that he always wore around his left wrist. Any time soon, nasty little Frankie Ferguson was going to get his comeuppance, for no one cheated Joshua and got away with it.

It had been on his previous visit to England that Frankie had pulled the wool over Joshua's eyes and, thereby, lost him a mint of money. The most annoying part of the whole con was that Joshua had always thought of himself as an astute and sharp operator, so to be bamboozled by an insider-trading scam had made him gasp at his own naivety. He would soon, however, get his revenge.

Seven financially disappointing days after his return and with the family as hard up as ever, Joshua's phone call had come for Frankie. "Hurry up and get out of that bed, Frankie! It's Joshua and you know he doesn't like to be kept waiting!" screamed Deirdre. Frankie blanched and his stomach did a somersault. He knew it was pay-back time and that he would have to face the music. He'd been keeping his fingers tightly crossed that perhaps some feeling of forgiveness might have touched Joshua's frosty heart, but obviously this had been a vain hope. His most sincere wish had been that the old man would die, which, as he was well past his sell-by date, would have come as no surprise to anyone.

Frankie took a taxi to Hackney – he always believed in living in style… well, he had, after all, flown first-class from Miami to Heathrow, which had certainly cost him a bob or two, but he had kept that snippet of information to himself, even removing the tags from his suitcase before he met his reception party. He didn't fancy becoming the Ferguson family's money pit.

There was a quick rap on the office door and Peter, who was almost as old as Joshua himself, ushered Frankie into the tobacco smog that pervaded the room. Through watery eyes buried among the deep, dried-up crevices carved into his ancient face, Joshua scrutinised Frankie, as though trying to read his soul. His voice creaked like an old door, but nevertheless he spoke succinctly so that there should be no doubt what was going to happen. He started to chew enthusiastically on his breakfast bagel, then slid his hand under his crumpled-up napkin and brought out the gun; the gentle whisper that issued from it ended Frankie's life. "You were a good-for-nothing, little thief, Frankie!" Joshua shouted to the four walls. Then a piece of bagel lodged in his throat, making him cough and stopping the laugh of triumph that welled up inside him.

Silently the door opened, causing him to flinch with shock, as he heard Deirdre Ferguson's voice. "Well, this is a fine mess you've got yourself into, isn't it, Joshua?" Deirdre was still a fine-looking woman, tall and statuesque, who at that moment, reminded him of an avenging angel. She was not as lovely as her sister had been, thought Joshua, that beautiful woman who had died years ago from some virus or other; no one had really known the exact cause. Deirdre hadn't seen Joshua for a long, long time and the years hadn't treated him kindly; he looked old enough to have been around when dinosaurs roamed the earth.

Deirdre looked down at Frankie's body and, now with the tears beginning to fall, softly said, "That was a very, very silly thing to do, Joshua. He may have been a good-for-nothing, little thief, but you were a good-for-nothing, little rapist who plainly didn't foresee the consequences of what you did all those years ago. Poor Frankie, perhaps if he'd been brought up by a loving father, he might have turned out to be a son of whom you could have been proud." She didn't have to say one word more for all to become crystal-clear.

Joshua knew exactly what she meant and his heart began to race at an alarming rate. Yes, it was true that he had used and abused her sister, but the idea of a child had never entered his head. That Frankie had been his one and only son was too shocking to contemplate: so much time wasted, so many experiences lost. As the pain went from his chest to his left arm, the recalcitrant piece of bagel worked its way once more up his windpipe so that he had no breath with which to fight against his ultimate fate.

Thus, both the Ferguson family and Joshua Goldberg had been denied the satisfaction they had sought from the second coming.

The family took some time to recover from the shock. Well, let's be honest, it's not very pleasant for one's house guest, however disappointing he'd been, to be murdered during his visit. Nevertheless, life gradually returned to normal. Until, that is, one morning at breakfast, when the postman slipped an envelope through the letterbox. It was Big Tiger who opened it but, being the slowest of Deirdre's children, it would have taken him half an hour to read it and another half an hour to work out what it meant, so Patrick, who was standing frying himself another egg, took it from him, glanced at it and then immediately, looking rather pale, sat down heavily.

By the time they'd finished hearing that rich, little

Frankie had left them a fortune in his will, fat was spitting from the pan and the egg was ruined.

So, after all, Big Tiger could spend hours in a nearby field shooting at tin cans with his fine, new air rifle, while Patrick lovingly polished his smart red, convertible, the only problem being that he was finding it very difficult to pass a driving test. Kevin sent the neighbours round the bend, forever revving up his motor bike and screeching through the streets. As for Tracey, she was now dolled up to the nines in her smart designer clothes: Versace, Chanel, Valentino – you name it, she'd got it. Sharon, spending most her spare time at the stables, was revelling in tending her horse, named Frankie, after her benefactor.

This all goes to show that tragedy can bring happiness, at least for the moment; until greed steps in and everyone starts squabbling among themselves over the money which, of course, they will. Nevertheless, despite a couple of deaths, it's not quite true to say that money is the root of all evil, because without it, it's all a damn poor show!

The Time-Shaper

Lying on his blanket on the stone floor, the cat stirred uneasily in his sleep. He loved the soothing ticking of the clocks, but he knew that at any second this peace would be interrupted abruptly. Sure, enough his eyes automatically opened right on time, for there came the sound of the striking of the hour when every clock in the room loudly sang out that yet another sixty minutes had gone forever.

He glared crossly with furrowed brows at the time-shaper seated at his work table. The table and the floor were dotted with a cluster of bronze clock-wheels that looked like tiny, pointed suns.

The cat, who was so very much more intelligent than his master, knew that the time-shaper was wasting his efforts making clocks and watches; they were all so predictable, tick…tock…tick…tock, one second automatically moving onto the next.

There was never any variation; it was all overwhelmingly repetitive, except when the timepiece was running fast or slow, but so methodical and accurate was his master that this rarely happened. He was such a boring young man that there was absolutely no room for flexibility, for imagination.

"Shame on you, cat. I know what you are thinking, but this is honest work – making sure that mankind knows to the minute what part of the day it is, helping everyone to keep their appointments, giving order to their lives. It's such a convenient mechanism."

The cat sat up and thoughtfully licked a paw. "No," it suddenly exclaimed, "that's just not true. And my duty is to make you understand your mistake."

It looked scornfully around the strange, octagonal room with a grandfather clock positioned against each wall, except where the only window opened onto dark, threatening trees. Each clock, beneath its face, had a curtained alcove behind which swung rhythmically its pendulum. In the same curtained space was a small, barred window and a manikin in period dress forever imprisoned in his time.

The cat stared hard at the time-shaper.

"Do you remember telling me to go outside because I had taken a piece of chicken from your plate? You said that I had to spend the next five minutes pondering on what I had done wrong. But I spent ages and ages out in the pouring rain. I asked why you had lied to me, but you swore that it had truly only been five minutes; don't you think that my time is somehow different from yours, that time has a mind of its own and does exactly what it wants with us?"

The time-shaper looked bemused, his huge eyes sunken in their sockets, his face and body so fragile that it was easy to perceive the skeleton beneath the paper-thin skin. He was diseased, dying and he would have loved to be able to play around with time, to stop the inevitable from happening. The cat was always talking about other dimensions where one was living out different lives, so that death was not really a problem for anyone. However, the cat was strong and healthy, so this did not overly concern him; it was he, the maker of clocks and watches, who was living out his last weeks.

"Time is an illusion," droned on the cat in his usual pedantic, pontificating manner. "It's always relative to something else. What's wrong with simply being guided by sunrises and sunsets, by the moon and the stars, by the ebb and flow of the tides. Why waste your time and your eyesight on such a fleeting, mechanical process?"

Suddenly his master, in an instant of enlightenment, of revelation, understood for the first time the cat's argument. This was manifested when, through the window, came a whirling ball flickering with the fire of insight and comprehension.

At that very same moment the manikins left their prisons and began to play with the watch wheels, bowling them backwards and forward along the floor. Here they were playing together, each from his own era; time had lost its boundaries of past, present and future.

The fiery ball eventually lost its force, spluttered into nothing and disappeared. The cat then turned towards the window to see if there was a follow-up, but all he saw was the wind shifting the trees, a moaning sound issuing from among their leaves. The manikins too had disappeared, each back to his own time, behind his own pendulum.

The cat's physical appearance is perhaps worth a mention. He was an odd-looking creature: normal black fur, but with very curly, woolly, grey feet that were out of proportion to the rest of him, a very curly, woolly, grey chest like that of an old man and with a mass of woolly, grey curls on top of his head. It was almost as though his body had at one time been undecided as to whether he was going to be a sheep or a cat.

The time-shaper's thinking had now broadened and so he asked the cat a very important question indeed. "Is it not possible to control time, indeed to borrow time, because I would definitely like to have a lot more of it, if it were at all possible?"

The cat turned his head away and pretended to ponder, but he already knew the solution to the problem. It would, however, be a case of playing now and paying later, of negotiating a deal, of bartering one commodity for another.

...Yes, there was a most satisfactory resolution to the conundrum: at least in the here and now, though perhaps not with the passing of that tricky little illusion called time.

"I think I can definitely help you out, master, so I shall call one of my business contacts." A deafening yowling suddenly issued from his mouth, which must have lasted for at least five minutes, but whose five minutes it was would have been difficult to quantify with any certainty.

Suddenly, looking in through the window was the Devil's Agent, a broker of time in cahoots with the one who allotted the years to the creatures who inhabited his universe. The cat was, in fact, rather frightened of her for she was a sharp cookie who stood no nonsense, so he knew that in the end things would not turn out well for his master. Time could not be fooled around with; a price would have to be paid.

The Agent stepped genteelly over the window sill and into the room. Dressed in a smart, black suit, sensible court shoes, a white blouse buttoned up to the neck, her dark hair dragged back into a tight bun, she straightened her skirt and felt ready to negotiate terms. Her brief case was stuffed with papers that would need to be signed when the deal had been agreed. On her wrist she wore an atomic watch and round her neck hung a uranium pendant-watch from the future so that there should be absolutely no error in what was about to happen. "Well, cat, he's nearly mine, isn't he? I can see death knocking at his door."

The cat had fared very well from their previous dealings and his net profit showed in the fact that he was now nearly five-hundred-years-old: his reward for selling souls to the Devil! How many years he would be allotted from this latest negotiation would have to be worked out. However, the Devil's Agent always played fair with him, so he knew that he would not be the loser. Her master, great Lucifer himself, would be inordinately pleased with the way things were going.

They both went and stood in front of the work-table

where the poor time-shaper was slumped with his head resting on a fine ormolu mantle clock, his arms hanging down loosely by his side, his eyes closed. He truly looked as though he were about to take his last breath.

The Devil's Agent prodded him in the back to rouse him from his slumber. He looked up, blinking his eyes, not understanding who the woman was and why she was there.

"I've come to save you, time-shaper, to make you feel better, to give you life. What would you say if I could promise you twenty more years of existence?"

"I'd do anything, absolutely anything for that to happen."

"Well, it's really all very simple. Just sign these papers and it will come to pass."

The cat quickly butted in. "And there is no reason to read them for, as your representative, I can assure you that everything is above board."

His master was such an innocent, a true lamb to the slaughter, so merely by pushing a quill pen into his hand the cat secured the deal. Both he and the Devil's Agent were very pleased at this outcome, as was the time-shaper whose flesh immediately regained its former healthy colour and whose quickly fattening muscles felt that they could run a marathon.

It was such an easy thing to accomplish: borrowing time, buying and selling lives, so the cat purred contentedly. Surely somewhere else in the universe he was a successful estate agent or car dealer or a commodities broker, something on the shady side, wheeling and dealing his whiskers off. Well, there were some things that you divulged and others that you kept to yourself.

"Right, cat, that's all settled then. In twenty years' time I shall come, on my master's behalf, to collect him. I shall arrive at exactly ten o'clock at night according to my uranium pendant watch. I am starting the stopwatch now."

Off she went, stepping over the window sill, giving the cat rather a frightening smile, which he didn't like one bit.

The time-shaper could not believe his luck; here he was feeling wonderfully healthy again and with twenty years of life in front of him. The cat stuck around even when he realised that the mathematician who lived in the triangular room next door too was dying, but rather than spreading his business interests over a wider area, he thought he'd be wiser keeping an eye on his master. The mathematician was always rushing off to church and calling in a priest to intercede for him, so the cat decided to keep an eye on the time-shaper: obviously a far better investment!

He wouldn't however, let the grass grow under his paws and kept a tight rein on the astronomer in the circular room at the end of the corridor. The star man was growing old and the cat thought there might soon be an opportunity there. Before this could happen however, time being the strange process that it was and meaning nothing to the Devil, in the twinkling of an eye the twenty years had gone. The woman was on the point of returning to garner the time-shaper's soul for the Devil's hellish kingdom.

At ten o'clock that evening all the clocks and watches chimed the hour loudly and the Devil's Agent stepped into the room. The cat's master was shaking with fear and disappointment. Where had all the time gone, he thought, why hadn't he used those precious years more wisely?

The woman stared at the cat who was glowering at her; there was something not quite right about him.

"So…?" he exclaimed. "What happens now?"

"Not only your master, but you too, should have read the papers more closely before you signed them. My great master and I have thought deeply about what to do with you both."

"No, this is absolutely nothing to do with me. I'm just a go-between like you. I've got other fish to fry; the astronomer along the corridor, for example."

"Sorry, cat, but your negotiating days are over. We need new blood, new ideas. Look at yourself in the mirror; you are changing and not for the better. After all these years you and your master are so tightly bound that it would seem an unkindness to separate you, but we are not going to kill or imprison you behind a pendulum in a grandfather clock. You are both coming with me"

"No, I don't want to do that. Take my master but leave me here. I've been tricked. You had this planned all along, didn't you?"

She regarded him critically; his whiskers and

pointed ears were still in good shape, but his woolly areas were now more prolific, and his mewing was more like the bleating of a sheep, which was rather worrying.

"So, are you both ready?" she rasped. "Ready to travel faster than light down to the underworld where my master is waiting to harvest your souls, where you will serve him in the fiery pit for all time."

"But I have no soul. I'm a cat."

"Don't be silly! Of course, you have a soul and one that my master very much wants to add to his collection!"

The time-shaper wept unhappily.

The cat baaed pitifully.

The Devil's Agent had a damn good laugh.

Totally Divine

Julian was swanning around the select gathering of the movers and shakers of the New York interior-fashion business, elbows tucked in, hands flapping about prettily and hips swaying sinuously. He was in his element, knowing that he had made it after so much sweat and tears, although sweat might be a word that his sensitivity would not allow him to use.

Everyone there – all his fellow interior designers, that is – were totally divine, at least on the surface, but bitchiness and soaring ambition at any cost was the name of the game. You had always to watch your back and never trust anyone as you went from party to party; the same shallow, false conversations, the eternal gossiping and pulling people's reputations to shreds, the same kissing the air on both cheeks of everyone you met to show that you were European savvy.

Insincere nothings, idle compliments that had not been given a second thought filled the air. "*Where on earth, sweet one, did you buy that marvellous creation?*" "*Darling heart, you look wonderful!*"

All this from lips that smiled and simpered, but whose thoughts were probably litigious.

Julian's eyes travelled across the rather tackily decorated room and alighted on his partner, his friend, his lover, that tricky little bitch universally referred to by everyone as Pale George, with his beautiful, blond hair and skin so colourless that it was as though he had never seen the sun. Pale George was his fellow designer, and also his project manager, who made sure that any undertaking ran smoothly. Tucked under Pale George's arm was Minnie, really the only sweet soul in the whole gathering: a black pug of doubtful provenance, for she was a rescue dog obtained at a charitable event in aid of homeless animals. Wearing her best pink, satin dress with its tulle tutu skirt, her nails were painted blue and a pretty bow sat on top of her head. All this was topped off by a sparkling Swarkovski crystal collar.

How ridiculous the poor little thing looked thought Madam Bella. This, however, was a clear case of the pot calling the kettle black, for she was the hostess of this impressive event, a highlight in the cultural calendar of New York, but was not one whose dress sense should ever have been copied. With her screamingly over-hennaed hair, pale-faced as death, looking, indeed like some latter-day Elizabeth the First, Madam Bella came tottering over on ridiculously high heels, her thin, withered hands decorated with rings the size of knuckle dusters.

"You poor little bumble bee," she said to Minnie. "Why on earth do those silly boys dress you like this?"

She was really too waspish and hurtful for her own

good, too doped up with the medication that just about managed to keep her sane. Pale George, grinding his teeth in anger, dutifully kissed the air twice, taking the opportunity to take a good look at the deep ravines in her skin. He was too vain to wear specs, but could never get used to contact lenses, so this was a chance to have a really close inspection. Why on earth didn't she have Botox or fillers like Julian, or even a face-lift like him?

"Madam Bella, darling, each time I see you, I truly gasp in amazement at how so many, many passing years have left you virtually unscathed."

She gave him a sharp look. Was he being impertinent? She thought he probably was.

"By the way, dearest heart, perhaps I should explain to you that we dress Minnie like this because we like it and honestly don't give a damn what anyone else thinks."

Yes, he was definitely being impertinent, but he'd pay for it.

Julian, even from the other side of the room, could sense the tension and minced over to pour oil on troubled waters. There ensued a group hug and a lot of faux kissing sounds, so that for the moment the tetchiness disappeared.

Then Pale George wandered away to work the room and left them to it. As they passed the loaded buffet table, Minnie's eyes grew even bigger and more bulbous than nature had made them, but there was no time to stop to give her a little treat, for Pale George had a nice, fat fish of the human kind to fry. The truth was that poor Julian was just about to be sent to the cleaners: the seeds of betrayal were being sown.

Another truth was that Pale George, so he thought, was the more talented of the two: so much more flair, so much more imagination, so much more taste when it came to choosing fabrics and furniture. Without his input the business would simply sink into anonymity. However, things were afoot about which Julian was in total ignorance, so let him enjoy this final evening before his name would be forever deleted from the 'A' guest list of gatherings like this.

A whispered, prolonged conversation then ensued between Pale George and one of Shanghai's greats, in other words Mr Tse Kiang, corpulent, clever and highly talented. Think Mao Tse-tung and you have him but, not being too proud to wear them, with the addition of spectacles.

Almost trying to speak without moving his lips, Pale George, to his credit felt a modicum of shame at what he was doing, but he didn't really need Julian in any aspect of his life, particularly in business. He so wanted to work in Shanghai under the auspices of the billionaire entrepreneur: how cool that would be! He was a traitor, but no different from the others in that room with their burning egos.

"Well, George," pronounced Mr Tse Kiang finally, "I really feel we can have a good and mutually beneficial relationship."

News of the betrayal quickly filtered through to Julian, for lip reading was quite an art in that gossiping jungle. So a few minutes later all hell was let loose and Julian screamed, he flounced, he pouted and he wept copious tears. "You little bitch, you bastard", he screeched, gnashing his teeth so fiercely that his ridiculously expensive cosmetic dental treatment was in danger of a melt-down. Pale George, however, was by this time too excited at the thought of Shanghai to be much moved by all these theatrics and so, with almost no emotion, watched as Julian patted his moist cheeks with rather a pretty hanky, tossed his head high in the air and strutted out of the room.

As for the rest of the spectators, they loved it, loved watching someone else's misfortune, for a good dose of what the Germans call schadenfreude always goes down well among people breaking their necks to struggle to the top of the tree. In one way or another, as is always the case with poseurs, there was a load of tension, conflict and jealousy floating around: offence taken for things that most people would forget in five minutes, grudges often harboured for years, bubbling under the surface. Can you guess from what you've read where emotions were the strongest and where tragedy was lurking, waiting to pounce?

Poor Minnie, her little dress was in tatters, her pretty bow lay soaking in a punch bowl and her lovingly painted nails were ragged. Her large eyes were forever closed. She lay lifeless on the table amid the gleaming glasses. The party was truly over, and the guests slunk away, for even they were shocked at the sight of the small pug lying dead. Such unnecessary cruelty they thought. The atrocity must have been committed in another part of the building, because she would not have gone quietly. How on earth would poor Pale George feel to have this happen after such an otherwise successful evening? Had it been Julian's way of taking vengeance, they wondered? Had he, or perhaps a well-rewarded barman, arranged Minnie on the table? Julian, however, was nowhere to be seen. Neither was Pale George.

Madam Bella suffered from what used to be called a touch of the vapours when she saw the sight and had to be revived with a stiff brandy.

"Poor, poor little darling! Poor little bumble bee! What a cruel world this is," she wept, her jewellery jingling and jangling in time with her sobbing.

Pale George entered the room, the blood drained from his face at the scene and he flung himself over Minnie's corpse, weeping and wailing incoherently. Such was the drama that most of the glasses ended up broken on the floor. Those that didn't, tinkled against each other desperately trying to keep their balance.

The murderer stealthily approached, wearing rubber-soled shoes so the victim had no warning before he saw the gun.

They were both in the street outside, where Pale George had gone to recover from the dreadful loss he had just suffered. His darling Minnie had gone, and he needed a breath of fresh air to help him.

George felt the gun in his back as he was shunted into the shadows. His head was swimming and he was finding it difficult to breathe. Despite the lure of Shanghai, he had momentarily wanted to join his pug wherever she had gone. Nevertheless, the instinct for survival is usually uppermost and he was not going to give in easily.

"Turn around and face me," said his aggressor. Pale George looked into those over-made-up eyes, saw the deep wrinkles and the scarlet lips.

"You!" he said to Madam Bella, barely able to swallow. "But why?"

"Because nobody, absolutely nobody ever speaks to me in the way that you did this evening, especially someone of your persuasion. I am the queen bee of New York society and you are a mere nothing."

"And Minnie? Was that you?"

"Of course, it was me. The little ballerina in her dancing costume was a travesty of good taste. You should have accepted more graciously my opinion of her." Madam Bella raised the gun so that it was pointing directly between Pale George's eyes.

Gathering his courage, George answered, "I really think, Madam Bella, that you should put that gun down."

"Do you? Do you really think that's what I should do? Wrong! Very wrong!" Then she pulled the trigger and that was the end of Pale George and his grandiose future. He fell onto the damp pavement and his blood seeped into the cracks.

Perhaps as his spirit left his body, a transformed and glorified Minnie was waiting to accompany him towards his destination.

"You know, Mr Tse Kiang, it really would be so much better if your apartment were more visually surrounded with an oriental ambiance – a touch of China overlooking Central Park would be just too, too divine."

The Shanghai entrepreneur was wondering why he had not chosen Julian from the get-go; he was so much more on his wave length than Pale George had ever been. Added to which he had wonderful biceps. Such is the fickleness of human nature.

So Julian went to Shanghai, Madam Bella went to prison and George, paler than ever, went to the mortuary. As for the spectators of the evening, well, they felt awfully privileged because, darlings, they now had oodles, simply oodles of glorious gossip to spread about. Their cell phones would be on overdrive as every detail reached the four corners of the wonderfully designed homes of New York.

White Noise

It always began in the same fashion: a distant wailing in her ears like a siren, signalling that she should close her eyes to concentrate and shut out the sight of the mumbling, slumbering people around her. So, the old woman obeyed the call and entered the scene that was etched in her thoughts. She watched two fragmenting, white, female figures on the decaying walls; pale bricks showing under the flaking plaster. Indeed, so degraded were the walls that two holes had appeared in them, through which shone a brilliant light illuminating a torn carpet; it resembled stubby grass more than textile.

A fat, ginger-striped cat eyed her crossly from the surface of the disintegrating painted wall, electric sparks like miniature stars flashing from its body. Both cat and sparkling decoration were in good condition, their paint as though newly created. What always held her attention most however, whenever this image entered her mind, was that one of the fading figures was holding a perfect, brightly-painted violin in her hand, but no sounds of music ever came from it.

Anyone else would probably have described all this as enchanting, reminiscent perhaps of the strange beauty left when Vesuvius had rained down upon Pompeii. The old woman, however, just shook her head, and away flew the vision that was gradually taking up more and more space in her thoughts; it was enigmatic, fascinating, but she had no idea of its meaning and it annoyed her that she was always forced to heed its call.

Her mind then wandered off into different realms. It had hardly been worth the bother of being born, she thought: all that pushing and shoving for hours on end by her poor mother – just for this! What was the point of it all? Here she was in a lonely, joyless universe that was expanding forever. Eventually everyone would be left shipwrecked against their will in a vast emptiness that even the existence of dark matter would fail to make more welcoming.

She personally had never felt the call of motherhood; to procreate would undoubtedly have forced any poor child carrying her genes to suffer the same dark and dreary life that she had led. As for a man to enable this to occur – yes, she'd endured that hell among all her other sufferings – so much pummelling and pounding that merely ended with a few groans and grunts from someone she hardly knew. Where was the joy in that?

Her thoughts randomly returned to the poor, silent violin – what chance did it stand against the continual hissing, crackling and even the occasional roar that came from the cosmos, against the droning of white noise that had pervaded the universe from the very beginning of time? The boring, sizzling signals from space were a clear indication to her that this was not intended to be a place of joy: such a sombre sound against which to live out our drab lives. There was no music of the spheres here. In other universes, within their own private bubbles of existence, perhaps the background was of tinkling bells, sweet chords, sublime melodies. Nevertheless, she suspected that this would not change her way of thinking and that, sooner or later, misery would set in, just as it always did. She simply did not understand the concept of what people thought of as joy, though a vague notion came into her head when she watched them laughing and smiling at things that caused her to weep. Couldn't they understand that the strange emotion was ephemeral, so short-lived as to be not worth experiencing.

Joy is not the destiny of our existence. The pursuit of happiness is a useless enterprise. To laugh at the misfortunes of others, to revel in the blood and gore of road-kill, of motorway accidents and to feel envy when others had their share of this so-called joy; is this really the best that humankind can manage?

She was different, however, from the rest of the world. She knew that her brain cells were wrongly wired, that they were mixed up and confused and that the equation that should result in joy had been omitted.

Depression had been her lot from the moment of birth – hence all the pills and potions that were stuffed into her aging body in this hell-hole of an old people's home. Did she want a cup of tea, did she want meat or fish for lunch, would she like a magazine to read? No, she didn't want anything – just to be left in peace, just to be allowed to be alone with her own thoughts and, ultimately, to die.

A smartly-dressed old man entered the room where they were all dozing and drooling; someone she had not seen before. He was carrying a silver-topped walking stick and slowly limped over to where she was sitting.

"Would you mind terribly if I sat down beside you? I promise not to disturb you, but I'm only here for the afternoon and would so enjoy your company. Please continue with whatever you were thinking about – and I will think my thoughts."

She nodded her head vaguely, not saying a word; she had never been good at social interaction or at making idle conversation. She watched him out of the corner of her eye and wished that he would go away. It was as though he were intruding on her space.

She then heard the squeaking wheels of the tea trolley coming nearer and felt a pressure on her arm.

"Forgive me, but they want to know if you would like a drink of some sort. I believe milky coffee is your preference, is it not?" he laughed gently. She irritably shrugged his hand away from her arm. How dare he touch her! What business of his was it to guess at her favourite drink – though, in fact, he had surmised correctly?

He handed her the cup and saucer. She felt like knocking it to the ground, but then remembered her manners, just hoping, for some unaccountable reason, that she wouldn't slurp, gulp or dribble in front of him. Fortunately, he accepted a cup of tea himself so that any lack of social graces on her part would hopefully be less noticeable.

Once all the cups and saucers had been removed and the promised silence between them maintained, she could feel him turning to look at her. She hated it: so rude, so intrusive. Nevertheless, she didn't feel threatened and suspected that, if she could only manage to put her drugged-up mind to it, she would find that he had a good heart, someone to whom she could unburden herself. In fact, someone much more useful to her than all the therapists and psychologists who for so many years had listened to her sad thoughts. She intuited that one of the things she most needed was to show more charity, so when he next spoke to her she tried her best to be attentive.

"I just want to ask you a very simple question. If you could have just one wish granted what would it be?"

She was surprised by his words and even more surprised at the speed with which she answered him. She had never craved for this before, because she had always scorned it as not worth having. "I would like to find joy," she said.

The old man took her hand and began to hum a tune. This time there was no wailing in her ears, no warning signal came, but she was so tired that she just had to close her eyes and once more, unexpectedly, saw the two figures. Their outlines were more frail and ragged than ever as the white paint fell onto the floor. They were very gradually disappearing but, suddenly, they folded over slowly from the top and slid downwards, ending up as a pile of dust.

The cat and the violin, however, were still looking fine and dandy. The cat meowed, stepped down from its spot on the wall where the artist had placed it and padded towards the violin, leaving marks in the white dust. It stretched up a plump paw and took down the violin. Then it placed its chubby jaw on the beautifully carved wood, and, with its claw firmly around the bow, began to play. Swaying with the music, eyes closed in ecstasy, the star-like sparks dancing in tempo, the cat's face became wet with tears of emotion. The notes that floated into the air were as sweet as honey, as blissful as paradise. The cat smiled at her dreamily and, for the first time ever, the old woman understood the miracle of joy.

The white dust then gathered together, until the two figures re-formed into the perfection they must have been when first painted. Their heads turned towards her so that they could watch as she disappeared into her next life with a smile of joy on her face while the old man held her hand.

Womankind

There were so many of them: Mary with baby Jesus, Isis with baby Horus, even God and the Holy Spirit. Patricia believed these last two were of interchangeable gender. There was Marilyn Monroe, Princess Di, Greta Garbo, Maggie Thatcher and even Jayne Mansfield who had been decapitated in a car accident – all women who, in one way or another, were worshipped and who, for better or worse, had made a name for themselves – and they were just the tip of the iceberg.

Women were at the top of the evolutionary tree thought Patricia, who was an intelligent, attractive woman, a lecturer in Classics at Severn and Avon University; she was no slouch.

She had grown tired of the exclusivity of men: their secret societies and their old boys' network. She was upset by the Illuminati, by Rosicrucians, the College of Cardinals, by Freemasonry and so on and so forth – nasty little gatherings where women were mainly forbidden.

What about the equality of the sexes? Could men really ignore the fact that there were so many female monarchs and prime ministers dotted throughout the world?

However, in Patricia's cosy, country cottage great changes were about to get underway, a new world order was about to emerge. Over morning coffee, as Patricia passed around a plate of home-made, brightly coloured cupcakes to her cronies, a new secret society was gestating. Including Patricia, there were five in attendance on this momentous occasion, the nucleus of what would, in a very short time, take the world by storm. This was a meeting for women and about women only. Men were out, out, out! They were totally forbidden! Verboten! They had ruled the roost for long enough.

The Brillianti was to be the new title of this women's secret society, and oaths would be sworn to ensure that the secrecy would continue. What the punishment would be for breaking the oath had not yet been decided but, thought Patricia, it would be pretty nasty.

"Right, ladies, let's get this meeting underway, shall we? This is an historic event matched only by Jesus' choosing of his disciples."

"But they were men, Patricia!"

"Precisely, Minnie. Personally, however, I think that Mary Magdalen was the chief disciple; this, of course, has been kept under wraps."

The group giggled at this and Patricia thought, not for the first time, that they were perhaps not the brightest stars in the firmament and not taking things as seriously as they might. Nevertheless, they were all she had to work with, for her female colleagues at the University had been singularly unimpressed by her revolutionary ideas. Her easiest route would have been to recruit members from the Women's Institute, but she suspected that some other halves were Freemasons and there may have been a conflict of interests. She did not, however, realise that her chosen group was there simply for want of something better to do. They had thought that it might all be a bit of a laugh, especially with dotty Patricia in charge.

"We are going to prepare the way so that others might follow," she announced like some latter-day prophet. "I think it is important, therefore, that we be suitably attired for our meetings so that a feeling of gravitas should pervade our proceedings. We are not going to dress ourselves in little aprons like waitresses in a café as some male societies do and neither are we going to wear spotless, white robes which seem to be in fashion in esoteric societies, for we all bear the stain of the sinner."

They were finding it hard not to laugh aloud at this. Of course, they were all sinners and what fun it was. They wouldn't want it any other way, especially Julia who was a real little raver and who would certainly not have been at the meeting if Patricia had known what a flibberty-gibbet she was.

"Can I suggest that perhaps we should wear an Ancient Egyptian garment, because isn't it true that these societies have their roots in Ancient Egypt and even before that?"

Patricia was rather surprised to hear this from Phyllis whom she had thought of as the most uninformed of the group. Evidently there was hope for them yet!

As they all loved creating costumes for fancy dress parties, this suggestion was met with enthusiasm and the meeting had to be brought to order. They had visions of looking like Cleopatra, the Elizabeth Taylor version that is, covered in gold and lapis lazuli, albeit of the bling kind, their chiffon dresses wafting in a warm, perfumed, aeolian breeze.

It was for Patricia to decide upon the emblem for the Brillianti. There would be no skulls, crossbones, roses, squares or compasses: nothing of that ilk. The all-seeing eye, as a reminder that she would be keeping a sharp watch on each one of them, might be a good idea; she had even considered a pyramid, now that an Egyptian-styled costume had been mooted.

In the end, she decided upon a hangman's noose, to remind them of what might happen if they betrayed the group's existence. Under this emblem would be the figure of a serpent or a lizard because, for some unfathomable reason, the thought had entered her mind that she might one day become a shape-shifter and imagined herself slithering into all sorts of hidden places to seek out the truth. Erica, who belonged to a painting group, was given the task of transforming the hangman's noose and the reptile into a suitable design.

Thus, the first official meeting of the Brillianti ended. Patricia, Julia, Minnie, Phyllis and Erica swore an oath of secrecy. One day, when more established, their existence could filter out to the world. Now, however, silence and discretion were the watch-words.

Returning to the University of Severn and Avon, after such a momentous weekend, was something of a let-down for Patricia. She knew that she was being watched carefully by her department and that her hopes of being appointed to the Chair of Classics were receding quickly. For a long time, both her colleagues and her students had found her somewhat strange, but now her behaviour and her ideas were becoming down-right weird, if not outrageous. The academic world was used to its eccentrics, but she was going beyond the pale.

Seminars were becoming a complete waste of time because all she did for most of the hour was to sit at the long, oval table constantly moving her notes, pens, diary and smartphone from one place to the other, never satisfied with the result, but with everything always beautifully aligned. Her students just chatted to one another while this was going on and occasionally asked her questions to which she would give only the vaguest of replies.

The department realised that she needed a break of some sort. Perhaps a year's sabbatical might be a good idea: time for her to rest, read and perhaps, eventually, to begin to write another of her perceptive papers on some obscure aspect of classical history. The groves of academe, or as she would have termed them, the *Silvas Academi,* were really all that she had ever known.

It was in this way that poor Patricia was, for the moment at least, removed from her tenure, her hopes of more academic honours probably blighted for ever.

Everyone thought that she received the news with surprising stoicism, but then they did not realise that her greatest achievement was yet to be realised, for her ideas of a new world order had now advanced since their inception. She would be the female version of Jesus. The women of the world would one day worship her. On the day of her death there would be many more floral offerings than the few odd flowers placed outside Kensington Palace.

So, in truth, she was not really disappointed by this turn of events, for now she could stay at home, think about the rules and rituals of the Brillianti and perhaps garner more members. What an opportunity this was! One that could surely not be missed! Secrecy, however, was definitely the key to success, at least for the moment!

During the couple of days it took Patricia to clear out all her books and files, things had been happening on the home front, for the Brillianti had taken a dangerous step: they were talking, they were breaking their sworn oath to say nothing.

For Julia it was through pillow talk that she broke her promise. After making love, she regaled her boyfriend with Patricia's strange ideas. She was a tittle tattler and any small pieces of news that she heard were usually quickly passed on.

Her boyfriend had found the story quite interesting, for his father had just been invited to become a Freemason. He would tell his father this snippet of gossip when he next saw him, especially the remark about waitresses' aprons!

"Wait till dad hears that one!" he laughed.

Minnie, in her pearls and tweed suit with her hair newly permed, told her gentleman friend all about it after a rather boozy lunch; not being much of a drinker, her tongue had soon been loosened. Harvey worked as a solicitor in the village and, yes, he had realised that Patricia was not well, for she had changed her will and left everything to the Brillianti with no explanation as to what this was, but she had been adamant about her decision. So, this information would shine some light on what she had done and the reason for it. His fellow solicitors would be interested to know the details.

Phyllis made the serious mistake of introducing the subject during a parents' evening. When little Jimmy's parents heard the story, they were shocked and thought that Patricia needed to seek professional help before she was put in a straitjacket. In fact, they were not far off the mark, for help was desperately needed and very soon every parent in the village knew the details of what was happening. Of course, like Chinese whispers it would all change in the telling.

"This is feminism gone mad – literally," commented little Jimmy's father.

Erica enjoyed painting the emblem of the Brillianti: the hangman's noose and the serpent. She was so pleased with it that she could not resist showing it to the rest of her painting group and then, of course, she had to explain its meaning to everyone.

So, everything that was supposed to be kept secret was revealed.

When Patricia returned home she was appalled to receive a phone call from the Orange Oak Express, which was the local evening paper. She could not believe that they actually wanted to interview her about her new secret society. She put the phone down without replying and flopped onto the sofa, feeling sick and dizzy.

Those bitches really should not have done it, should not have opened their mouths, should not have broken their solemn oath, should not have betrayed her. They would pay dearly for their loose lips. She hadn't chosen a hangman's noose as the emblem for nothing.

Then, she decided to try out the shape-shifting skills that she was certain she possessed. Sure enough, as she focused her mind, she watched her hand grow scaly and turn green. She looked in the mirror, and there was a serpent's face staring back at her, its forked, venomous tongue shooting in and out of its mouth. She was now a sly, slithery snake that could kill without being detected ...but for some reason this did not seem practical and she decided instead to hold a meeting with her betrayers. She just hoped that she could think herself back into a more recognisable form before then.

The next day she awoke to find the village covered

in snow, so she crept out into the garden in her wellies carrying four nooses, which she attached to four stout branches. There were no neighbours to boggle about this and, even if there were, they would surely understand. Well, any sane person would, wouldn't they? Hanging from gallows was a just punishment for treachery, and if it was good enough for Judas, though self-inflicted, it was good enough for Phyllis, Julia, Erica and Minnie.

The meeting was convened and despite the snow and the chill in the air, all four turned up. The gall, the cheek of it! You wouldn't credit that people could behave like that and sit there as if butter wouldn't melt in their mouths! So straight for the jugular went Patricia. There was no point in hanging around, she thought.

"Well, ladies, to say I am disappointed and angry with each one of you is to put it mildly. It didn't need Sherlock Holmes to trace the source of the treachery."

"Patricia, can we help ourselves to the cake?" said Phyllis completely ignoring the tirade.

"Of course, you can. And as it's such a cold day I have added some brandy to your coffee." There was a frisson of pleasure at this from the four of them. Oh, yes, she had read her victims well!

Soon their eyes would begin to close as the narcotic took effect, its taste hidden by the brandy.

Once they were all out for the count, she grabbed Minnie by the ankles and dragged her into the snow. There was no resistance from her at all, so a path was made towards the nooses and Minnie was placed under one of them. The same path was taken three more times so that there should be as little disturbance in the snow as possible. By now, Patricia was feeling tired from all her physical effort and sat on top of Julia's prone form to recover her breath.

Then came the most difficult part – hauling them all up to the nooses, but she was a strong woman and where there's a will there's a way.

She stood looking at the four corpses suspended from the branches, their necks twisted, their mouths open. Truth to tell, Patricia was a little disappointed because the scene was not as dramatic as she had imagined. She had pictured them swinging theatrically in the wind but, actually, their feet were only inches off the ground. That was all that she'd been able to manage, so the effect had been spoiled. However, it did please her that their faces were swollen and congested and she was quite taken by Erica's purple, protruding tongue.

Yet the scene was still lacking a little something, until she had a flash of inspiration... She cut their wrists and the deep red blood seeped down onto the snow, glowing wonderfully against the pristine whiteness. She loved it. It was now all so perfect. She had got her revenge.

Patricia became known as the Noose Lady. Deemed to be mentally unfit to be tried, it was proclaimed that no change to the ruling was to be expected. She is therefore incarcerated in a psychiatric hospital where she will spend the rest of her life. She is not, however, downhearted, for she spends many a happy hour still planning her new world order and trying to interest other inmates in her ideas, with little success, as you can imagine.

Her shape-shifting has come on by leaps and bounds. Her latest success is a black cat, and she enjoys nothing more than gazing at her long-clawed paws, stroking her fine whiskers and scratching behind her immaculately pointed ears

Ironically her most prized possession is the little white apron made of lamb's wool that she insists on wearing every day around her waist. How she got it, no one knows, but she tells everyone that it signifies purity. and innocence.

Little Brat

"Why aren't you eating your blancmange, Tillie?"

"I want jelly! I want jelly," wailed Tillie, banging her spoon insistently on the table.

"But you love blancmange and I can't remember your ever having refused it before."

"Well, we had it yesterday at school for pudding. Anyway, I want jelly"

"Tillie, there's no harm in having something two days running. And stop banging your spoon like that! It's very rude"

"There's something funny about the blancmange. I don't want it. Won't eat it!"

"How can you possibly think that? There's absolutely nothing wrong with it."

"Oh, yes, there is. It's got poison in it."

"Poison! You silly, little girl."

"It's true …and you put it there!" Tillie rose from her chair, and theatrically pointing an accusing finger at Mummy, backed away, yelling petulantly, "Murderess! Murderess! Murderess!"

"That was not a very nice thing to say to Mummy, was it?"

That was Tillie all over, however, already a difficult diva even at six-years-old: forever flouncing and pouting, always expecting to get her own way. Although as they say, '*out of the mouth of babes and sucklings*'! It was true. Her mummy really was trying to do away with Tillie, but the plan was only at the experimental stage. Tillie's dish of blancmange had contained two milligrams of ground lorazepam, which wouldn't kill her, especially as she'd only had a couple of spoonsful, but hopefully would make her dopey; for Tillie's mummy, a quiet Tillie would be like heaven but until her clinical tests reached perfection she would obviously have to proceed with caution.

However, Tillie's mother couldn't stand the little brat: no maternal love there. One of the main reasons for this was jealousy, for Tillie was plainly the apple of her daddy's eye: his precious cherub, his chug-a-lug, his feisty little love-bug. Really! What a silly daddy he was! He certainly never used such endearments to Tillie's mummy, which was why she was so embittered. By the way, just so you know, Mummy's name was Myra.

Tillie's eyes were already beginning to droop and she was starting to yawn, so her mummy quickly wrote down the very first entry in her black Death Book, noting down the time and the effects the lorazepam was having on Tillie. It would make much more interesting reading, of course, when she reached the arsenic stage, because that was a colourless, odourless poison that, with any luck, Tillie would be unable to detect.

Feeling a bit wobbly, Tillie sat down again at the kitchen table, staring at Mummy through glazed eyes.

"When Daddy comes home can he have a spoonful of my blancmange?"

"Does that mean that you want me to kill Daddy as well?"

Tillie looked flustered, turned red and giggled. The *'as well'* bit, luckily failed to register. "No, I don't," she mumbled. "Feisty love-bug loves daddy!"

"If, I mean, *when* you grow up what would you like to be, Tillie?" Mummy Myra thought that this would take Tillie's mind off murders and poisoning. Nevertheless, she shouldn't have gone in that direction, because this innocent, little question was going to lead to all sorts of horrors.

"I want to be a pop star, just like Madonna."

"Not like Madonna, Tillie. You don't want to look cheap and tacky!"

"But Madonna is not like that; she's pretty and I like her songs:"

"No, no, no, Tillie!"

"Yes, yes, yes, Mummy! Anyway, Daddy likes Madonna."

"Daddy certainly does not like Madonna. You know perfectly well that he likes Tchaikovsky and Johann Strauss."

"But I saw him kissing her the other night."

"Where, Tillie, where?"

"On the landing, outside your bedroom."

"Outside my bedroom! And where was I!"

"You had gone to play bridge"

"You're a brat and a damned little liar."

Tillie, however, had not lied and when Daddy returned home she heard a terrible row going on the sitting room. It seemed it was confession time for Daddy. '*Madonna*', whose name was really Poppy, was at this moment holed up in a love-flat just around the corner: convenient, though perhaps a little stupid of Daddy to have purchased somewhere so near for his shenanigans. Poppy had got into deep trouble when she had dared to turn up at the house, knowing that Tillie's mother was at her bridge group.

"You stupid woman! What if Tillie had caught sight of you? She prattles on about everything she sees!"

"But she didn't see me, did she?"

Although, while she and Daddy, whose name, by the way, was Robert, had been kissing she thought she had glimpsed a little figure lurking behind a large potted palm. Tillie did an awful lot of lurking: here, there and everywhere, liking always to know what was going on.

When Daddy, carrying a stiff drink in his hand, came upon Tillie, she was sitting at the top of the stairs, her head resting on her lap. She was wearing her very favourite dress, a little blue number in tulle with frills on the bodice; not the sort of thing he thought she would have chosen, for Tillie was something of a fashionista. Whenever she and Mummy went out shopping there was always a clash of wills clothes-wise. Tillie the tantrum queen was known to every fashion shop in town!

He shook her and she looked up at him blurrily. After a quick gulp of his whisky, Daddy managed a weak, though not very sincere, smile.

"And how's my little love-bug this evening? I hear you've been telling Mummy all about Madonna."

"It was Madonna! I said it was, but Mummy said I was a little liar." She started to grizzle.

"Of course, it wasn't Madonna, you silly girl! That was my good friend Poppy. And I want you to like her, Tillie."

"But why, Daddy, why do I have to like her? Tillie managed to mumble.

"Because Mummy and I have decided that Poppy is going to move in here as your nanny."

Mum-Myra was naturally furious at this new turn of events, but it was either that or Daddy would sell the precious horses he'd given her, that she loved far more than she loved either Tillie or Daddy.

Daddy, because he had plenty of money, being a big wheel in the government and working for some rather iffy charities, had no intention of giving up Poppy; like Tillie, he always wanted everything his own way. His liaison with Poppy would certainly not be ending any time soon.

"Poppy, why are you here? I'm a big girl now and I don't need you to look after me. Mrs Crawful say that

I'm the best in the whole class at looking after myself. I even look after the class rabbit. He's called Tribbles and I'm the one that feeds him and cleans out his hutch. He eats ever such a lot and makes ever such a lot of mess."

"Now, look here, Tillie, this is what your Daddy wants and so this is what's going to happen. Got it, Tillie?" she said, not unkindly.

"Got it, Poppy!" replied Tillie, giving a salute and gazing closely at Poppy's golden hair and her thick eye-makeup. She decided to borrow Mummy's makeup tomorrow and see if she could get the same effect.

Mummy, meanwhile was in a terrible state, and spent much of her time in the stables, weeping into Douglas's beautiful neck or lying in the straw by Dimple's side. She had, for the moment, abandoned her thoughts of disposing of Tillie and her attitude problem. The killing arrows were now aimed in a different direction, in fact in two directions; silly Daddy and that little whore, Poppy. They'd both better watch out, especially at meal times!

She still wondered about the love-flat and hoped that he wasn't going to keep it on as a convenient meeting place for any other woman who might catch his fancy. She knew that, like most men, he had strayed now and then from the straight and narrow, but nothing to match this in intensity.

Tillie was getting on mummy's nerves, on Poppy's nerves, even on Daddy's nerves, for the gilt had gone off the gingerbread where the love-bug was concerned. All they ever heard from her was, *'No, I don't want to ...No, you can't make me ...No, I don't like it ...I hate you'*, and even *'...Sod off, Poppy, Sod off, Mummy ...Sod off, Daddy.'*

What a difficult, mouthy little girl she was!

One morning while sitting in the kitchen, smoking a strong spliff with a nice, black cup of coffee, Robert asked Myra a very important question. "Did you really put lorazepam in Tillie's blancmange?"

"Yes, Robert, I did."

"You haven't by any chance got some left, have you?"

"I have indeed," she replied brightly, having, she hoped, caught his drift.

"Enough that could be used progressively, without arousing suspicion from, for example, Mrs Crawful or from her piano teacher?"

"Thank goodness," thought mummy. She had understood his meaning perfectly.

Later, meeting the resident whore on the landing, Mummy said to her, "Poppy, do you know where to obtain the sort of substance that might be useful at a later stage for you know what?"

Poppy looked up at her, smiled happily and replied. "I certainly do. No probs there!"

It all sounds pretty awful, doesn't it? So coldly premeditated, three prospective murderers in cahoots without ever really talking directly about how they were going to achieve their end.

The affair finally, however, came to a head a few weeks later when, after a particularly stressful day, all three simultaneously, but independently of each other, sprinkled a healthy dose of arsenic onto Tillie's mashed potato.

The victim's name had for a long time now, hardly passed their lips, but she had been like a constant presence even when at school, as though her complaining and whinging had entered the soul of the house and impregnated its walls. The jury at the murder trial was revolted by the whole event, but then they hadn't ever shared a house with Tillie. It had been the discovery in a kitchen cupboard of Mummy's black Death Book that had put the final nail in their coffin, its final entry reading *Mission accomplished.* The accused were vilified and crucified by the press, because, quite rightly, no one ever takes kindly to child murder.

Only Mrs Crawful and Tillie's piano teacher felt some sympathy with the offenders – in fact, they thought that they might well have lent a helping hand if they'd realised what was going on.

Pumpkin Baby

Introvert, timid and unorthodox was Lady Dotty: but also beautiful – Cleopatra could not have held a candle to her. You would not have known it, however, for her perfectly shaped face was covered in spots, her cute, retroussé nose red and runny with the snuffles, her eyes swollen from the tears shed for the unfortunate heroine of the novel she had just been reading, newly dead from consumption.

On her lap, wrapped in a cosy, crocheted blanket was an orange pumpkin that Lady Dotty was nurturing and loving as though it were her child, which in a way it was. With a pen-knife she had carved a large, smiling mouth onto Pumpkin Baby's surface so that she always had a cheerful face looking up at her. Technically speaking, the poor pumpkin babe was blind and fighting for breath for Dotty had not thought to give her eyes or a nose. She was also going to endure a silent life, for no ears were to be seen.

Every day at this hour Dotty sat in the conservatory surrounded by succulent plants and palms; there she watched the sun rising above the horizon. Her pumpkin babe and the lovely sun were not dissimilar, she thought, each bringing light and happiness into her life.

A knock at the door interrupted her thoughts. "Come in!" she commanded and in came the breakfast trolley pushed by her personal maid who was an elderly, long-suffering soul who loved her mistress and now had opened up her heart to the infant pumpkin.

"Good morning, Elaine."

"Good morning, Lady Dotty. How are we today? While you eat your breakfast, shall I wash Pumpkin Baby's face? I've brought some lovely, scented soap that will make her skin glow." Lady Dotty smiled happily as she tucked into her huge breakfast. Was she mad? No, certainly not – merely eccentric and needy, with a strong creative imagination.

Pumpkin Baby had been born and bred on the family estate. She was the chosen one, the recipient of all this affection, because she was a reject. She had been left intact, no invasive surgery performed on her, her flesh not scooped out of her body; she would never shine with an inner light, illuminating the darkness of the Halloween night as a jack-o'-lantern.

Lady Dotty had felt sorrow seeing this poor, round, living thing with no obvious job to do, apart from one day playing a starring rôle in a pumpkin pie or a pumpkin soup, so the pumpkin babe went home with Lady Dotty to the Manor House. There she was washed tenderly and the green tendrils on the top of her head were twisted and curled around Elaine's fingers to make her even more cute.

Elaine knew that no one must learn of her

mistress's strange compulsion to play mother to a pumpkin. One of the reasons for this was that Dotty's family, in spite of her undoubted beauty, ignored her somewhat because of her very odd ways and this would really take the biscuit. They did, however, use her, to fulfil social engagements in town that they didn't want to undertake; now, for example, the livestock market, which it was essential to patronise to keep up the Manor House's good relations with the farming community. She hated to see the bartering of living creatures, like slaves of a past era, and she didn't want to think that most of them were eventually destined for the abattoir.

So, with a heavy heart, Lady Dotty relinquished Pumpkin Baby into the safe hands of Elaine. The make-up was slapped on and the spots hidden. Her snuffles had now cleared up and she was dressed to kill – a very chic, very county look, nothing too flashy, but obviously very expensive – a vision in black and fawn and smelling discreetly of Coco Chanel.

By this time, it was raining heavily, which only increased Lady Dotty's reluctance to go to her engagement. A certain section of the farmers and their wives would fawn all over her hoping for invitations to glittering, social events. She hated this and didn't want to waste time with such people, when she could be with her darling Pumpkin Baby.

As she descended the grand stairway, her mother, tall and autocratic, looked her up and down critically; she passed muster and was allowed to leave without comment. Waiting at the foot of the stone steps was the impressive car with the chauffeur holding the door open for her. Only Elaine would ever know that Lady Dotty did not return until the next evening.

She first saw him as he was studying the sheep pen intently, wondering if he could possibly steal one without being caught. He looked like a gypsy with his black boots, tight, brown, twill trousers, and white shirt, with a red kerchief around his neck and a silver ring in one ear. From that moment, however, she would always think of him as her gypsy king. According to him, his real name was Sean, but there would always be some doubt in her mind about that, but a gypsy he most definitely was. The sight of him had made her heart leap, for to call him good-looking was the understatement of the year. He was a truly swashbuckling, testosterone-fuelled hunk of manhood and she had fallen for him totally.

When he turned, he saw her standing under her smart, black-striped umbrella and was immediately attracted: a high-end woman by the look of her. "Hello, beautiful one. What are you doing here? I would not have thought that smelly animals and squelching mud were quite your thing."

Peculiar as ever, she spoke in terms that would have shocked her family and, even she, was amazed by the words that came out of her mouth. "You'd be surprised by what I like," she said, giving him a saucy wink. "Perhaps later today, if you're a good boy, I might show you!"

"That's an offer I simply can't refuse," replied the gypsy king.

Lady Dotty told the chauffeur that he would not be needed again that day and that he was to keep mum about this, so it would never reach the ears of her family and meant that she was as free as a bird to do exactly what she pleased. Later therefore, as promised, on the damp grass, under the starlight, with the branches of a tree moving in the night breeze above them, she certainly did do as she pleased. Beloved Pumpkin Baby was for the moment forgotten in the first flowering of sexual love that she had ever experienced.

It was not until the early evening of the next day that the gypsy king walked out of her life forever, promising eternal love and arranging to see her the following month at the livestock market.

The following evening she eventually arrived back at the Manor House. It was a devastating return. She found Elaine holding the pumpkin babe wrapped in her shawl, but it was too late. The orange skin had overheated and changed colour; it had reacted to the sun's hot rays and was now soft and mouldy with pumpkin juice leaking from its interior.

Guilt that she had not been there at the end erupted from Lady Dotty like a pan boiling over. She seized the dead beloved and hurled her at Elaine. The defunct pumpkin exploded, Its squashy, rotten flesh covering Elaine's face and hair whose pristine uniform was now ready for the washing machine.

It was a dreadful few weeks for both Lady Dotty

and Elaine who was so hurt that her mistress had taken her grief out on her. Fancy ending up plastered in the little one's bodily fluids! Why couldn't Dotty have put her little darling in a cardboard box and just given her a decent burial?

Lady Dotty was so upset that she hadn't been thinking clearly. She was now even more distressed, because, despite the gypsy king knowing her telephone number, he was strangely silent. There had been no response to her written messages explaining that a tragedy of a private nature had befallen her and had been responsible for her absence from the last few livestock markets.

What with one thing and another, her spots had worsened with a vengeance and even the thickest make-up was impervious to them. With her immune system weakened, her snuffles had now returned so she was feeling a real mess. It was a very low point in Dotty's life; nevertheless, not as low as it was going to become.

Now, it won't strain anyone's imagination to know what was happening, when I tell you that she was gaining weight and feeling sick in the mornings. Even her mother was beginning to look at her suspiciously.

Lady Dotty's family was always to wonder why the baby was usually dressed in orange and her nursery painted the same colour. Just another of Dotty's peculiarities they all thought. She would never talk about the baby's father, but she loved his daughter to distraction.

Nonetheless, there would always be a place in her heart for the little, orange angel who now, she was sure, was hanging on a lush vine with a crown of gorgeous tendrils on the top of her sweet head, in a beautiful vegetable garden in paradise.

Ralphie

Venal, forever seeking women to use and then abandon, Ralphie's bad reputation never proved to be a hindrance, for they all loved him: his dark, good looks: his wild ways. He was a country lad, born and bred: rough-spoken, never slow to use his fists or his tongue to cause pain to other people, friend or foe. Pub fights, street brawls, nasty expletive-ridden vocal arguments it was all the same to him, as long as he was the winner, which ninety-per-cent of the time he was.

He might sound out of control, but he had a native intelligence telling him that there was a big world waiting for him outside the rural setting where he fed the pigs, milked cows and tilled the earth. It was in the far-off horizon where he would prosper and make his dreams come true. Despite only a few sparse days of schooling, his willingness to learn made him an able pupil, for he wanted desperately to succeed.

"Come here, you little sod, so I can give you a damn good hiding!" …this from the so-called father figure in one of the many homes where he was farmed out. Whichever place fostered him, a family or an institution, the reaction to him was always the same. This was not surprising because at times he was a small version of the devil incarnate.

His chance of any love had disappeared at only two years' old when his parents, walking across the fields towards home, were killed: victims of a random shooting that also did away with three of their neighbours. The effect of this on Ralphie would have needed regression therapy to reveal, for he had fallen screaming from his mother's arms as she was hit, and he was the only surviving witness. Harsh times were ahead for little Ralphie, but his innate strength made him rise above it all. His world was hostile and so this is what he became.

He seemed to spend most of his childhood being punished for misbehaviour, but he had gathered plenty of friends, either because they feared his bullying or because they admired his daredevilry.

Eventually he was employed in a cement works as a quarryman, which he enjoyed because it was a tough job for a real man, always covered in dust and streaming with sweat. He was required to have a good level of physical fitness and to be able to work as part of a team. The latter, of course, didn't work out well in that, after one punch-up too many, he was given his marching orders.

However, the cement works closed not long after. Not only he, but most of his mates and most of the men from his village found themselves on the dole. It was a bad time for them all, especially those with families.

Ralphie, fared better than most though, for pilfering and other nefarious goings-on became his way of life. On the way, he got to know some very unsavoury people who, in the future, would prove to be extremely useful acquaintances. By this time, he was living hidden in a barn.

"Do you love me, Ralphie?" asked Sarah as they snuggled in the hay. "Will you always love me? We could get married, if you want to!" It went without saying that he didn't love her for it was an emotion that he had never experienced. Unfortunately, Sarah, size twenty, flirty, flashy and lots of fun, had a special reason for wanting to know the answer to this, for at nineteen years of age and with all his life in front of him he had unwisely planted his seed within Sarah's womb where it had begun to grow.

"I'm pregnant, Ralphie. Isn't that wonderful, so we'll have to get married, won't we?"

Ralphie's muffled answer to her question was lost as he nuzzled his head in her breasts, but he realised full well that this news spelled big, big trouble

Despite appearances, Sarah lived a sad little life. Her parents were very puritanical and strict with her, their only daughter, and impressed upon her the importance of leading a moral existence. There was no television in their house, no frivolous magazines, no swearing, no taking God's name in vain. Poor Sarah, a flabby, unattractive girl, forbidden to wear makeup or to make the best of her appearance, thought she might as well be living in a convent. It was only late in the evening, when the front door shut quietly behind her, with all her cheap, gaudy clothes and makeup stuffed into a duffle bag, that she became her true self: naughty and daring.

Three months later the scene was set, and the hour of reckoning had arrived. Centre stage of the shabby little sitting room stood Mr Smyth, Sarah's father, and in front of him was Ralphie, his huge muscles flexing as he ground his victim's foot into the carpet and clasped his throat tightly. Stage left, trembled a white-faced, doe-eyed Mrs Smyth who had, never before, heard such language uttered within those four walls, especially coming out of her husband's mouth. Stage right, the log fire burned brightly and sitting in front of it was Sarah, her swollen stomach showing her parlous condition, feeling sick from the heat of the stuffy room. The dialogue was blunt and to the point, with no words minced.

"You dirty little sod, taking advantage of an innocent girl, having carnal knowledge of my lovely daughter. This is a God-fearing house," gasped Mr Smyth trying to remove Ralphie's hands from his throat, "and it will only be when you're both married and living here that any more goings-on of that sort will be acceptable in His eyes."

"Damn God!" shouted Ralphie. "She better be getting an abortion for there will certainly be no wedding. Just look at her. Who'd want to marry that?"

"But I'm all right when hidden in the hay aren't I, Ralphie?" sobbed Sarah, both her red nose and what was dripping from it, making her even more unattractive.

"There will certainly be no abortion" declared her father, "but there will most certainly be a marriage. Tomorrow I shall have a few words with the vicar, for the sooner this is sorted out the better."

This had been Ralphie's first encounter with Sarah's parents who were, of course, completely blind to their daughter's sluttish ways. He had certainly not taken her virginity and, with a reputation like hers, he was amazed that some busybody had not dropped a quiet word in their direction. Anybody could be the father. Nevertheless, he felt pressured and caught in a trap of his own making, so something had to be done, but he'd weigh up the pros and cons of that little problem during the three weeks' respite that the reading of the banns would give him.

Back in the barn he thought that he would fall asleep at once, leaving the problem until it was daybreak; instead he lay there for most of the night in the rustling hay and pondered. He had thought of a solution, even while arguing with Sarah's father, but he couldn't, wouldn't do that; even he who cared for no one couldn't sink to such depths. Or could he? He could always just flee, of course, but that was not definitive enough.

He then had vague thoughts of pushing Sarah down a flight of stairs, just hard enough so that the little foetus would die, thus not causing any problems. However, this was a hit-and-miss solution, so he had another think.

The nasty little plan was therefore abandoned, but worse was to follow. This time it would not be about his lack of control, it would be his quick temper and ready fists that were at fault, not his hormones.

After weeks of heavy rain, the weather had finally dried up, so instead of lying on his bed of hay reading, he decided to take a walk under the magnificent, white moon despite the ground still being wet and slushy under his feet. Anyone following him would need a compelling desire to do so.

Behind him, illuminated by moonlight, came a wraith-like figure with a bulging stomach and clad in waterproofs and Wellingtons.

"Hey you! I want a word with you."

Upon hearing her, Ralphie turned around and saw the white-faced, silly, little girl who had become the stuff of nightmares.

"Go away. Don't you come near me, you tramp."

"What did you call me? That's not very nice, is it, especially as we're getting married next Tuesday at 12 o'clock, only a week from today. It's a lovely surprise for you, isn't it, Ralphie? The vicar's just rung my dad with the good news, so you better get down to the charity shop – get yourself some glad rags for the grand occasion – dad will go bananas if you turn up looking like you usually do." Sarah came close to him. "Aren't

I getting a little kiss, then? Just think, very soon we're going to have a lifetime of kisses!"

She put her hand around his neck and he punched her in the shoulder. She screamed with shock, lost her balance and fell into the mud. By this time Ralphie was beside himself with anger, so he stamped on her and on the fast-growing foetus, time and time again, so that they eventually disappeared into the mire almost, but not completely, hidden from view.

He didn't stop there because Sarah had to disappear once and for all. Grabbing a stout branch, he ground it into the mound her body had formed and the earth was soon churned up; no one, at first glance, would realise that anything untoward had taken place.

So, on Tuesday at twelve o'clock there was no wedding. There was a post-mortem.

Rather a coincidence! Did God perhaps have some sort of weird sense of humour, wondered the vicar, who knew that soon he would be officiating at the funeral? Finding the missing girl, the police discovered so many clues on the body and at the murder site, that there was no doubt what had happened to her and who was responsible.

False name, false passport, false anything he needed, even a comfortable safe-house with every mod-con where he hid from the police; all this thanks to his group of corrupt and villainous buddies who saw great promise in him. This service, of course, came at a price and payback time would inevitably arrive. It had taken quite a time to arrange, but finally everything was in place, and at last he was on a cargo ship arriving in Miami, a truly different world. He was fascinated by the containers stacked upon the dockside, gazing in wonder at the islands and inlets with magnificent mansions such as he'd never seen before, surprised by the beauty of the palm trees that he'd known only from photos. This did indeed seem to be the promised land, and thus began his American dream

He had arrived in Miami on his birthday and, after various daunting interviews with some rather sinister characters from a well-known criminal family, he was soon on his way to where he wanted to be. He was already a wanted murderer and, being an obvious tough guy would, therefore, not be overly sensitive about some of the things he would be asked to do.

So, starting at the very bottom of the ladder he became a henchman of Luigi Testa, not someone with whom you would want to argue, if you had any sense. To begin his career, Ralphie was a fetcher and carrier and it doesn't take much imagination to know what he was fetching and carrying. As he made his way up the organisation, he inevitably treated himself to many of the luxuries he was now able to afford: high-class prostitutes, designer clothes, restaurants, cars – everything of the highest quality. He didn't however flaunt his life-style and was always discreet both in his work and play. In some miraculous way, despite all the cruel and highly illegal jobs he carried out, he was never caught. He had learned to curb his ambition; his skills were recognised, but, on the other hand, he didn't engender envy in his fellow criminals. Neither did he arouse much interest from the police, though they undoubtedly knew about him, but only as a shady, shadowy character.

Dressed in jeans and a T-shirt, with his arms resting on the railing, Ralphie looked down upon the boats in Bayside, his favourite area of Miami. The little restaurants there were nothing to write home about, but would do for this evening; he was alone so he could please himself. Suddenly, he felt the back of his T-shirt held fast as someone fell to the ground behind him.

"I'm so very sorry, but I slipped and you were the nearest thing to grab hold of."

Then a very unexpected emotion hit Ralphie fair and square in the centre of his heart. Love's arrow had reached its mark. As he looked down at this gorgeous woman, it was love at first sight: her red hair, her green eyes with one or two wrinkles beginning to show, her lovely South American accent, they were all totally irresistible. The mature woman at her very best! Laura was this goddess's name.

Of course, drinks and dinner followed as did many weeks of discreet meetings: days in the sun, nights in each other's arms. The usual, Barbara Cartland type romance. There was, however, no happy ending, no wedding on some Caribbean island, no relationship that would last a lifetime: just love that would go on for ever through eternity.

Outside it was a dull, cloudy evening and inside the

sumptuous room the only object that was spotlighted was the gun being directed at Ralphie.

"Don't be afraid, Ralphie, I won't kill you today. That would be far too easy. No, I'll make you wait so that never again will you feel safe. You will always be looking around wondering when death will finally find you. Today is your last taste of life in the safe lane." Sitting at his ornate, baroque-style desk, the torturer Luigi Testa spoke to his victim Ralphie.

"This is what happens to people who try to double-cross me …however today's entertainment is not yet over. I have another little surprise for you, so sit down, Ralphie, and make yourself comfortable."

Luigi pressed the buzzer under his desk and the door opened. Enrico, the newest henchman on the block, stood with a red-headed woman whose mouth was taped and whose wrists were tied together with rope. Ralphie gasped and he could feel his heart pounding as her green eyes stared into his.

"Let me introduce you to Laura, my wife. I suspect she failed to give you that little piece of information. She's mine, Ralphie, only mine and I'm very, very possessive over my goods and chattels. I don't care for someone who thinks he can muscle in on what belongs to me, or, indeed, for a wife who thinks she can play fast and loose with Luigi Testa."

The gun now changed direction and was aimed at Laura. It gave an ear-shattering report and left a very deep hole in Laura's head, causing her brains to fly out and splatter over the wall forming a fascinating, modernistic design. The expensive light fittings that she herself had once chosen didn't fare too well either.

All this sounds as if there had been no reaction from Ralphie or Laura – but she had struggled violently and made pitiful mewling sounds, while he had shouted the single word *'NO'* so loudly and desperately that it must have echoed the length and breadth of Florida. The tears flowing down his cheeks would have needed more than a lifetime to dry. In this way ended Ralphie's career as a member of the mob.

Passing the barn where he had rolled Sarah in the hay, he crossed the fields where his parents had died and arrived at the spot where, many years ago, he had trodden into the mud Sarah and someone's unborn child. No longer did he want to live with this terrible fear that he always carried with him and he certainly couldn't survive without Laura, the only person who had ever touched his heart.

A couple of days later his body was found lying in the same hay loft, where all those years ago, he had slept the sleep of the unrighteous. An empty bottle of liquid fertiliser was clutched in his hand; an agonisingly painful death, ensuring that he would never grow strong and resilient like the fruits and vegetables he had once fed and tended. His destiny had been to wither and fade into eternal nothingness.

The Battle of Bosworth

She ducked as the vase of daffodils smashed deafeningly against the mirror behind her, so bringing yet another seven years of bad luck upon them – as though they hadn't enough already!

"You bastard!" she screamed, as she picked pieces of glass out of her hair.

"And why is that, Maisie? Why am I a bastard? Well, the answer, of course, is because you're a cow, that's why, so count yourself lucky I didn't knock your bloody teeth out!"

Back and forth, forwards and backwards went the screams and insults: ugly faces screwed up in anger, tiger lips drawn back as they snarled at each other!

It's been like that since I was about eight-years-old, which was, I suppose, when the rot first set in for my parents, marriage-wise. A slight indiscretion on my father's part had been the catalyst for the ensuing, long drawn-out, battle. So far, it's been the *Nine Years' War,* although judging by its present intensity it might, in duration, even outstrip the Thirty Years' War – the period, by the way, being covered in my A-Level History Course! That is, if the wear and tear on our nerves allows us to last that long!

"I wonder what common little whore has managed to capture your fancy this time!" An uppercut to my father's chin misses its mark.

"Anyone would be preferable to you, you raddled old slut!" he shouts as he grabs her wrists to stop a further onslaught. It all sounds like a rather bad episode of *Eastenders*, doesn't it, but I can assure you that it really isn't like that here at all – not here, not in leafy Hampstead!

However, ten seconds later a plate whizzes through the air to reach its final resting place on the floor. Not, I have to say, one of the gilt-edged plates from my mother's favourite dinner service. Not even my father would be brave enough for that – the fall-out would be the Blitz, Hiroshima and Armageddon all rolled into one!

The way I tell it might suggest that this kerfuffle, which takes place on average, I suppose, about every two weeks, has its amusing side, but this is just not so! Really, it's all very sad, very undignified and very noisy. Heaven only knows what the neighbours must think, especially in the summer with all the windows wide open! I sometimes squirm with embarrassment at it all, but once they're in full-flight it's impossible to stop them.

However, at last, a temporary truce has been called in this wonderfully equipped and expensive battlefield of a kitchen in salubrious Bosworth Field Court. We sit here eating our supper under the watchful eye of

Jasmine, the live-in, all-purpose dogsbody of the last four years. The way my father ogles her I wonder how far her domestic duties really extend; droit de seigneur, I think you might call it!

No real conversation is ever made around our supper table, whether in here or in the dining room, which is surprising, considering how vocal everything becomes in the heat of battle. Sometimes there's complete silence, except, of course, for the non-stop background music, which I'll explain about in a moment. However, on the more stimulating of evenings the occasional noteworthy remark *is* bandied about, such as: *'How is your soup, Tabitha?'*…Tabitha – that's me – or, *'I have an awful feeling it's going to rain tomorrow!'* and so on!

All rather bland, isn't it, but that totally sums up life in this house, except, of course, when the Cold War erupts into fully-fledged skirmishes. The furnishings and the décor throughout the house, including my bedroom, are bland: bland, sterile, colourless. All this reflecting my mother's desire to create a tasteful, anonymous habitat where she can impress her clients with her good taste. My mother is an interior designer and, for fear of offending the sensibilities of her clients, she resorts to this awful nothingness in which we have to live. Even my school uniform is, by chance, in varying shades of fawn and white, so there really is no hope for me, colour-wise.

"You must fully understand, Tabitha, that nothing here must clash, so I'm sorry but you really can't have red cushions and red curtains in your room. This house is my showroom and what would people think if I were to show them in here? And please ask Jasmine to remove those awful posters from the wall. I know how much you love the Portuguese football team – and yes, they certainly are very dishy – but I'm afraid they have to go!"

The trouble with the fortnightly outbreaks of artistic temperament, which is how they both like to think of these little episodes, is that one is never completely sure when the fighting will resume, because the time frame is not infallible. Every minute one tends to be on tenterhooks, which is not helpful, believe me, when one is studying hard to gain grades good enough for entry to Cambridge.

More than anything in this world I crave peace and quiet, but I'm just not getting it, am I? No way…! Especially, when, added to all this, we have Bach, Handel and bloody Vivaldi blaring out all day – the Baroque lot! For my mother, however, this type of music is considered a totally suitable background for her negotiations. All day long nothing but musical frills and furbelows, those damned cellos, violins, harpsichords and trumpets churning it out non-stop. Good taste gone mad! What's wrong with a nice bit of silence once in a while? However, I suppose it does hide the paucity of conversation that exists between my parents…

Good grief! Not already, surely? …Yes, hell has suddenly broken out again. In record time the troops have recouped their strength and are now lined up once more in battle formation; the King and Queen are ready to slug it out again, with me as the poor little pawn in the centre! I can hear the ranting and raving as I sit in the little room along from the kitchen where I'm ironically trying to study '*War and Peace*' – 'A' Level English Lit!

"You little sod, Barry. A captain of industry you may be, but your brain is somewhere in the region of your groin, like most men. Castration is what you need!"

"Bitch Maisie! Maisie the bitch! You're creative if nothing else, you ugly, old harridan – a very decorative scratch, I may say, all over my car!" Oh dear, his precious and very expensive BMW convertible – black with black leather seats – every potential playboy's dream machine. No wonder he's not happy...!

Anyway, that's enough of Tabitha and her ramblings for a while. Let's go instead to peep at Barry in his place of work, shall we? Definitely a bit of a lad is our Barry – when it comes to women, that is – which makes poor Maisie's outbursts rather more understandable; although, if she but knew it, it is only she who, for better or for worse, draws out any true passion from him.

You've only really met him, so far, in his rôle as an aggressive husband, but out in the wide, wide world he's a lamb, so easy to deal with, so easy to manipulate – a bit weak and woolly really – at least when it comes to women! Be that as it may, his romantic infatuations are never overwhelmingly serious, and he's never yet suffered a broken heart when things have inevitably run their course and come to an end.

On the other hand, of course, he's an absolute wizard in the sphere of business and has made a mint of money selling second-hand cars, hence the lovely house in Hampstead and all the other material goodies that the family possesses. It just shows you how many different facets to our characters we all have. Believe me when I say that nothing is more complicated in this universe than what goes on in the human mind!

"Come on, Sylvia," he says jauntily to his secretary, perching one rather substantial buttock upon her desk. "I think it's time we went and had a little coffee, don't you? And maybe a little something extra?" …this last with a wink and the sort of look he imagines the wicked squire in a melodrama would give! Nothing like a nice bit of rough and tumble in the stationary cupboard to set the mid-morning pulse racing! Perhaps, however, not too wise an idea if Barry has forgotten to take his blood pressure pills at breakfast, but the pleasure far outweighs any risk. Nothing kinky you understand – that's more Jasmine's forte with her fluffy pink handcuffs, which she keeps hidden conveniently under her mattress. At one time, he used to think of himself rather as a sort of sex god, but Maisie soon put him straight about that one after his first extramarital fling!

Sylvia, his ever-willing secretary, is what Maisie would have described as a bit of fluff; rather a plump girl, very well-endowed in the chest area – to which Barry is especially partial – with platinum hair and a great deal of makeup, particularly on her botoxed lips: the red bright enough to stop the traffic.

"Ooh, Barry," lisps Sylvia, "there's only time for coffee. Your wife's coming in to look at the new Mercedes. Had you forgotten?" Hardly any mileage on the clock – a beautiful silver – sleek and elegant; in other words, just Maisie's cup of tea!

"I forget everything when you're around, Sylvia, my little darling," answers Barry, automatically oozing his usual dose of insincerity. "Anyway, she doesn't need a new car, just the occasional smile on her face."

"Oh, poor, poor Barry. And all *you* need is a just a bit of TLC." She straightens his tie and gives him a little peck on the cheek.

No sooner has this tender little scene taken place than Maisie herself strides in, hair newly highlighted, enveloped in her favourite, red-fox fur jacket… but, unfortunately, at that very moment one of the mechanics has just driven Barry's beautiful, black car into the workshop to have the scratches removed, with which she has so imaginatively adorned it. Not surprisingly, the atmosphere is just the teeniest, weeniest bit frosty.

"Whenever I see you two, you always seem to be having coffee breaks. Actually, how much coffee do you both drink in a day? I should think that, between you, you keep the economy of Columbia in a very healthy state! No biscuits? Sylvia, be a pet and pop down to Mr Patel's and buy some. Something with dark chocolate on."

So off goes Sylvia, Barry's eyes firmly fixed on her shapely rear-end, while Maisie, watching him closely, decides that today she will undoubtedly buy the sexiest, most expensive car in the show room – and that Mercedes would seem to fit the bill ideally! So, Barry really has little choice but to instruct Harold, his main man, to drive the car on to the forecourt so that Maisie can have a test drive. Well, it's either that or a further engagement in the war, which would not be a good idea – especially as other people were within earshot.

"I think I'm going to like this car very much indeed. You will come with me for a little drive, won't you, Barry? Rather you than Harold, nice as he is!"

So off they go. Fifteen minutes later, with two pairs of hands struggling to have control of the wheel, they return to the garage, the battle once again in full cry. The lovely, silver, power-machine sits on the forecourt for another ten minutes, but, of course, by the time Maisie and Barry emerge from it, Maisie has a new car and Barry has a swollen eye…!

Very soon, however, back in Bosworth Field Court the truth about Barry's latest little bit of shenanigans is about to be revealed …and, no, it has nothing to do with the curvaceous Sylvia! Oh dear, poor Barry, poor Maisie and, especially, poor Jasmine! The three of them are in the kitchen when suddenly things take a very bad turn for the worse. The details are not nearly as important as the outcome, so we'll just leave those to your imagination! Suffice to say that in her little study along the corridor poor Tabitha, still struggling with War and Peace, suddenly hears an ear-piercing scream; as she runs to the kitchen, she catches her mother's final comment on the subject... *"Well, one thing's for sure, Barry, you certainly won't be having it off again with Jasmine, will you?"*

Opening the kitchen door carefully, in case there are any dangerous missiles flying around, Tabitha sees Jasmine lying on the beautiful, pale, tiled floor with her mother's favourite carving knife stuck in the side of her neck, bleeding profusely from what she assumes is the jugular vein – *O-Level Human Biology!* Poor Jasmine, in nine years the first direct casualty of the war ...but not indirectly the last!

This is all a bit of a shame because, apart from being dead, it means that there's not an awful lot more that I'm going to tell you about Jasmine. Quite a funny little person she was, truth to tell, with one or two rather strange habits that were very much to Barry's taste. However, it's only by going through the trial in detail that you would be able to glean more information about her and about their relationship, and as we're not going to do that, this, I'm afraid, is all you're going to learn – no salacious details for those of you who like that sort of thing – sorry!

Barry, the stuffing well and truly knocked out of him, suddenly has to sit down with his head between his knees. Well, it's not every day that you discover that your wife is capable of murder, plus, of course, the fact that there is rather a lot of blood around, the sight of which always makes him feel a bit queasy. Maisie, meanwhile, has fainted and so, what with one thing or another, it's left to Tabitha to ring the police station and call for the boys in blue!

"Now what have we here, Mr York? A touch of the domestics by the look of it!" remarks Sergeant Jenkins to Barry as he awaits reinforcements from headquarters. The sergeant, by the way, came out of the affair very well, having made sure that there was no contamination of the crime scene and that all the physical evidence was in good order…

Well, after all, he'd watched the whole of the O.J. trial avidly and was very aware of the difficulties in that area if things weren't done according to the book!

So, even during the initial enquiry, there was no doubt at all as to what had taken place and who was the chief suspect.

Poor Maisie, she really should have kept her cool and not done it!

However, a statement had to be made and she made it, which is why she ended up in jail for six years! Sylvia, of course, thought that this was her big chance and, that with Maisie safely out of the way, everything would have a lovely romance-filled, chick-lit ending but she'd misread her man, for what did he do, but go out in Maisie's wonderful Mercedes and drive, with great deliberation, into an oak tree?

He just couldn't stand the prospect of a Maisie-less existence, you see.

Yes, well, we all know that six years isn't forever and that there were, of course, visiting times, but it just wasn't the same, was it…?

However, what of Tabitha, you may be asking? Well, I have to tell you that I just adore Cambridge …all this wonderful peace and quiet where I can study uninterrupted, with only Josh Groban cooing softly in the background. I'm actually quite famous around the university and frequently find myself invited to the most wonderful parties for I am popular, and, indeed, notorious, among both my fellow students and among – well, especially among the university staff. Why, many is the porter who has led me up those historic, fascinating little stairways to pass the night with an eminent philosopher or a world-famous physicist! My notoriety, of course, stems from the fact that I have a murderess for a mother, a suicide for a father and that I'm also the owner of a highly successful second-hand car business. My fortnightly visits to Holloway in my snazzy, little sports car also do nothing to spoil my reputation as somewhat of a goer.

My unfortunate mother, however – poor mummy – is having a less enjoyable time, especially as her cell is such a very bright, coloured-filled living space; the vivid red cushions and bedspread provided, of course, by yours truly! She is now a lonely, cowed, bullied, self-harming creature – though I do believe that Daddy's main man, Harry, is waiting somewhere in the wings to take over Barry's place. I don't think he is fully aware, however, of who actually rules the roost money-wise and I think he will find himself severely disappointed when he does.   Personally,

I believe, to quote from Victor Hugo, in whose work I am particularly interested at the moment, *'Tout est pour le mieux dans le meilleur des mondes'* – or, for those of you whose French isn't too hot, *'all is for the best in the best of all possible worlds.'* Very soon it will be the end of term and I shall be off to spend a very peaceful, non-aggressive vacation in Bosworth Field Court. Poor Barry! Poor Maisie! Poor Jasmine! ...Lucky me!

Anticipation

It was such a beautiful day, she thought, as she opened the bedroom curtains. The early morning sun shone directly onto her face and filled her with such happiness that she almost felt like jumping for joy – except, of course, that she was far too fat to attempt it. Today was the day when the long, thrilling sense of anticipation would finally reach its climax.

She wrapped her faded, grey dressing gown around her plump frame and went downstairs to potter about in the kitchen – making the tea, making the toast, switching on the radio. Andrew Lloyd Webber? Was it him – or was it somebody else? She simply couldn't remember! Well, whoever it was she loved his music, loved *'Les Mis'* – and here they were playing her favourite – *'I Dreamed a Dream'*. Surely an omen for what was going to happen later, for today her dream was going to be fulfilled, wasn't it?

She was fifty years old – never had a man, never had sex. Hadn't really had time, had she? Her life had been filled with looking after her cantankerous, demanding mother, as well as working all the hours God sent: cleaning other people's houses, cleaning their own, keeping the weeds at bay in their tiny garden, etcetera, etcetera… Now, that mother was dead, however, the house and garden could look after themselves. So, men and sex awaited her – beckoned to her – about bloody time too!

Disappointingly, things hadn't quite worked out as she had hoped. She had tried in her own little way to let it be known that she was available, but after so much lack of practice she just wasn't very good at the chat-up line, the flirting, the come-hither body language that other women obviously found so easy. In fact, she didn't have much opportunity to meet new men and the ones that she did meet were either married or unsuitable candidates because she did have her standards and knew just what she wanted.

Walking down the street she had got into the habit of looking at men to see if they were looking at her and the unfortunate answer had been a resounding *NO*. Mainly because their eyes were focused on somebody half her age, half her weight and twice as attractive, so one day she took a long look at herself in the mirror. Her hair perhaps was a little over-permed, her skin dry, uncared-for… Maybe just a tad of lipstick would help.

She had then looked at her nails and felt a sense of shock. They were awful; no cuticles, rag nails, cut with a pair of ordinary scissors; she didn't even possess a nail file! As for her feet – well, what a disaster! Come the great reveal what would a man think of those – no enticing, scarlet nail varnish there, just fleshy, sausage-like toes with ugly, yellow nails embedded in them.

Her body wasn't too bad – athough a bit wrinkly on the arms and thighs, and she had to admit that her rear-end was so pitted it looked as though it had suffered a meteor attack ...but her boobs were good – still firm, still smooth. No children, of course, and thus there was not a stretch-mark to be seen. The excess weight, unfortunately, would have to be dealt with later – there was certainly no time now!

Richard was his name – the man she was going to meet. Something in the city apparently – blond hair, six-foot-tall, interested in wining and dining and reading – widowed with no children. He couldn't sound more perfect, could he?

It was for him, for Richard, for her Richard, as she had begun to think of him, that she had undergone a great makeover this last week. The grey, poodle hair had gone and when she looked in the mirror she now saw this surprising woman with her blonde, straight, sleekly-cut bob. Her skin was exfoliated and moisturised, perfumed and pampered ...and as for her nails, well, a good pedicure and manicure had soon sorted those out, so much so that she must have spent minutes at a time gazing at them in amazement – they just didn't seem to belong to her at all.

She had seen his ad in the personal column of The Telegraph, which she'd glanced through quickly while cleaning Mrs Humbert's sitting room. Ever since then she had purchased the newspaper herself, so that she could perhaps appear to know more than she really did. *'I read yesterday in The Telegraph,'* she could hear herself saying to him, *'all about that terrible business in Japan – what do you think of that? – such a tragedy and on such a large scale.'*

Perhaps she could even venture a political remark, which would be okay as long as he didn't quiz her on it; because, in fact, she knew damn all about politics or about anything else for that matter – except, of course, for EastEnders or Corrie. Luckily, like him, she absolutely loved reading – the great Barbara Cartland, the wonderful Norah Lofts and all those gorgeous, gorgeous Mills and Boons! As for *'Fifty Shades of Grey'* – well, what a shocking book, but she'd simply adored every single word of it! Now, finally, she would live her own romance, experience her own torrid love scenes.

She just hoped that he didn't suffer from bad breath or BO or any other embarrassing condition because that would put a bit of a damper on things, wouldn't it? However, surely anyone who read The Telegraph would not have problems of that sort. The Mail, perhaps! The Mirror, maybe! The Telegraph, never!

At 8'clock that evening she found herself opening the door of Finnegan's Wake, dressed to the nines and plastered with makeup; rather over-the-top perhaps, but really quite acceptable. She looked around anxiously – he wasn't at the bar, he wasn't at any of the tables. Where was he? – please God, she hadn't been stood up! – the let-down would be more than she could bear. However, as she passed the table in the corner she heard a voice. "Phyllida? I'm here! It's me – Richard!"

Her heart gave a lurch and she turned her head to the right. In the shadows, she saw a man. He stood up and held his hand out towards her. Five-foot-seven, dark, greasy hair, smelling of cigarette smoke; surely a reject from casting for EastEnders! Not like her Richard at all.

"I know what you're thinking, love, but we all tell porky pies, don't we? Sit down and have a drink – you'll soon feel better."

So she did – sit down, that is – too shocked and too disappointed to do anything else. She just sat there staring at him. What could she say, what kind of conversation were they going to have? However, she needn't have worried about that, because three hours later he was still talking – about his racing greyhound, about his caravanning holidays, about his racing greyhound, about his work at the local aircraft factory, about his racing greyhound. Why didn't he just build a bloody temple to the bloody greyhound and be done with it?

Not once – not once, did he ask her a single question about herself. She might as well have been a cardboard cut-out, for all the notice he took of her – except for keeping her wine glass filled. Never ever had she been so bored – and she stared at his little piggy eyes behind the rimless spectacles, stared at his awful, green, tightly-buttoned tweed jacket, at his green and white flowery shirt, at his green pullover, at his tightly-knotted green and white striped tie – he must have been so suffocatingly warm under all those layers of greenness. So much enjoyable anticipation, for what? – for this, for this... well...!

She suspected that he was deaf, because when she did venture to say something he merely screwed his face up and turned his left ear towards her. In fact, she thought that she was probably dining with the blind as well as the deaf the way he'd read the menu, his nose virtually touching the paper.

Everything, in the fullness of time, comes to an end and finally they left the restaurant. Next to the restaurant was an alleyway, at the entrance to which they stood to shelter from the rain that had been falling all evening. Please, please, don't let him start to fumble me or try to kiss me she thought, but no sooner had this passed through her mind than she suddenly felt his arm encircling her shoulder.

She tried to move away, but was too firmly within his grasp. His arm then moved around her neck so that she found herself in what she would have recognised as a chin lock if she'd been able to think more clearly. She'd always loved watching the wrestling on the telly and knew the name of most of the holds. His hands clasped firmly together, she was then dragged helplessly into the darkness and, so tight was the hold, that she could feel herself beginning to choke. He threw her to the ground... and the rape began.

Bruised and bleeding, she eventually managed to crawl along the wet ground towards the street – though Richard was by this time long gone, never to be seen again, never to be identified – an insignificant, little man who had ruined her life, blighted her dreams. The day that had begun so auspiciously had turned into a nightmare.

While she was safely tucked up in hospital with her beautiful nails torn, her face scratched and ugly, her virginity stolen from her, the police, under the damp night sky, began to search the alleyway for clues. Before long, behind the stinking, overflowing dustbins, they found the body of a tall, well-dressed, blond-haired man who was later identified as Richard Sargeant. Under his body, they found what must have started out as a most beautiful bunch of pink roses and, not far away, lay an old copy of The Telegraph with an item in the personal column circled in red ink.

Poor Richard Sargeant, he really should have been less communicative with the odd, little man with whom he had shared a taxi.

Aqua Tofana

Her name was Malvia: shrewish, sharp-featured and ugly with evil intent. Nevertheless, she was not the only one by far who, at that moment, was negotiating a death.

Every woman in Naples knew that men were born promiscuous and they wanted their revenge. That was why so many of them resorted, like Malvia, to seeking the services of an alchemist or someone connected with the occult arts.

Malvia's rage had no bounds, but would soon be appeased by lovely Aqua Tofana, tasteless and odourless. For those with murder on their mind this magical liquid, carefully-calculated, was so slow-acting that the fatal moment could be planned and guaranteed to take effect weeks, months and even a year ahead.

The victim would just gradually weaken and languish, until death would eventually claim him. It was not a dramatic end, for there was no pain and the symptoms were negligible, so that the perpetrator could feel reasonably sure that blame would not fall on his shoulders.

At that time, Malvia did not possess the secret of how to make Aqua Tofana, but it was bruited about by the gossips of Naples that it contained oddities like toad flax, extract of snapdragon, a solution of pennywort. Its basic ingredient, not surprisingly, was claimed to be arsenic.

Malvia had thrown on a black, hooded cloak to go about her dark task. On the front door of the apothecary's shop, a shabby, unloved building, she tapped four times, quickly, as instructed, all the while looking around surreptitiously to see if anyone was watching. She was so obviously furtive that she would have fooled no one.

The door creaked open as the ageing, arthritic apothecary's talons held it ajar for her. Malvia silently slipped into the room of mysterious secrets and magic.

"Well," croaked the apothecary, wasting no time, "what have you got for me?"

From inside her cloak she took a richly embroidered purse. She opened its drawstring and poured a veritable shower of gold rings, bracelets and necklaces onto the table.

He held each piece up to the flickering candle, estimating its value.

"I think this could well buy you what you want, Signora."

His lips parted in what could have been a smile or a grimace but, with his brown rotting teeth, it was difficult to tell.

"It is Aqua Tofana that you are wanting, is it not?"

"Of course! What else?

"For how many people?"

"For two bitches," she snarled between gritted teeth, in her mind damning Benedetta and Valentina's souls to hell.

Before they settled down to the real business of the day, the making of a phial of Aqua Tofana, Malvia removed her cloak and leaned upon the table, provocatively showing off her breasts for the delectation of the ancient apothecary. The immediate prospect of being able to rid herself of her rivals was almost a sexual response, for her lover, darling Lorenzo, would soon be hers again. Within, she was in a frenzy of ecstasy and excitement.

In her ornate, green dress with its blue frills and bows and with her red hair hanging down over her ears in thick ringlets, she felt she had accorded the apothecary an honour by her presence. Nevertheless, she needed his knowledge desperately.

His room was unclean, unswept, and he was grubby, but he had ceded to her the best chair in the room: a well-used, shiny, velvet affair that did not smell very fresh. She was too excited, however, to sit in it and simply leaned shoulder to shoulder against the apothecary, surrounded by his retorts and glass instruments of all shapes and sizes, with, at her feet, an untidy pile of books. For some unaccountable reason, the apothecary's feet were resting on a pair of bellows.

She watched so very carefully as he prepared the mixture, each time asking the name of the ingredient and the quantity used. She had a good memory and would not forget any small detail.

When he had finished his work, the apothecary handed her a pretty, blue phial.

"Hide this, Signora, hide it well among your perfumes and love philtres. Nothing must connect this to me. I do not wish to end my days in a dungeon being tortured."

In a spontaneous rush of gratitude and sexual confusion Malvia kissed him full on the lips. He had vouchsafed her his knowledge, but, of course, she now knew the secret of Aqua Tofana and would have no further use for him. She, in her turn, wanted nothing to connect her to the apothecary, but she would think of a solution for that later. For now, the phial was concealed among the folds of her dress in yet another finely-crafted purse.

Thanks to him, Benedetta and Valentina were doomed and, at a time of her choosing, would start to wilt and fade. Lorenzo's days of philandering with these two she-devils were over. They were nothing. They were low-life. Whereas she, Malvia, was at court, only as a lady-in-waiting, but nevertheless she was a person of some substance. Where Lorenzo had found Benedetta and Valentina she had no idea.

Out she went into the street, her hooded cloak again protecting her from prying eyes, but there was no one to see her. She breathed in the fresh air to erase the claustrophobia of the apothecary's stuffy room, with its strange smell of flowers and powders and chemicals.

Tonight, she would go with her brother to the opera at the Teatro San Carlo: listen to the music of Pergolesi. She would enter a dream world of beauty, taking her mind off how and when to administer the Aqua Tofana; tomorrow she would return to her plan for murder and revenge.

The next business in hand was to locate the whereabouts of the two foxy minxes, which was not a difficult task as they were somewhat notorious: indeed, a pair of very naughty girls!

So, in a scarlet, hooded cloak, with her hands gloved and hiding her face behind a beaded, hook-nosed carnival mask, Malvia was completely unrecognisable as she entered Il Mandolino. It was a rough and ready, smoke-begrimed tavern frequented by all types of thieves and swindlers. Because it was carnival time she was not the only one wearing a mask, so she felt anonymous, safe and sexless.

She soon espied her victims seated by the blazing fire, quaffing their ale from pewter tankards. Before you could whisper *Aqua Tofana* the ale had assumed a very different quality. The liquid had been carefully measured out beforehand and within a very short time the hussies would go to meet their maker. After the debilitating two weeks there would be a funeral and Lorenzo could weep and wail for all he was worth, but nothing would bring them back. He would again be hers: Lorenzo and Malvia walking into the sunset.

Malvia smiled at her strange disguise in the mirror

as she made her way out. "My, you are a bad girl!" she said with satisfaction.

She also thought it would be prudent, while she was at it, to dispose of the apothecary: a dangerous, unsavoury old man who, while he remained alive, was a threat to her. He could identify her if she ever came under suspicion, he could tell the authorities of Naples about her, word might even reach the ears of the King of Naples, probably leading to her dismissal from court. Worse still, she might find herself in prison, tortured and then, as a blessed relief, swinging from the gallows.

By the time she again donned her disguise and stood in the darkness outside the apothecary's house, both Benedetta and Valentina had died on the exact day that she had planned.

She was carrying in her hand a beautiful, multicoloured nosegay of flowers. She tapped on the door, this time less timorously. She could hear the scraping back of his chair and his shuffling footsteps as the apothecary slowly made his way to the door. Again, the gnarled claw, with its long, yellow nails was the first thing she saw. In the other claw, he held a candle.

It went through her mind that he might call himself an apothecary, but he was also a sorcerer skilled in the black arts. Heaven only knew what all the bottles in his strange room might contain.

As she glanced over his shoulder, she saw strange, wispy shadows moving around that put the fear of God into her. She just wanted to be away from there as quickly as possible.

"Did it work, Signora? Did the Lady Aqua Tofana do her work well? Were you pleased with her?" Malvia was disturbed, her heart beating loudly in her chest. He had recognised her.

"Yes, everything went according to plan, which is why I have brought you a small token of my gratitude. I believe you like flowers, so this nosegay is for you with my thanks."

"I thank you, Signora. It is not often that I receive such a gesture for my work." As she handed over the nosegay, a sleight of hand quickly took place and she removed the top from a phial. As he buried his face in the flowers to smell their scent, poisonous fumes were released. Not Aqua Tofana, but another wonder potion from the black arts.

The apothecary or alchemist or whatever he was looked her hard in the face, his almost black eyes seeming to bore into hers so deeply that she feared he could read her mind. She needn't have worried, however, for a rattling sound suddenly came from his throat and he slowly slumped to the floor.

She quickly retrieved the nosegay, pulled the door hard behind her and disappeared into the night.

If you should be wondering about Lorenzo, well he too is dead, another victim of Aqua Tofana administered by Malvia.

His death took only a day, but she kept him well away from other people because she wanted to explain to him why he was ailing. That was part of her revenge.

"I've become tired of you, Lorenzo," she said, gazing at his pale face with its dark shadows under the eyes. "In the past, you were all I wanted. But times have changed, and I've changed. You betrayed me. You let me down. I can't forget. I can't forgive. You don't know her, but last night I joined you in marriage to Lady Aqua Tofana and, by this evening, you will make her a widow."

"And who the hell is Lady Aqua Tofana?"

Malvia then described the disadvantages of such a union to Lorenzo. "Now I've told you all about her, you can spend a few hours thinking about your sins and cleansing your soul. As I've given you this luxury, I shall feel no guilt whatsoever over your death."

"You bitch," he moaned from his deathbed. He hadn't the strength to say more or to argue with her, dying, hours later, silently and unprotestingly. He just drifted away into the hereafter; his last sight of this world was Malvia's smiling face.

The city was a constant hotbed of intrigue and death. There were all sorts of disreputable groups of people dealing in poisons and magic potions, even within monasteries and convents. It was, indeed, from a cleric that Malvia had purchased the lethal concoction that the apothecary had breathed in. Now that she knew exactly how to make Aqua Tofana, Malvia saw no reason not to take advantage of her knowledge. The dispensing of poisons was a profitable business, but it was prudent not to have too many clients, for fear of arousing suspicion.

Malvia herself kept a low profile and it was her brother who was the front man, negotiating and bartering. Their life changed dramatically as they became wealthy. Malvia took numerous lovers some of whom were quickly disposed of, in what was becoming her usual manner.

The house they purchased was magnificent, its gardens manicured and decorated in great style. There were lovely views over the Bay of Naples, but what particularly delighted Malvia was her bedroom where she entertained her lovers. It was a little paradise of gold-leaf decoration with an abundance of cherubs, nymphs and shepherdesses – beautiful mirrors, richly woven sofas and chairs and a magnificent curtained bed: all for her delectation.

The curtains of Malvia's bed were closed to keep out the draught that somehow always seemed to find its way through the windows and doors of that splendid room.

For once she was alone. Her latest lover had been called to the court of the King of Naples where, only five short years ago, Malvia had served as a lady-in-waiting.

She was almost asleep, but suddenly sensed the curtain being disturbed. Opening her eyes she came face to face with a long-fingered hand with dirty nails, outlined in the moonlight that had filtered through the curtain. It was holding a dagger.

"I know that you are more than a little surprised to see me again, Signora. Dead? A ghost? No, I'm no phantom, nor a figment of your imagination, nor a dream. Nothing so dramatic as that! Just plain flesh and blood, I'm afraid. Malvia could hardly breathe, could hardly think. *How? Why? It could not be true.*

"Touch the dagger, touch my hand, if you dare!" She gasped and did as the apothecary asked. It really was him, but she had killed him, had seen him die!

"I am not a fool, Signora and have many enemies. You were an amateur at murder. But I have ways of reading men's and, indeed, women's intentions, so I was prepared for any eventuality. A potion on my belt, for example, that will give me time to seek out the appropriate antidote! I am also a consummate actor, and many is the time I have played a death scene."
Malvia was struck dumb in shock and confusion; she could not even beg for her life.

"You tried to ruin me by using the secret ingredients of my beautiful Lady Aqua Tofana. My mistake... I didn't realise how devious and sly you are. But I have always sworn that one day I would take my revenge, for, as the proverb says, it is a dish best served cold. Today therefore, when with all your wealth you've so much more to enjoy and, of course, so much more to lose, I will take your life. But Aqua Tofana is too good for you... I will use cold steel instead!"

Words just wouldn't leave her lips and so, like

Lorenzo she went silently and unprotestingly to her death as the apothecary slid the sharpest of daggers through her heart.

Hybrid Dream

It was that strange dream again. Once dreamed, never forgotten! So weird that, on waking, it would stay with me the whole day! I had no idea of its meaning...

Dark, vaulted passageways led to a claustrophobic, circular piazza of terracotta-tiled paving in front of the smartest, snazziest emporium in the city. It was through those passageways that we, fashionable women, with our elaborately coiffed hair decorated in leaves, made our way to make our purchases. In fact, the stylish building was our life-line, for without it we simply couldn't function.

The whole scene was in shadow and the only illumination came from within the emporium which, as you will see, was forbidden to me because of my own stupidity.

We women were all similar, with bits and pieces that were inanimate or mechanical. I knew that I, together with the others, was a hybrid, but strangely I still felt very feminine.

I had no feet, which didn't seem at all odd; just wheels that were rather old and needed replacing, for they creaked, squeaked and shed rusty flakes. When I moved, I would occasionally have to come to a stop and hold onto a wall. Well, it was either that or fall over onto the paving!

Every dream began with a group of us, each one suffering from severe mechanical failure, making our way towards the purveyor of replacement parts. We were all falling to pieces in one way or another; there was a constant trail of women waiting for repairs. Women entered the emporium ailing, failing and silent, and exited from it restored to full health, happy and chattering away to each other.

There were all types of breakdowns: mechanical hands, hearts and so on and so forth.

Rotting wheels, however, were particularly disfiguring and inconvenient. A good pair of small wheels instead of feet, or one larger wheel instead of legs, depending on the style you had chosen, were essential for a fast, exciting life. You could whiz along at no end of a pace and never miss an important social event.

Everyone, that is, except me, because I was totally incapable of crossing the threshold of the emporium; I simply froze. It wasn't because of fear or the fact that I was tottering. Mentally and physically I seemed to turn to stone. In fact, I don't know why it was, but this is where the dream always ended, which meant that I was forever damaged goods, and that is how I always felt on waking.

I was so jealous of them all. I just needed a new pair of wheels – a very simple process that only took about five minutes, so expert were the assistants. A small adjustment was all that was necessary for me to be perfect, because in my stylish gown I looked so good and so elegant you wouldn't have believed it.

We all wore lovely, floaty, shape-enhancing little numbers – more or less identical, but we could choose from a rather limited range of two colours, all that seemed to be available in the dream place. I, for example, was an amazingly beautiful vision in red, while most of my companions had opted for green, which I would never have chosen.

On one particular day I awoke from the dream in what might be termed a bit of a state for, during my waking hours, I was going to do something really, really stupid.

On the front of my wardrobe hung a wedding dress with its sweetheart neckline and its mermaid silhouette, just like the ones I had seen a hundred times on '*Say Yes to the Dress*': not a great intellectual experience but, nevertheless, my favourite television programme. Draped over a chair was the veil.

In my humble opinion, if you are still unmarried at the age of thirty-five, you have missed the boat. I say this with an apology to anyone who is still floundering about on a sea of hope. Therefore, I had felt a great sense of urgency to rectify the problem and Cosmo was my solution. He was a pet, a darling, but he didn't really rock my boat, or anything else, for that matter.

The hour of reckoning was fast approaching, for it was at high noon that the deed would be done, and the knot tied forever: that is until death or, more probably, divorce parted us. To be a divorcée sounded to me a bit racy and I quite liked the thought of it: especially as I would be a very desirable woman, rich from my divorce settlement and unbelievably beautiful.

It was a very tense situation for me, for a great deal of time, effort and money had been spent planning this day. On principle, I never go into churches, except for christenings, weddings and funerals. However, I wanted the best and I wanted the kudos of the Dean of Westdash performing the ceremony, so a church it must be. A wedding on some sun-drenched beach in the Caribbean just did not have the same appeal.

Cosmo's family was a bit of a joke for someone like me who had pretensions to be the lady I was in my dream: needless to say, without the wheels. They were true countryfolk, the kind that chewed straw, looked big and ungainly and sounded like Long John Silver. However, they had become super rich from manufacturing farm machinery and having plenty of business savvy, which was not unconnected with my choice of Cosmo for a husband.

I awaited the arrival of my sister, Amy, who was going to help me get ready, and of Uncle Chester who was to give me away. In my hybrid body in my hybrid dream, I had seen my reflection in the emporium window and knew I looked absolutely tip-top. For some unknown reason however, this beauty didn't translate itself to the cheval mirror in my bedroom, for dressed in my lovely, white gown with poor Amy doing her best, I looked just like any other bride. In fact, there was a distinctly hang-dog expression about me. Was it perhaps because Cosmo, though sweet as a cup-cake, was simply not what I had visualised all those years in my silly, sentimental daydreaming?

I was shoved, sniffling slightly and feeling decidedly second best, by Uncle Chester into the wedding car that, with its plethora of red and pink ribbons, looked much more festive than I was feeling.

As we were being driven towards the church, my ankles began to ache and my hands to shake so hard that it was a wonder that the petals from my bouquet of wild flowers did not all fall onto the floor of the car. When I finally emerged from what felt like a tumbrel going to the guillotine, shooting pains in my feet made it almost impossible to walk. It was only by holding on to Uncle Chester's arm that I was able to make it up the path.

I suddenly saw, in all its horror, the church's medieval, stone arch, its wooden doors wide open with the Dean of Westdash, a true figure of doom, waiting to receive me. Dimly behind him my eyes took in the interior: its stained-glass windows, the gathering of guests, the floral decorations and, almost hidden, Cosmo and his brother standing at the altar.

My stomach did a somersault and there was no way that I was going to put one foot across that threshold. I had frozen. I told Uncle Chester that I had changed my mind, that it was all a terrible mistake but he, with a determined smile on his face, forcibly yanked me inside.

I walked easily and painlessly up the aisle, for everything had changed. Waiting for me was Cosmo, my best friend in the whole world. Why hadn't I realised before that no one else would do? This was reality, not some never-to-be attained fantasy, which, even if it had been fulfilled, would probably have been a great disappointment.

The ceremony was meaningful and our vows heartfelt. Finally, I felt beautiful and even the Dean of Westdash gave me a saucy wink. From that day forth, whenever I returned to my hybrid dream, I always left the great emporium a new woman, spinning along on my little silver wheels prepared for anything. Now I was a glorious vision in green and my mind open to new ideas. Because it had taken me a long time to cross the threshold and it had all been such a struggle for me, the assistants treated me with great courtesy and I felt very much at home. I loved going inside and having a browse around to see what mechanical parts were available: springs, cogs, wheels, axles, ball bearings; they were all there for our convenience.

Now that I knew I was free to come and go as I pleased, I loved to linger outside the emporium in the piazza under the pretty tree that stood in the centre. I would admire myself in the hand mirror that we all kept in our gown pocket and knew that now there was nothing hang-dog about me.

Blue Imperfection

The wizard stood and contemplated the emptiness around him; there were still one or two fragments left over from his very first experiment, but nothing of any importance, so he was really starting from scratch. This would be his umpteenth attempt and would be completely different from what had been created before, but if it did not succeed he would just have to come to terms with being alone.

Thinking very deeply and letting his imagination take flight, he suddenly clicked his fingers to set the process in motion. This was the momentous culmination of his thoughts. An instant before there had been nothing and now there was everything. For the wizard there was no conception of time, but in a second he was surrounded by a tumultuous noise, followed by great swathes of mist and colour that then began to form the swirling galaxies, the stars and the planets and all he had seen in his mind's eye. "My goodness me, it's done! I've done it," he shouted, waving his wand furiously and causing the solar winds to moan and groan as they were buffeted about in space.

He thought it all looked terribly impressive, but

there was a definite glitch somewhere in the equation that he had formulated, something was not quite right, for it all seemed far too chaotic. On some planets great fiery eruptions were coming from beneath the ground, while others had no smooth knitted-together surfaces; instead there were huge areas of rocks that clashed against each other and caused the ground to swell and rise, to form mountains and hills. Not at all what he had intended; he'd wanted tidiness and uniformity. What displeased him most, however, were the worm holes and the black holes that were completely unplanned and unnecessary. Where had they come from? "I'm really not very good at this," he thought and began to walk around what he had created to see if he could perhaps manage to resurrect from his failure a veritable jewel of perfection and beauty.

In an instant of pure inspiration, he then envisaged something called time and decided that he would go right back to the beginning to gather up his rejected, left-over fragments. Having done this, he resolved that he was going to make from them the most glorious object in the whole of his creation; a gorgeous, red sphere, a vibrant ruby, where he might put living creatures with whom he could perhaps communicate. He thought deeply about its attributes, deciding that it would be mainly a warm desert world with patches of water where lush palms and exotic flowers would grow. He then put creatures in this tropical paradise, surely a home that would bring them happiness. An exciting, interesting place; not totally watery, gaseous or rocky like some of his other inventions.

Having given the planet form, he then wandered about trying to think where to place it. Then, suddenly, on an outer spiral of a galaxy, he spied the perfect spot, just the right distance from a star. Carefully the wizard set the sphere down within its orbit, determining always to keep a special eye on it.

The living spirit of the universe was watching the wizard very carefully and holding its breath as to the outcome, not having much confidence in his abilities creation-wise. Sure enough, three seconds later, the creatures had all died from heat stroke and lack of water. What a blunderer he was proving to be. "Get your act together, magic man!" the universal consciousness whispered to him.

"I simply don't understand what happened" he replied. "Everything was on line for success; the maths was right and I'm sure I put it in the best possible place."

All of this meant, of course, that he would have to go back to the drawing board to find the ideal design for his perfect planet. He knew that whatever he created must be placed – roughly – in the same vicinity as the red planet, because he was certain that his positional equation had been correct. It must, therefore, be another factor that had caused the error to occur. His favourite colour was blue, so why had he created something that was red? "Perhaps it was the colour that caused the problems. I must be losing my marbles," he said out loud. The universal consciousness was too polite to reply, but agreed completely with the second part of his assessment.

Once more it was launch day and holding the beautiful, blue globe, that sparkled like an emerald, he confidently, lovingly, put it next to his failed dream, that barren red orb that he had created with so much care. This brilliant, blue sphere, its inhabitants walking proudly on two legs, was so perfect that he knew in his heart that his aim had been achieved. It was a world of waterfalls and great oceans, ponds and streams, with ice floating on its surface and rain falling from its skies; a watery world, but dotted with dry land of every variety to please every taste.

Unfortunately, he had hardly turned his back when, glancing over his shoulder, he could see that there was something very wrong with his masterpiece: emanations of aggression and ill-will were arising from it; terrible events were taking place on its surface; natural disasters abounded. Sadly, there was only one thing he could now do: remove it from its solar system and throw it into a black hole, never to be seen again. So black holes did have a purpose; perhaps they were where all the rubbish in the universe was supposed to go.

Evidently, he was never going to have anyone with whom he could communicate. Yet, you would have thought, with all he had so far achieved, that he would persevere, but he simply didn't have the backbone or the stamina for this. Having a low concentration level, he was now bored and decided that he needed to diversify, have new interests upon which to focus. Perhaps now he would consider making something dark and mysterious, matter that would make his universe more stable and stop each part of it from flying away, which it was now doing.

He would, however, on the other hand, have to think about releasing an energy that would prevent everything from being boringly static. He would make these two forces invisible so that his beautiful design would not look too cluttered. He thus had his work cut out for him on both fronts. At least it would keep him out of mischief was the thought uppermost in the mind of the great omnipresent consciousness.

While he was thinking over those new ideas, the wizard suddenly came to a momentous decision that would make a difference to everyone. He realised the stupidity of tossing the blue orb into a black hole. Why bother, when those very imperfect creatures in their imperfect home would sooner or later, left to their own devices, destroy themselves without any help from him?

So, this is how the wizard left the situation and how it continues to this day. The universal consciousness, that unseen spirit that reputedly pervades everything, does not seem much involved nowadays because no one, least of all the wizard, ever listens to it.

Too Tightly Bound

He'd been there many times before. He knew that much, but he simply couldn't remember how it all ended. Perhaps each ending was different, though he didn't think this was the case. So, as usual, he stood bolt upright unable to do anything else. If he moved his elbows even a fraction, the hard stone surrounding him prevented further movement.

The darkness, the clattering of footsteps above him, the clanging of metal upon metal were all unbearable. He would like, if it had been at all possible, to have killed himself there and then, anything to have escaped the suspense and the terror. Now he heard voices, deep and gruff above him and could just make out the flickering light of a candle. He was unable to see the source of this because his head was firmly gripped by the wall, which became narrower the higher it went but, by lifting his eyes as far as they would go, he knew that there was a grill above him.

Eventually, he managed to utter some sort of cry for help, but the answer was overwhelming silence as though the world had forgotten him. He closed his eyes wanting to sleep, for surely, he couldn't possibly really be there. His breathing gradually became deeper and more regular. As the seconds passed an inner darkness began to overwhelm him and he gratefully sank into it.

The moon and the stars shone through the window as Dougie lay gazing at them, with a wonder that never failed to excite him. He was relieved to have awoken from his nightmare and looked at the clock. It was only two in the morning so, if he wished, he could continue watching this glory for hours. He snuggled down under his luxurious duvet with, as always, his arms digging into his sides and smiled. Suddenly, however, his moments of pleasure were shattered by the sound of his mother's imperiously creaking voice descending loud and clear from her eyrie high up in the eaves of the house. Sharp-beaked, sharp-eyed old buzzard!

There was never any respite from her presence, but he was comforted knowing that her frail mind would soon, start to go downhill very quickly. Once she had gone completely batty, he could have her placed in a home where she could drool and mumble her life away. At present he was afraid to upset her because she was still lucid enough to take it into her head to instruct Peterson, Handley and Handley to change her will ...and what a great pity that would be after all his patience!

"Dougie, Dougie are you deaf?

"Unfortunately, you bloody old crow, I'm not," he muttered under his breath.

"I want some water, Dougie, but I'd like it today,

not tomorrow. If it's not too much trouble!"

Down Dougie went obediently to the beautiful, all mod-cons kitchen grumbling to himself what he'd like to do to her; it would be something very painful and something that would take a very long time. Stick her in a dark cupboard, that's what he'd like to do. Tightly put a rough rope around her until her breath almost stopped and she couldn't move.

As Dougie was filling the glass, his hand suddenly slipped and let the beautiful object fall onto the floor where it smashed into a hundred pieces. His memory had been jolted and he didn't like it one bit.

Dougie bent down and began to pick up the shards, but, having always been rather ham-fisted, his fingers were soon cut and oozing with blood. Actually, he quite enjoyed the pain, so he slowly made a deep gash across the palm of his right hand and shivered from the sheer pleasure of it. He smiled and went to the window, opened the shutter and gazed again at the moon and stars. He lifted his bleeding hands, his elbows firmly tucked into his sides, and showed them to the night sky.

"What do you think of this then! No, I haven't murdered her, but it's satisfying to imagine that I could have done it. Anyway, I'm sure as you peep into people's houses you must all have glimpsed much worse things than a dead, raddled old bitch."

As he made his way upstairs with a couple of sleeping-pills well mixed in a fresh glass of water, he could hear more complaining. "I trust you didn't put any ice in the water, Dougie. You know it doesn't do a delicate stomach like mine any good."

At least during the week, when Dougie had to be out of the house, there was a life-line near at hand in the form of Milly. She was such an obliging neighbour who, fortunately, mother considered to be on the same social level. Because there was no permanent help, the little spinster was at her beck and call all day, but certainly stood no nonsense.

Unfortunately, any staff that managed to pass muster at an interview, sooner or later became so thoroughly fed up with mother that they rarely lasted more than a week or so and poor Milly was becoming somewhat of a fixture in the house but, of course, she always went home at night and then the burden became his.

"Here you are, mother ...your water!"

"About time too, Dougie. I can't fathom out why it always takes you so long to perform the simplest of tasks, but then you've never been the brightest of boys, have you?" He was forty-six years old, for God's sake, and stupid was the last word that could ever be applied to him! He bit his lower lip and looked at her red-veined face with loathing. She was propped up on pink, frilly pillows in her sumptuously-large bed, staring at him through dark, steely eyes. She really was like a buzzard ...and that nose, well, it was a true hooked beak, wasn't it?

He continued to watch the old biddy noisily slurping her water and, as her eyes grew heavy, he sat down in her wheel chair, putting his feet on the bed. He could feel the warm mound of Maxi, her cat, underneath the blanket and, smiling with anticipation, took out of his pocket a piece of sharp, broken glass that he'd saved.

Seated in the most humble though still stunning office, was Dougie Brewster who had joined Bigwig, Bolster and Bigwig as an associate just two years ago and was the latest incumbent in the firm. He was highly thought of and already had been given a wink and a nod that, if things went according to plan, he could eventually expect to become a partner. It didn't hurt that his name too began with a B and would thus fit in well: Bigwig, Bigwig, Bolster, and Brewster had a good ring to it, the sort of name that would stick in the memory of potential clients.

He sat there grinning, thinking about his mother, who at that moment, was sitting at home only half a mile away from the office with her darling boy dead in her arms. Her face was awash with tears and her breath coming in short, tortured gasps from her heaving breast. Her beloved Maxi, what could have happened to him? She stroked the grey fur that covered his huge, overweight body and kissed his lovely ears No longer would she hear his purring and snoring as he slept all night under the eiderdown at her feet.

"He's had a wonderful life," said Milly, "and he was, after all, eighteen years old, which is a good age for any cat. Just think that he's now in the place where all good cats go."

"But it's so cruel and life will never be the same without him," she sobbed and wheezed.

By now Dougie's mother was tearing at her hair and wailing loudly, the lifeless cat lying on her knees with his head and front paws drooping towards the floor, his chubby back paws and thick tail flat out on the sofa. It was all rather like a bad village-hall production of a Greek tragedy.

What Milly and Dougie's mother had failed to notice, however, was the hole in Maxi's body that led directly to his heart. The blood that had issued from this wound had been carefully cleaned away and the thick, grey fur brushed over it… The piece of glass had been meticulously sanitized for further use.

The funeral took place later that evening, the burial spot under a fir tree carefully chosen after Dougie's mother had made a sombre tour of the garden in her wheel chair. The handyman-cum-gardener had dug the hole.

On Dougie's return from the office, the solemn proceedings began. "Bring out your dead," muttered Dougie sarcastically as his mother proceeded slowly towards the grave side. She bore on her lap the deceased, wrapped in his day blanket, with his favourite fluffy hedgehog between his front paws. She insisted on committing the body into the ground herself, with the result that it was flung rather than placed in its final resting place. The blanket unwrapped itself and showed the hapless Maxi with his large teeth bared in a rictus smile, but fortunately Dougie's mother saw nothing through her tears.

Dougie, with his handkerchief in front of his mouth obviously trying to stifle his grief, looked the epitome of sorrow. How deceptive appearances can be! How wicked he had been and what fun it all was, he thought, especially his mother's suffering! By now the decibel level of the weeping issuing from his mother's throat had increased by leaps and bounds and he was not surprised to see her wriggle her way out of her wheelchair and cast herself upon the hallowed turf.

Prue was a legal assistant at Bigwig, Bolster & Bigwig, a somewhat plain girl with golden hair who had her sights firmly fixed on Dougie. She was at that very moment stalking outside Dougie's house, just within earshot of the funeral.

She approached the tall, thick hedge that surrounded the garden. The only way she could have a close glimpse of this Shangri La, without approaching the imposing iron gate and thus running the risk of being seen, was to scramble through the hedge.

This was not an easy task and her arms became scratched and her hair full of leaves and twigs. Once she was able to look through the hedge she was amazed to see an old lady lying on the lawn beating her fists on the grass, wailing for all she was worth. A wheelchair was behind her, so she had obviously either hurled herself out of it or someone had tipped her out on purpose.

The old dear was surrounded by a small group of people: there was Dougie shaking with emotion, a young man with a spade in his hand and an elderly lady. They approached the distraught, prone figure and tried to haul her upright, but she was so overweight that they were unable to manage it. Suddenly, however, Prue became the centre of attention, for Dougie, always on the alert, had seen the leaves of the hedge trembling and knew that it boded ill. He went over to investigate, and, at lightning speed, Prue found herself being yanked into the midst of the funeral party.

A miracle of Biblical proportions then took place as Dougie's mother, gazing wide-eyed at Prue, stopped her audition for the Old Vic, turned off the waterworks and slowly staggered onto her feet, the soil from the tomb dropping from her black dress, and plonked herself back into her wheelchair.

Dougie's mother knew with total certainty that this blonde-haired vision who had suddenly appeared magically among them was a sign sent from Heaven to tell her that all was well with Maxi and they would meet again one day.

Dougie was beside himself with annoyance at this sneaky trespassing into his private life. He was just about to send Prue on her way when mother trundled over the lawn, grabbed the girl's hand and led her into the house to enjoy the wake, comprising tea, cucumber sandwiches and cake. Prue, glancing quickly at Dougie's face knew that tomorrow she would have to face his wrath for her temerity, but she didn't doubt that this would not be a problem.

Dougie's mother was enchanted to hear that girl's name was Prudence. What else could it possibly be; you could see that she radiated the virtues of wisdom and good sense.

As the polite tea party progressed Dougie's fingers enjoyably played with the shard of glass that he had put into his jacket pocket before going to work that morning. This meant that he couldn't possibly hand out the sandwiches that were sitting daintily on the beautiful china plate or pour from the solid silver teapot, for they and the spotless, white cloth, would all have been dotted with blood. Thank goodness that Milly was there to do this task.

The conversation was all on so vague a level that no one was any the wiser about Dougie and Prue working in the same legal firm. All that was gleaned about her, once she'd sussed out what had caused all the palaver, was how much she adored cats, especially grey ones. Indeed, she firmly averred that she would give her life to save a cat. Dougie's mother's eyes brimmed over yet again especially when Prue, the little liar, said what a coincidence it was that her brother's name was Maxi.

Everyone at the office knew that Dougie was rather weird and sometimes went into what they called his creepy mode. Only Prue, however, knew that he was also dishonest and corrupt, moving money away from Bigwig, Bolster & Bigwig that ended up in his own private account in some tax haven: in his case, the

Cayman Islands. She should really have been an accountant, for she always made it her business to examine everyone's financial situation; it was almost a hobby.

"Don't you ever again, Miss Henson, try and poke your nose into my private life, or your job will well and truly be on the line.

She immediately opened her tote bag, whipped out several papers filled with numbers, which were thrust in front of his eyes for perusal. Dougie immediately collapsed onto a sofa as, in the distance, lightning flashed and thunder rolled. Prue glanced at the rain drops that were beginning to lash against the windows. The muffled sound was repeated like approaching cymbals and, as a grey cotton-wool army of menacing clouds moved over the farmland, Dougie went off again into a world of his own.

This was a scenario that hadn't been played out before ...not a familiar experience and, therefore, it was all the more frightening for its novelty. He could hear cymbals and drums in the distance, but he literally felt too empty to appreciate their rhythm, for he knew intuitively that his brain and lungs, his liver and stomach had all been taken from him; only his heart remained so that later on it could be weighed by the spirits of the underworld. Tightly bound in white linen, the feeling of claustrophobia was overwhelming, not helped by the pungent smell of herbs and spices, of resin and fresh flowers with which his shroud had been anointed. The coffin was so narrow that even if his wrappings had been removed his arms would still have been imprisoned. He could hear the tinkling amulets and glass beads that had been placed among the layers of linen. He knew without any doubt that he was dead: as a dodo.

Dr Silas Schreiber MD was quickly sent for and diagnosed the patient as a burnt-out case, a victim to overwork and family problems, but one that would eventually flicker back to life.

The doctor, the senior partner Mr Bigwig and Prue all tried to uncross his arms, but it was a real challenge, for it was as though they were glued firmly to his chest. Eventually, however, his eyes began to focus and his limbs to relax. Prue leaned over and discreetly stroked his hand. She whispered into his ear. "You need someone to love you, Dougie, someone who will take care of you." She shivered when she saw his reaction to this, for such a look of intense dislike passed across his face that it was a wonder that she hadn't turned to stone. Nevertheless, she wouldn't give up. Let him get used to the idea, especially as his batty old mother had obviously taken such a shine to her.

An ambulance arrived and Dougie was loaded on board, while Prue was being physically restrained from accompanying him by Mr Bigwig who had long ago fathomed out her little game and who, in truth, thought she was a piece of all right and ripe for the picking himself.

The private hospital was comfortable, even

luxurious and Dougie's room like that of a smart hotel.

The nursing staff found Dougie rather weird, for when they tucked him into his bed he always complained vociferously and insisted that his arms should be inside the covers and that the sheets and blankets were laid as tightly as possible around him.

"I want to feel hemmed in, chained," he explained, "as if I'm in prison. It makes me feel safe."

"But, Mr Brewster, we do it for your own comfort."

"Listen," he said, "this is what I want, and this is what you will do."

He also insisted that no one should move the piece of broken glass that he kept on his bedside table.

Wonderful floral displays and magnums of champagne arrived as did many visitors from the law firm. The senior partners did not want the prestigious hospital to think that one of its associates had been abandoned. This would not do their reputation as a caring firm any good.

One day when she was helping to bath her, Milly was shocked to the see the state of the soles of Dougie's mother's feet, which were covered in suppurating sores and ulcers and little moist, bleeding cuts. Milly made a terrible fuss and tried to question Dougie's mother closely on where these awful wounds had come from, but of course she hadn't the foggiest idea.

By now Dougie had been discharged from the hospital, so you will have guessed the name of the culprit and that the culprit had failed to keep his glass shard fully sterilised. In fact, so lackadaisical had he become that his own hand had swollen with infection. Indeed, he thought his thumb looked as though it might have developed gangrene and perhaps would have to be amputated – but he really enjoyed the pain, the throbbing, the stiffness in his muscles. He had bandaged his hand so tightly that the circulation was cut off and a severe coldness was affecting the end of his fingers. He spent much of his time surveying this mummy-like object that hung from the end of his arm, both elbows as usual tucked tightly into his sides.

Unfortunately, it was going to be more difficult to hurt his mother now that Milly had pushed her nose into where it wasn't wanted. However, Dougie would find a way to make his mother suffer as she had caused him to suffer. He would wear her down most cruelly and very, very slowly. She probably thought he couldn't possibly remember what she had done to him, but he did. He knew the bitch had broken him in both body and mind.

He should have started his war of attrition against her long ago so that, by now, it would have all been over, his revenge complete. The terrible visions had begun in earnest only recently, bringing sensations that had been long-buried in his subconscious, but now the memories were back and would not go away. He sat in her wheel chair with his feet on her bed, as he did every night, and moved the glass shard into his other hand, thinking deeply. He would not be bested.

There he was, floating between papyrus islands, watched on both sides by the creatures of the Nile. Hippopotamus, gazelles, graceful egrets and, of course, the menacing eyes of crocodiles all surveyed him with curiosity as he glided by in his boat of gold. They were the very same creatures that he'd seen painted on the walls of his pyramid. He knew, despite being entombed within the suffocating darkness of his coffin, his body bound in tightly wrapped linen bandages, that this scene was in the open air and that it was real. Was it perhaps that his spirit had left his body and could survey everything? Was he a pharaoh who had now become a god in the after world? He was not, however, such a fine god that he could ignore the stifling, enclosed space where he lay. He felt desperate and had to escape, though he knew it was not possible for he would be here for all eternity. With his eyes almost popping out of their sockets, a serious case of hysteria and panic was about to set in.

He was next aware of his own voice screaming and his lungs struggling for breath. Dr Schreiber was looking down upon him with a needle in his hand ready to sedate him, while two nurses held his arms. Once more he was in the familiar surroundings of a hospital room identical to the one he had occupied only a month or two ago.

When Prue entered his room the first thing she saw seemed to be a disembodied hand, its fingers crawling spider-like over the bedside table. Dougie was, of course, searching for his shard of glass and mumbling fretfully, but Prue didn't know of its existence.

As she looked at him she realised that he was so drugged that he was hardly able to move his lips and that his eyes couldn't focus upon her, gazing constantly, for the duration of her visit, at her right ear.

Not wishing to waste time, she plonked onto his chest a crumpled bag of left-over grapes and got down to business.

"Right, Dougie, this is the deal, this is how it's going to play out," she said like some broad from the Bronx. "You scratch my back and I'll scratch yours."

Drugged he may have been, but the awful truth gradually penetrated the fog and he knew that he was beaten.

"What did you say, Dougie? Was that a yes? I hope so, for that's the only possible answer. After all, you don't want all your hard work and prospects to go down the plug hole, do you? ...Right, now we've sorted that out, the only thing that remains is to tell your mother the good news. She'll love the prospect of all those baby Brewsters, won't she?"

Dougie groaned, and she could see tears falling down his cheeks, but whether of frustration or rage she didn't know. They certainly weren't tears of happiness, that's for sure. It was lucky for her that she didn't know what was going on in that twisted mind of his or she might not have been so smug, especially as his hand had just knocked over a plastic bottle of Lucozade in its desperate search for his precious piece of sharp glass.

His other hand, the one that he had treated so badly

was now cured, but the nursing staff still couldn't understand how it got into that terrible state.

Hanging upside down in the darkness with his feet grasping the rocky roof of the cave, he knew that others of his kind were with him so that he did not feel alone. He could smell their acrid scent and could sense their bodies swinging gently in the air. As he wrapped his leathery wings around himself, he felt the furriness of his warm body and fell asleep until dusk called, his mind filled with dreams of blood and fruit and insects. He was safe within this world and squeezed his wings more tightly to him for comfort.

As dusk descended, the bats within their cave began to stir and unfurled their leathery wings from around their bodies. Gradually they made their way out into the gloom to find food, while owls also, silent as the grave, were on the wing seeking nourishment. There was nothing they enjoyed more than a fresh meaty bat for supper and often caught them in flight.

Suddenly, he felt the air move around him and knew that he was doomed.

It was a damp March morning and moisture seemed to ooze through the stone walls of the church from the rain falling outside, making the funeral even sadder and more sombre than it was already. The ailing Dougie by this time had been long discharged from his hospital bed, long enough indeed to have become a murderer. He and his mother sat wheelchair to wheelchair on the second row – both equally spaced out and confused.

How the stalwart Milly had died was a mystery, except to Prue, the eternal spy, who had watched her demise as Dougie had pushed the frail, old dear into the garden pond. He wasn't going to allow the gentle Milly to have any suspicions over the lingering torture that he had planned for his mother.

Dougie's mother in her befuddled mind thought that Maxi lay in the coffin with his fluffy hedgehog at his side, while Dougie saw a small, black bat sitting on the wooden box and struggled to think why this should be.

Prue, not being one to miss an opportunity sat down behind him and whispered in his ear. "Don't forget *Crimewatch* will you, Dougie? I've not said a word yet, but if you don't soon buy me an extremely expensive engagement ring, I shall blab to the world what I know about your little financial games and about that other game we call murder."

Suddenly, Dougie's mother looking at Prue, tottered onto her feet, held out her arms towards her and shouted loudly in her strident voice, "Maxi's angel! You've come back to me! Do you bear a message from the Great Beyond? Oh, how is my little grey darling? Tell me, Prudence, tell me, I pray. Only you know the answer."

With her arms stretched out in supplication, it would have been a toss-up between Dougie's mother or Dame Judy for the Oscar. Like a script from an old melodrama the plea echoed to the very back seats of the church, made its way into the North Transept, into the South Transept, bounced up the stout pillars that supported the roof, even surprising the gargoyles that were looking down upon the scene; in fact, it was a wonder the noise didn't set the bells ringing in the belfry.

It doesn't take much for people's concentration to wander, so that now there was a faint sound of murmuring and whispering among the people gathered there, even an inappropriate nervous giggle or two. Until that is, the Dean began the solemn rite, and everyone remembered why they were there.

As the sun broke through the watery sky over the grave site, Dougie was suddenly aware that he and his wheelchair were surrounded by a strange circle of shards of glinting glass. Surely an optical illusion, but he knew that it was a part of his psyche – the old bag had seen to that. His very own personal prize shard was in the pocket of his mackintosh and he curled his fingers around it. He would, however, teach himself to forgo the pleasure of cutting himself – that would be something for high days and holidays. He smiled.

Standing slightly unsteadily near the sun-lit altar, with his hand again heavily bandaged, his elbows tucked in to his sides, a glazed-eyed Dougie awaited further torture, but it was better than being snitched on by Prue.

The organ burst forth with what, to Dougie, sounded like *The Dead March* and down the aisle tottered Prue, a dramatically lone figure, her red-soled Louboutin shoes peeping out from under a blush-coloured, mermaid-styled wedding dress which did her shape no favours. Dougie wished fervently that she, mermaid-like, would sink into the ocean and swim away. The word *kill,* kept repeating over and over in his head and now it began to beat time with his heart.

His mother sat on the front row, a great splodge of blusher on her cheeks and her eyes decorated by the bluest, most sparkling eye-shadow known to man or beast. When she caught sight of Prue, that portal to Maxi's abode, now in actual angel garb, she ignited with excitement and indeed, clasping her chest, her lungs almost paralysed, she suddenly stopped breathing and expired so quietly that no one knew she had died. Only Prue, always with eyes in the back of her head, realised what had happened, but decided that the deceased should sit there until the ceremony was over, for absolutely nothing was going to prevent this marriage taking place.

Dougie was glad that his mother had died, but he regretted that her suffering had not been as intense as he had wanted. However, having just one person to obsess over was far better than having two. So now he could direct all his feeling of hate towards Prue, although this didn't work out terribly well because his mental state was worsening. He had several more visions and dreams of horror, very quickly, one after the other, where he screamed out in the dark for help.

Dr. Schreiber, much to Prue's delight, recommended that he should be sent to a secure place where he would not harm himself or anyone else. The greatest difficulty for the nursing staff was parting him from his precious shard of glass – why did he want it, why did he need it and why did he like to be tightly bound in his blankets and sheets?

A rope kept his arms from moving as he was forced to walk over the broken glass that covered the path. He was not enjoying this one bit, for his feet were bleeding badly and, unusually for him, he had a bad feeling about the pain; something was not right.

On either side of him was a prancing, laughing, red-nosed circus clown who made sure that he did not deviate from the path. Ahead he could see palm trees bending over, their reflection clearly visible in a large, luxurious swimming pool, the bottom of which was decorated by a mosaic serpent, its body green and undulating. The clowns prodded him roughly, making him walk to the very edge of the pool, where all at once they pushed him in.

As he fell, the serpent hissed and, in a split second, rose up and had him in its grip. It squeezed and squeezed him until he could resist no longer, for he was now doubly tightly bound by rope and serpent.

He did not wake up again.

Doctor Schreiber pronounced Dougie dead at two o'clock in the afternoon of the sixth day of September, 2017 from heart failure.

"Darling Dougie! My sweet little baby! Mummy loves you so much. Please, don't ever change. I promise you that I will always make you happy."

Well, she would make damn sure that he never changed; he was such a bundle of cuteness. Thus, she wrapped him very, very tightly and roughly in swaddling clothes thinking that this would prevent his new, little baby body from growing; any more pressure would have done him permanent damage, but she wasn't to know that. To reinforce this, she then placed him in a small drawer, so that like seeds in a dark place, his growth would be stunted, and he would remain forever like a little doll.

Although she was already mentally disintegrating, and misunderstood the whole concept of maternal care, she still, however, had the sense to leave the drawer open slightly, so that he wouldn't suffocate. If something should happen to him, however, she would simply have him mummified, like her darling, dead cat, Fluffy, who had lived for years in the drawer above Dougie. That way she could always still hug and kiss her baby boy and, of course, he would not cry and grizzle, which he seemed to do for hours on end. It could all be very wearing.

A few days later, to ensure his happiness, she purposely dropped a wine glass on to the tiled kitchen floor, for she had read somewhere that to smash drinking glasses during a wedding ceremony would bring good luck. She, therefore, swept up the broken pieces and carefully placed them in the bottom of Dougie's drawer. Then she popped Dougie himself back on top of them. He was now surrounded by good luck. Needless to say, his soft skin gradually became badly infected, like a red, festering pin cushion, as the sharp glass pierced his wrappings. It was only the hiring of a nanny and, thence, the intervention of a doctor, plus some very strong pills for his mother, that saved Dougie, but his subconscious never forgot, never forgave, what she had done to him.

Acid Rain

A selection of Short Stories by Vonnie Giles.

Following Vonnie's successful contributions to the short story anthology 'Picked and Mixed', Vonnie was invited to publish a selection of her unique and quirky short stories. Acid Rain delves into her eclectic collection of dark and esoteric tales and promises to entertain and surprise.

Meet some of the darkest characters ever to send shivers into your dreams.

Paperback ISBN 978-1-908135-06-3

eBook ISBN 978-1-908135-17-9